Single Shot

Single Shot

RON ELLIS

First published in Great Britain in 2002 by
Allison & Busby Limited
Bon Marche Centre
241-251 Ferndale Road
Brixton, London SW9 8BJ
http://www.allisonandbusby.com

A catalogue record for this book is available from the British Library

ISBN 0 7490 0569 6

Printed and bound in Ebbw Vale,
by Creative Print & Design

To my wife Sue for her unwavering support

Ron Ellis lives in Southport where he works as a football reporter, broadcaster and lecturer. Originally studying to become a librarian, he became caught up in the Merseybeat scene of the 1960s and has been a record company promotions manager, a mobile DJ, a property developer and an actor amongst other things. Married with two grown-up daughters, in his spare time he enjoys songwriting, photography, painting and playing for his local quiz team. The author of twelve books, *Single Shot* is the sixth novel to feature Liverpool private eye and radio DJ Johnny Ace.

www.ronellis.co.uk

Prologue

The temperature was 75 degrees, about right for an afternoon in April. A warm breeze wafted in from the sea and the orange and lemon blossom was in full bloom. A bit different from Liverpool the day before.

I was sitting at an outside table at the Miramar Hotel overlooking the bay, drinking a glass of red wine and glancing through a copy of the local rag, the *Costa Blanca News*.

My plane had landed at Spain's Alicante Airport just a few hours earlier and I'd hired a car for the short journey to the town of Javea.

Javea is an unspoilt Spanish seaside resort on the edge of the Mediterranean. It's divided into three sections, a port, the town centre and a charming warren of narrow streets and ancient buildings called, would you believe, The Old Town.

It's a bit like nearby Benidorm must have been before it was discovered by Germans, lager louts and Judith Chalmers. I say unspoilt and so it is, architecturally speaking. No twenty storey hotels or apartments have appeared as yet.

The British, though, are arriving in droves; mostly retirees fleeing the floods, the frost and Blair's rip-off Britain, happily eking out their pensions in a sunny clime where petrol is nearly half the price and a three-course meal for two costs £12 with a bottle of decent wine thrown in.

Others have moved over permanently and created their own Little England. They watch English TV programmes, buy English papers, form bridge clubs, attend line-dancing classes and read articles on annuities and fitness for the over-sixties.

As most of these ex-pats are halfway to the grave, health is a big issue here. The papers seemed to be full of articles instructing readers how to ward off bowel cancer by special diet, remove wrinkles without cosmetic surgery and prevent your colostomy bag from ruining your golf swing, interspersed with enticing advertisements for stair lifts, nursing homes and Viagra.

Rather alarmingly, the best adverts were for the crematoriums, which were built like palaces. I suppose they were the only businesses with a guaranteed clientele.

Actually though, if The World Health Organisation is to be believed, the immigrants are worrying about nothing. The WHO says this is the third healthiest place on the planet to live. I don't know where Liverpool comes in the table but it isn't first or second, that's for sure. People of sixty retiring to this part of Spain can apparently happily expect to add at least another ten years to their life expectancy.

Unless, of course, somebody shoots them.

The headlines in the paper I was reading reported just such an incident. A man had been found the day before, slumped beside his swimming pool at his luxury villa, a bullet through his brain, his body being discovered by his Spanish cleaner.

I was in Javea to find a man called Carlos Botago, a wine merchant, antiques dealer and professional hit man. He lived in a villa five miles out of town in the shadow of a mountain known as Montgo, shaped like the head of an elephant.

Botago had been in England a few days before. I had been on his trail for some time and I almost apprehended him on the day he flew out of Manchester Airport but he took an earlier flight and I missed him.

But now I'd no need to look any further.

Carlos Botago was the dead man.

Chapter One

It had all started a month or so before, back on Merseyside. January, February and March had been three particularly cold and wet months in what seemed to have been an everlasting winter.

The television newsreels were full of pictures of floods and blizzards, and what with petrol strikes, NHS cock-ups, rising crime, race riots, corrupt politicians, stealth taxes, train cancellations, mad cow disease, foot and mouth and the fiasco of The Dome, no wonder half the population wished they were in Spain. Or Australia. Or anywhere except Britain.

Even Everton, after allowing their manager to spend fifty million pounds to buy new players, were yet again struggling at the wrong end of the Premiership table with relegation a distinct possibility.

There used to be this saying, "cometh the hour, cometh the man" but Tony Blair and Walter Smith were still respectively in charge so I guessed it didn't apply any more.

Jim Burroughs and I had had a quiet few months since the Joanna Smithson case and we were even debating whether to shut down for a couple of weeks and take a winter break when a Spanish lady came up to our Dale Street office one Tuesday afternoon towards the end of March with an intriguing story to tell.

Her name was Gabrielle Lorenzo and she was working as a consultant with a British pharmaceutical company based in Speke called DRP. It seemed competition in this field was pretty fierce with huge amounts of money at stake so it followed that industrial espionage was high on the agenda.

Ms Lorenzo had only been with the company for a few weeks but, in that time, she had learnt that somebody was sending results of top-secret tests of new drugs to an unknown competitor.

'How exactly did you find this out?' asked Jim.

She smiled. She was in her late thirties with lustrous black hair, a bronzed skin and dark eyes that shone beneath thick eyelashes. She was tall, around five foot nine, and slim enough to get away with wearing a bright scarlet trouser suit that would have made many women of her age look like a pear drop.

'Because I was looking for it. Let me put you in the picture, Mr. Ace. It's no coincidence that I'm here in Liverpool and with this particular firm.' She reached down for her handbag and extracted a business card, which she handed to me.

The name on the card read El Greco Detection, Alicante Province.

'As you see,' she continued, 'I represent a Spanish detective agency and I am in your country acting on behalf of a drug company in Alicante who have retained us to investigate a possible leak of some recent very hush-hush experiments.'

I raised my eyebrows.

'They concern a cure for Alzheimer's Disease,' she explained 'As you can imagine, there is a tremendous market potential out there for such a drug. With the life expectancy of the population increasing all the time, more and more people are being affected by dementia in one form or another.'

'So the company who's first to patent a cure can make a killing?'

'That's right. One of our operators was able to infiltrate the company and managed to identify the culprit but, before we could apprehend the man, he disappeared.'

'You think he may have been killed to make sure he didn't talk?'

'Who knows? He lived alone. We found out his address and searched his apartment but he'd left no trace. Maybe he'd already fled the country. All we know is that the information was sent by e-mail to someone in Liverpool and he himself has never been seen since.'

'How do you know it was sent to Liverpool? E-mails don't have addresses.'

'It was a co.uk address so I knew it was England but I was able to retrieve the reply and Liverpool was mentioned.'

'But no clue as to who sent it?'

'No.'

'Then how did you make the connection to DRP?

'They're the only company in the area working in a similar field to our Spanish clients. It therefore seemed a good place for me to start looking.'

'Which is why you came over to England, to check them out?'

'Correct. With their managing director's knowledge, of course. He was the only person at DRP that knew my real identity. He fixed me up with a 'consultancy' position so I could move around the office and factory and keep my eyes open.'

Jim interrupted. 'Hang on, you said when you first came in that it was DRP who were losing the information, not the other way round.'

'That's right. After I had examined their P.C. network, I discovered that DRP were in exactly the same position as the Alicante people. Someone was sending out information about their experiments too. Unfortunately, I haven't been able to find out yet to whom the information has been going or who in the company has been sending it.'

'If you're sure about this and you've told the company, why haven't they brought the police in?' asked Jim. I sometimes think he's on commission from his ex-colleagues.

'Because the credibility of the company would be ruined if competitors found out.'

'A bit like the banks keeping quiet about the massive sums they've lost to computer hackers, you mean?'

'Exactly. But I still believe that the person responsible is based in Liverpool and, if we could apprehend him, it might be a different story. They might then be willing to prosecute.'

'Someone receiving information from both companies, what sort of position would you expect him to have?'

'I'd say undoubtedly it must be someone in the medical profession and probably in the drug industry, possibly working with a research organisation. He'd have to know what he was looking for. You see, if someone with the right knowledge could get hold of these formulae, he could then take them to a company anywhere in the world and sell them on.'

'Would they buy them though, knowing they were stolen?'

'Come on, Mr. Ace, this is the real world. Okay, maybe one or two

15

companies would baulk at the idea but a good many more would be only too willing.'

'You seem to be progressing quite well in this enquiry. Why hand over the investigation to us now?'

'Because I think my cover has been blown. Last night, somebody made an attempt on my life.'

'What happened?'

'Someone fired a shot at me as I was walking down the street.'

'Did you see who it was?'

'No, it was dark and they were in a car.'

Jim looked horrified. 'Are you sure it wasn't just a car backfiring?'

She gave him a scathing look. 'I think I can tell the difference, thank you.'

'Did you tell the police?'

'I didn't see the point. But I think it wise for me to be out of here before they try again. I am too conspicuous now in your city. It is better I hand over the job to somebody like yourselves with local knowledge who might be better placed to work from inside the company.

And who was just as likely to be shot if they got found out.

'What does DRP stand for?' I asked.

'Derek Routledge Pharmaceuticals .'

'Derek Routledge being the MD?'

She shook her head. 'No, his son Rupert. The old man retired last year. Needless to say, Rupert Routledge would offer you full co-operation. In fact, I have already spoken to him about you and he'll be available to see you tomorrow morning if you agree to take on the enquiry.'

'If we were to take this on,' asked Jim, who was ever practical when it came to money, 'who would be picking up the tab?'

'Initially, you would send the bills to my firm and we would pass them on to our client in Alicante.' She smiled. 'You needn't worry. The fee is assured. We are talking blue-chip companies here.'

Jim looked satisfied. 'Sounds fair enough to me.'

'I've compiled a dossier,' she said. She pulled out a lilac plastic

16

file from her briefcase and handed it to me. 'Everything I have been able to discover so far is in here.'

I opened it and glanced through the papers. I was impressed. She'd written out a summary of her progress together with a list of relevant names, addresses and phone numbers and code numbers of the stolen formulae.

'Looks fine to me.' I told her we would give the matter our full attention.

'I'm going back to Alicante tomorrow,' she said, 'but here's my mobile number. You can reach me any time on that.'

'Could be a nice money-spinner, this,' said Jim, when Ms Lorenzo had left. 'A cut above some of our other cases. Corporate clients, that's the market we ought to be aiming at, Johnny. I like it.'

'A bit classier than our other case, I'll admit.'

Our other case concerned a stalker.

Chapter Two

The client was a large lady in her early fifties called Dorothy Grove, who was convinced somebody from a local singles club, Simply Single, was following her.

Ms Grove, as she insisted on being called, had joined the club early in the New Year, having parted company with her husband the previous Spring.

She'd been married twice. Her first husband had escaped to the Middle East and never returned whilst his successor had seemingly ended up in the bankruptcy court after she had taken him through an acrimonious divorce and cleaned him out. Now she was anxious to find a speedy replacement to enable her to continue enjoying the high standard of living to which she'd become accustomed.

She'd found Simply Single from an advert in the *Liverpool Echo* and persuaded a friend to go along with her. The group met every Tuesday evening in the function room of a pub on Queens Drive. It hadn't really been her sort of scene, drinks and a disco, but she'd quite enjoyed it and, although she hadn't met anybody there whom she wanted to go out with, she'd made friends with a couple of women, both recently bereaved, and was prepared to give it another chance.

And then, on her second visit, the stalker.

'This wasn't at all what I expected when I joined the club, Mr. Ace. I just wanted to find a partner.'

I didn't reckon it was going to be easy for her. Even disregarding her facial hair and a chin Jimmy Hill would have died for, she was a formidable woman who would have frightened off most men who came within a hundred yards of her, stalkers notwithstanding. But I didn't tell her any of this. She was a paying customer.

'Someone has followed me home twice now, last week and again last night,' she told us when she came to the office. 'It must be one of the men from the meeting although I didn't see his face.'

'You walk to the meetings then?'

'I only live a couple of streets away. No sense in wasting petrol.'

'You're sure he was following you?' Jim asked.

'Oh yes, when I stopped, he stopped. I heard his footsteps distinctly.'

'But you didn't see him?'

'No. He must have stepped into somebody's gateway or behind a tree.'

'And you didn't think to go back and challenge him?' Her size alone would have made most potential attackers think twice.

'And risk being raped on a public highway?'

Privately, I thought that would be wishful thinking and, to be honest, I didn't take her claim too seriously but I asked her the usual questions. Had anyone got a grudge against her? Had she any enemies? Could they have mistaken her for someone else? Might she not be imagining it?

All her answers were in the negative.

'You know, it could have been somebody who wanted to ask you out but was too shy,' suggested Jim. 'Followed you home but couldn't pluck up the courage to talk to you.'

I could see he was as dubious as I was about taking on the case, which, in a way, was understandable. Having been a DI with Merseyside Police, Jim had been in the front line of major crime; drug-dealing, murders, race riots, you name it. He was hardly likely to get excited by the romantic imaginings of a frustrated divorcee like Dorothy Grove.

'I think not.' Ms Grove was undeterred. 'He's a stalker all right and I want you to come along to the next meeting and ferret him out. Shouldn't be too difficult.'

She saw us hesitate but before we could object, she played her trump card. 'I can write you a cheque now for £200 if you like, with a further £500 when you nail him. Will that be enough?

Before Jim could contradict me, I told her it would be fine. Maybe it wasn't exactly the stuff of *Miami Vice* but the bills had to be paid. Not that we needed the money. I own some houses in Liverpool 8 and Liverpool 17, which I've turned into flats, and Jim has his pension from the Force. But what's the point in working for

19

nothing? I watched Ms Grove sign the cheque and assured her we'd be there at the club's next get-together.

All that had been six days ago and now the Simply Single group was due to meet that night. Gabrielle Lorenzo would have to be put on the back burner for the next few hours.

Jim was reluctant to go. 'I think it should be you, Johnny.'

'Too risky, Jim. Anyone might recognise me from the radio programme.' I do the six to seven slot on local radio, a phone-in programme with my own choice of records in between, which can mean anything from Billie Holiday to Shane McGowan with maybe a bit of The Cramps or Ethan Allen thrown into the mix. Cult listening for real music lovers.

'They don't see your face on the radio.'

'Maybe not but my picture never seems to be out of the papers.'

'Don't be so bloody arrogant. Comb your hair a bit different and put a pair of glasses on and nobody will know you.'

'I still say it should be you. You're older and look like a lonely widower.' In truth, he still looked like the policeman he once was, tall and straight backed with steel grey hair and an authoritative manner.

'They might just as easily recognise me from one of our gigs.' Jim plays bass guitar in The Chocolate Lavatory, a group that was part of Merseybeat folklore in the sixties and who had misguidedly reformed a couple of years ago to play charity gigs for The Merseycats.

They still play all the same stuff like 'Teenager in Love' and 'Sweet Little Sixteen' that they played in the sixties. Not much musical advancement there. It's like The Beach Boys. I find it very hard to take seriously a bunch of balding pensioners singing 'Be True to Your School'. It's OK to sing jazz or country or blues when you're renewing your bus pass for the third time but rock'n'roll is like punk or dance. Young people's music and of its time. Ask your kids.

'It's really not my scene,' went on Jim. 'I know what they're like, those places. A load of sad bastards who have a few bevies and a bop and hope that before closing time they'll get lucky and find themselves a lifelong companion or, failing that, at least end up with a convivial leg-over to see them through until the following week.'

'I take it that's a no then?'

'What do you think?'

'Don't be so bloody pessimistic. It could be chocka with trendy babes looking for a life-enriching experience with a mature man.'

'Like Dorothy Grove you mean?

'...or a night of hot passion with the bloke of their dreams.'

'That lets us out then. I still say it's more likely the place'll be full of perverts.'

In the end, we agreed to go to the meeting together, posing as two divorced and lonely middle-aged men in search of someone to share our affections. It couldn't have been more inappropriate. Jim had been happily married to Rosemary for nearly thirty years and my girlfriend, Maria, had recently given birth to our first baby, Victoria.

I didn't tell Maria where I was going to, other than I was out on a case. She knew I'd discuss it with her when I was ready. A night at a singles club might not have gone down too well. She was already having difficulty accepting that I still occasionally saw Hilary, my ex long-time girlfriend, albeit on a platonic basis.

Well, mostly on a platonic basis, although there'd been a couple of occasions when we lapsed into our old routine of wild passion which I wasn't too proud about.

'I still can't imagine a more depressing way to spend a night,' said Jim.

Had I known the horrific way the evening was to end, I'd have agreed with him.

Chapter Three

First of all, I had the show to do. There'd been a lot in the papers recently about illegal immigrants flooding into the country from Eastern Europe and being put up in posh hotels whilst they waited for their generous handouts from the Government. Council tenants waiting in vain for repairs to be done in their houses were naturally resentful of this and made their feelings known.

As an act of solidarity with the British taxpayer, I played a record for the unwelcome incomers. Ken, my producer went apoplectic, storming into the studio.

'What do you think you're doing playing that?'

'What's wrong with it? It's The Beatles.'

'I know it's The Beatles. It's the title, that's what's wrong with it. Do you think it's a good idea to dedicate that particular track to the refugees? 'Get Back (to where you once belonged')!' 'Ken was only in his early thirties but he made Victor Meldrew look young. 'You'll have the Human Rights people on our backs.'

'Not refugees, Ken, illegal immigrants. There's a difference. I patted his tweed-jacketed shoulder. 'Don't worry, everyone in the country agrees with me, just wait and see. Don't you read the Letters pages in the papers?'

Sure enough, all the phone lines were lighting up with listeners saying 'about bloody time too'. All good controversial stuff.

'We never had this trouble when Shady Spencer was here,' moaned Ken. 'I don't know why they got rid of him.' Shady had been made redundant in the last outbreak of cost-cutting at the station.

'Downsized I believe?' I nodded sympathetically. Rumour had it he'd got a job playing the background muzak in Tescos. Perfect for him. In later years he might graduate to Chapels of Rest.

After the show, I drove out to Queens Drive and the Simply Single meeting, collecting Jim on the way.

If Maria had seen the talent on display, she'd have realised she'd nothing to worry about.

'Katie Johnson could have given this lot a run for their money,' I commented, as Jim got the drinks in at the bar. A disco was set up at the corner of the square dance floor and the DJ, no spring chicken himself, was playing Alma Cogan's 'Sugartime', circa 1958. He'd got the age group summed up all right.

'Katie who?'

'Don't you remember the old Ealing film, *The Ladykillers*? With Alec Guinness and Herbert Lom and Peter Sellers, the one where they tried to kill the old lady with the parrot'

'By swinging it at her do you mean?'

I ignored the comment. 'Well, Katie Johnson played the old lady, Mrs. Wilberforce.'

'So?'

'I'm just saying, she must have been eighty at the time and she'd knock spots off any of this lot.'

A lady came up to the bar beside us and ordered two rum and peps. She turned to look at us and winked lasciviously. I placed her in her early seventies. She was wearing a lemon mini skirt that revealed acres of crinkly thigh.

'You're new here aren't you?' she smiled. 'I'm Vera.'

Jim held out his hand. 'James,' he said, 'and this is John.' He spoke with a flat Lancashire accent that I hadn't heard him use before.

She shook both our hands and smiled again. Her white plastic teeth were too perfect for the rest of her face, which years of excessive sunburn had turned leathery like a pre-war football. Dixie Dean would have felt at home kissing her.

'Do you live locally, boys?' I felt the "boys" was overdoing it.

'St. 'elens,' answered Jim in his new voice.

'My late husband originated in Prescot. Eccleston Park to be precise.' Just so we'd know she wasn't common. She went on to give us a potted obituary.

At the other side of the room, I could see Ms Grove, looking more than usually bulky in a pair of oversized beige Crimpelene trousers. It reminded me of my days on the "rubber chicken" circuit in the Seventies, drumming with The Cruzads in our later days. 'Yellow

River' and 'The Wigan Slosh' every night. An experience I wanted to forget.

'I'm with my friend, Celia,' Vera told us as she collected her drinks. 'Over in the far corner.' She gesticulated to a lady of similar vintage who was wearing a pair of brass curtain hook earrings of the sort that became obsolete at the end of the fifties along with hula-hoops, panty-girdles and those elasticised rubber bras that I used to trap my fingers in on the back row of the cinema in my teenage years. 'Would you care to join us?'

I noticed Celia sported a walking stick.

'Later maybe,' replied Jim. 'I'm expecting a friend and here she is.'

Ms Grove hove into view and Jim turned to greet her. Vera gave our client a vicious glare and went off to join her septuagenarian friend.

'Have you seen anyone yet who looks like your stalker?' Jim asked her.

'How could I do that when I never actually saw him?' Acid tones.

I looked around the room. Most of the men were in their forties and fifties, dressed in tweed jackets and cavalry twill trousers like extras from a Terrence Rattigan film. The women, if anything, looked somewhat older.

I got a gin and tonic in for Ms Grove and the three of us sat down to discuss strategy. We arranged that she would leave alone at the end of the evening and Jim and I would follow separately, some distance behind, hopefully stalking the stalker. If, indeed, there was one. Simple stuff but Ms Grove looked doubtful.

'What if he attacks me?'

I still felt she was worrying unnecessarily. Even if there had been a stalker, attacking her didn't seem to have been high on his list of priorities so far, but I felt I should reassure her. 'We'll be right behind you.'

'Just make sure he doesn't get away.'

The opening bars of Guy Mitchell's 'She Wears Red Feathers' signalled the next dance. A small man with a thin moustache sidled up to our table, nodded briefly to us and invited Ms Grove onto the floor where they set off on a foxtrot. We watched from the bar as he pushed her round the room, panting heavily. As he barely reached her shoulder, it looked like she was holding him up.

At the opposite side of the dance floor, I saw Vera being propelled round by a refugee from the Addams Family. Her friend Celia was sitting alone. She waved cheekily.

'Christ! It's grotesque.' Jim took a sip of his beer and wiped his mouth with the back of his hand. 'Imagine going back to her place for a jump. She'd have a dressing table full of suppositories and elastic stockings. The sooner we wrap this up the better. We can get on with a proper job. What do you reckon to the Spanish lady, then?'

'I want to study all these notes she's left us then I'll go down and see Rupert Routledge tomorrow. When it comes to working there though, I've still got the problem that someone in the place will recognise me.'

'I was thinking about that. You could say you're doing a programme on the company. That would give you an excuse to nose around the different departments.'

'Maybe.' My eyes followed the client's progress. 'You know, Jim, I can't believe someone's really stalking that.'

'Stalkers are strange people, Johnny. One case we had a few years ago, this bloke suddenly started receiving abuse by e-mail, each one getting more and more threatening. "We know where you live, we're watching your house, we know where your kids go to school", that kind of thing and ending up with death threats. He was a nervous wreck within a fortnight.'

'What did the police do?'

'Told him to change the locks, then we got our anorak boys onto it. '

'Did they get him?'

'Within twenty-four hours. Traced him through the credit card he used to pay for his ISP and do you know what? It was a bloke he'd been at school with twelve years before and had never seen since. Hardly spoke to him at school come to that.'

'Then why…?'

'Our man had a website, he was in business on his own. The stalker came across it one day, recognised his old school buddy and thought "why the fuck has he got all that and I'm on the dole?"'

'And that was it? Nothing else?'

'Nothing. Just good old fashioned envy.'

'What did he get?'

'A warning.'

Guy Mitchell finished his song and the dancers cleared the floor. Ms Grove walked sharply away from her partner and came back to us.

'He asks me up every week. An odious little man.'

'Don't you think you'd be better joining an evening class,' suggested Jim. 'A woman of your intelligence. Wasting your time with this lot I would have thought. Bunch of no-hopers.'

'You're quite right of course. I have done them in the past but this academic term is nearly over. I intend to start Greek Philosophy in September.'

We stuck it out for another hour during which Ms Grove danced with three other men, all of whom she seemed to know. In between, she sat with a couple of women whom I assumed were her new-found friends. At ten thirty, people started to drift away.

'They're probably all going for the last bus,' observed Jim.

Ms Grove disentangled herself from her last partner and came over. 'I'm ready to leave now.'

'Right,' said Jim. 'We'll be right behind you.'

'You will keep me in your sights?'

'Don't worry, we're masters of surveillance,' Jim reassured her.

We accompanied her to the cloakroom to collect her coat, a camel haired creation with a brown fur collar, then we hung back as she left the pub and walked up Queens Drive towards her house, two streets away.

A couple of men went out of the pub after her. One walked the opposite way but the second took the same direction as Ms Grove. Straight up Queens Drive.

'Here we go,' I told Jim. 'I'll go after that one. You wait and see if anyone else comes out.'

I gave them both a full minute; they were not walking fast, then set off behind them. I saw Ms. Grove turn left round the first corner, some two hundred yards down the road. The man was a hundred or so yards behind her. I kept a similar distance behind him.

As he came to the corner, he too turned left. I quickened my pace. I was still fifty yards from the corner when suddenly there was a loud noise like a car backfiring and a squeal of tyres. As I reached Ms Grove's road, a silver Hyundai Lantra came racing towards me, screeched to a brief halt at the junction then wheeled right into Queens Drive in the direction of the pub.

I looked up the road. The pavement ahead of me was deserted. There was no sign of Ms Grove, or of the man following her. I broke into a run.

As I advanced a few yards, I caught sight of something in the distance lying in the gutter. As I came up closer, I recognised the fur collar and knew it was Ms Grove. She was laid face downwards and was not moving. My first reaction was that she'd tripped and knocked herself out falling. I bent over, lifted her by the shoulders and turned her round.

It was then I saw the bullet hole in the middle of her forehead.

Chapter Four

'Killed by a single shot.' Detective Inspector Colin Warnett pronounced the verdict. 'Appropriate that.'

'How do you mean?' I said.

'Well, she was on a Singles night.'

They call it the police's idea of black humour. Prevents them becoming too emotionally involved although, nowadays, the popular option for officers seems to be to sue the Force for post traumatic stress and claim a few grand compensation, early retirement on full pension and a course of one to one counselling with a social worker of your choice.

At two in the morning, I wasn't in the mood for jokes.

We were in the Interview Room at St Ann Street Police Station. Immediately I'd found the body, I'd dialled 999 on my mobile and, to their credit, the police were on the scene within five minutes. I also called Jim, who came straight over from the pub, and after Forensic had done their stuff and Ms Grove was removed to the mortuary, the officer in charge of the investigation invited Jim and I to follow him to the station to make a statement.

Jim didn't know DI Warnett. He'd been gone from the force for over twelve months so, as far as Warnett was concerned, he was history, whatever his former rank.

Warnett himself was a much younger man, barely out of his thirties but his face bore a grim expression that suggested he'd already become disenchanted with the world. No wonder, given the job he had.

He listened while I gave him my version of the evening's events, explaining that we had been working as Ms Grove's minders. He didn't seem impressed by this.

'This silver Lantra you saw, I take it you didn't get the registration number?'

'Fraid not.' I said. One-nil to him.

Warnett sighed. 'What I want to know is, what was it this woman was so frightened of that she hired you in the first place?' He didn't add that we had made a lamentable mess of the task but the implication was there, unspoken.

'She thought she was being stalked.'

Warnett's face hardened in disbelief. 'Stalked? Come on. Why would anyone stalk her? She wasn't famous, she wasn't young, she certainly wasn't pretty.'

'But someone was following her nonetheless.'

'So you say. But where is he now?'

'My guess is he was picked up in the Lantra.'

'But that presupposes that this was a carefully planned killing.'

'Exactly. I think it was. It certainly wasn't a robbery. Her handbag was still by the body and there were no signs of a struggle to suggest she was being molested in any way.'

Warnett bristled. 'Right. So give me one reason why a professional assassin would want to kill an ordinary middle-aged widow?'

Jim and I exchanged glances. 'Pass.' It was a mystery to us too. I realised we knew very little about Dorothy Grove.

The Inspector tried another tack. 'How did you meet her in the first place?'

'She came to see us a week ago saying she was being followed home from this Singles club so we went along to check out her complaint. Tonight was only the second time we'd met her.'

'How much do you know about her?'

'Other than she's twice divorced, nothing.'

'What about her job? Where does her income come from? Who's the next of kin?'

'At a guess I'd say she was living off her alimony. As for jobs or relations, I've no idea.'

Warnett was obviously not happy but realised there was nothing more we could tell him.

'You understand your part in any of this is finished now. However, I might need to talk to you both later.'

'You know where to find us.'

'Gone two o'clock,' Jim said as we left the police station. 'Rosemary'll kill me.'

I couldn't see Maria being too pleased either.

Since Victoria was born fifteen months ago, I'd been spending most of my nights at her flat in Blundellsands. Lately she'd been on at me to sell my apartment in Waterloo Dock and get a place together but I wasn't comfortable with this. I needed my own space. Didn't all men? My apartment was the modern equivalent of the garden shed or allotment. A private refuge. Maria couldn't see this and it had become an ongoing item for discussion.

'At least we can concentrate on the drug company case now,' Jim said.

'How do you mean?'

'Well Ms Grove's murder is out of our hands. Let Warnett and his lot get on with it. It's his case now.' He grinned. 'Good job we got the money up front.'

'Hang on. We were supposed to be protecting the poor woman so at least we should try to find the bloke who killed her.'

'Bollocks. It's the police's job and they've told us they don't want us interfering. Besides, nobody's going to pay us to investigate. We've had two hundred quid, more than covered our expenses so let's leave it alone, eh Johnny. We've got enough on as it is.'

Financially, I supposed he was right although I wasn't happy about it. Morally, I felt we owed it to her, but this wasn't the time to argue about it.

I tried not to disturb Maria when I got in but I reckoned without Roly who took his guard dog duties seriously. Hardly had I put my key in the lock before he bounded to the front door barking furiously, waking Maria and the baby.

There had been a time early in our relationship when, if I came in late, Maria would get up and make me a drink but those days were well gone.

She stirred sleepily as I started to undress beside the bed. 'What time is this?'

'Half past two.'

'Where've you been?' Maybe she didn't say it accusingly but it came out pretty close to that. Years of living on my own and pleasing myself hadn't prepared me for nocturnal versions of The Inquisition. Or was I being touchy?

'I told you, on a case.'

'Till two in the morning?' I paused in the act of removing my trousers. Waterloo Dock was looking good at this point. I always figured that whatever else, my time was my own. But I answered defensively.

'A woman got shot tonight.'

That quietened her.

'She'd hired us to protect her.' I briefly ran over the details. Somehow, I omitted to mention the pub was running a Singles Night but why risk further aggravation?

Maria was awake properly now and turned over to look at me.

'Who would want to stalk some old woman never mind shoot her?'

'If we knew that…' I said. I finished undressing and climbed into bed beside her.

And that was the trouble. I did want to know but, as Jim had rightly pointed out, it was out of our hands and we had enough on as it was.

And by the next morning, there were new events to occupy us.

Chapter Five

I arrived at the office in Dale Street at 10.15 to find Jim already there and with a visitor.

Mike Bennett was a DI with Merseyside Police and our paths had crossed on a couple of occasions in the past.

'Hi, Johnny,' he said. 'How's things? Still got the mutt I see.'

Roly trotted in behind me and allowed himself to be dutifully patted.

'I'm not so bad, Mike. Still playing tennis?'

'The odd game, that's all. My knees aren't what they were.'

'What brings you here then?'

'I've got a problem,' he said. He swivelled his chair round to face me. 'I was just telling Jim here, I've turned my badge in.'

'You've left the force? I never knew this. When did it happen?'

'Only a couple of weeks ago. Tell the truth, I'd had enough. The job isn't what it was.'

'Is any job nowadays?'

'The Selina Stark murder was the last straw.'

'You were involved in that?' I was surprised.

The Selina Stark case had made national headlines. She was a Liverpool girl who'd started out as a singer with a group called X-L-NT who'd a couple of big dance hits before they split up.

The two other members faded into obscurity but Selina blossomed. She was a good talker, with a winning grin and a Scouse accent. Cilla Black Mark Two. She appeared on numerous TV chat shows, compered several charity events and eventually won her own series presenting a fashion programme. Definitely a star on the rise until, one afternoon over twelve months ago, she was found murdered in the city centre.

The public was aghast and expected an immediate arrest but it didn't happen. Weeks went by and opinion was divided as to why such a popular, high profile star had been murdered at all. Favourite option was a stalker, another Mark Chapman, a weirdo obsessed with a celebrity. But there was also talk of a professional killing although nobody had come up with a good reason why there should be a contract out on someone who was, after all, nothing more than a TV personality. Selina Stark was hardly Mafia business.

'I wasn't involved directly, no, but indirectly. You know the story I take it?'

'Everybody knows the story."

'She was found in an alley off Temple Street with a bullet through her head.'

'So I believe. Killed by a single shot, you might say.'

'What?'

'Nothing. Private joke. Go on.'

'Needless to say, the Force got the blame.'

I remembered. After much public criticism in the papers of the ineffectuality of the police, a 36-year-old man from Toxteth, whom the police described as a certified psychopath, was eventually arrested. It was maintained that he had been stalking Selina for months.

'Wayne Paladin his real name was, but he used to call himself Fatty Arbuckle after the 1920s film star. Changed his name by deed poll. He had some sort of fixation about Arbukle.'

'Wasn't Arbuckle the one who was involved in an orgy at a hotel party where a girl died?'

'That's him. The prosecution claimed she was crushed to death beneath his excessive bulk as he raped her.'

'That's right. He was so heavy he burst her bladder apparently.'

'As it happens, that wasn't true. It turned out to be an extortion scam and the case was thrown out, but mud sticks Johnny, as you know, and poor Roscoe Arbuckle was ruined. However, *our* Fatty Arbuckle, alias Mr. Paladin, had already been found guilty of rape in the past, not to mention attempted murder, indecent assault, abduction of minors and GBH.'

'Give a dog a bad name,' I murmured. Roly growled in the corner.

Jim glared at me. 'So what's the problem, Mike? You're not saying he didn't do it?'

33

Mike Bennett spoke quietly. 'That's precisely what I am saying, Jim. Wayne Paladin didn't kill Selina Stark. He was fitted up.'

'Who by?'

'Scotland Yard, Special Branch, MI5, who knows?

'But he was found guilty at the Old Bailey.'

'Oh yes. Twelve good men and true.'

'On what evidence?'

'All circumstantial. They never found the actual weapon but Fatty had once belonged to a gun club. Guilty by association, you see. Then they found pictures of Selina in his flat, her face ringed in magazines, and letters written to her describing what he'd like to do to her and, I'm telling you, it wasn't pleasant.'

'But he didn't post them?'

'If he did, she never told anyone. Then there was CCTV footage showing him hanging outside the TV studios the week before her death. What more do you want? The jury were certainly convinced, and the judge. He recommended that Paladin should serve at least 25 years.'

'And you're saying he's not guilty?'

'Oh, don't misunderstand me, he'd be capable of it. I know Fatty well. I've pulled him in a few times and, I reckon that he deserves every one of those twenty five years, that is in the unlikely event the other inmates don't finish him off before then. But he didn't kill Selina Stark, which means the man who did is free to kill again. And that is what bothers me.'

'But if he didn't do it, why would the police frame him?'

'Public pressure. The girl had been dead for five months and no sign of a result, which was bad PR at a time when the police were asking for more taxpayers' money from the Government. They needed to make an arrest and quickly, especially after the Jill Dando case and how long that took. Paladin was the perfect fall guy. We'd been wanting him put away for some time. There'd been a couple of really nasty incidents that we knew he'd been involved in but we couldn't prove so this way we…'

'Killed two birds with one stone. Very tidy.' Jim looked as if he approved. 'Good for the clean-up statistics too.'

'That too.'

'There's still people who say that that Barry George bloke didn't kill Jill Dando,' I mused.

'I don't know about that, but this one I do know.'

'How can you say that for certain, Mike?'

'Because, Johnny, within ten minutes of Selina Stark's official time of death, I saw Fatty, Wayne Paladin, out on an industrial estate in Speke. He was having a slash outside Palace Chemicals. Fond of pulling his plonker out was Fatty, for whatever reason. I mean, the bloke was thick as pigshit, mental capacity of a backward giraffe. But that means that, short of hiring a helicopter, there's no way he could have been in Temple Street when she was shot.'

'Didn't he tell them that?'

'Of course, but he had no witnesses to back him up.'

'He had you. Why didn't you say something?'

Mike Bennett sighed. 'Let me just say, it was suggested to me that I must have been mistaken in what I saw on a misty night, after eighteen unbroken hours on duty and with nobody to corroborate my story. I suppose, in the end, I didn't want to lose my pension.'

'And that's when you decided to pack the job in?'

'That's right.'

Jim shot me a warning glance. 'More than that, Johnny. Mike intends to find the real killer and he wants us to help him.'

'Why bother?' I said. 'Getting Paladin off the streets seems a good idea to me. At least he can't harm anyone else.'

'Maybe not but the man who killed Selina Stark can. There's a murderer left free to walk the streets and kill again and this offends my sense of justice, which was the reason I joined the police in the first place.'

I could see his point but I didn't think we were best placed to help him. 'If the cream of the country's detectives with all their resources haven't been able to find him, a fat chance we'd have. I take it they've given up looking?'

'Unofficially yes. They say they're keeping a watching brief but it's all baloney. As far as the Force is concerned, the case is closed.'

'The thing is, Mike, we've got this drug company job at the

moment which is likely to keep us busy for a while. Industrial espionage.' I told him about Gabrielle Lorenzo and Derek Routledge Pharmaceuticals. 'Which means I'm not sure we can take on anything else right now. In fact, I shall have to leave you both in a minute, I've got a meeting with Rupert Routledge at twelve o'clock.'

'We'll sort something out, Johnny, don't worry.'

I abandoned the two retired officers to their discussion, with Roly to keep them company. The drug company case was one that would need all my attention and I didn't want to get sidetracked by Mike Bennett's obsessions although I knew how he felt. I felt the same way about Dorothy Grove's killer.

At the same time, I knew there was every chance that Jim would get us sucked into it. What I could not have foreseen was the danger that would bring.

Chapter Six

DRP was situated within a mile of Liverpool Airport or the John Lennon Airport as it was soon to be called. I could think of more suitable people to name the airport after, people who might have been considered to have done more for the city. Bessie Braddock, for example, or John Moores. Or Pete Best.

The building was a three-storey block, constructed predominately of glass with landscaped gardens around a car park at the front. I parked the RAV4 close to the reception and went inside. The vestibule was large and airy, air-conditioned with minimalist furniture and a display of tropical plants beside the entrance. The receptionist at the desk, an Asian girl with a jewel in her nose, was busy at the switchboard.

As soon as she'd finished, I handed her a card. 'I've called to see Rupert Routledge. He is expecting me.'

She glanced at the card. 'Take a seat, Mr. Ace. I'll let Mr. Routledge know you're here.' She gesticulated to a black leather couch with uncomfortable stainless steel arms. On a glass-topped coffee table in front of it were copies of *The Economist* and *Time*. I'd hardly time to open one of them when the receptionist called me to take the lift up to the second floor where someone would meet me.

That someone was Rupert Routledge himself. He was a soft-faced man, in his early forties, already running to fat, pale and with small eyes like currants in an underdone Spotted Dick. A blond Bobby Charlton strand covered the top of his head.

'Mr Ace?' His voice was high, good for a doo-wop group but the wrong timbre for a managing director. I shook his hand firmly. I'd squeezed firmer dishcloths.

'Mr. Routledge.'

He led me to his office. The window behind his desk overlooked the car park. On the desk were two aluminium-framed photographs of small children, obese replicas of their father, one male, the other a girl. No sign of Mrs. Routledge.

'Do sit down,' He gesticulated to the black leather chair in front of his desk. It matched the one in reception. Probably part of a job lot. 'Ms Lorenzo has briefed me about your visit.'

'I've been examining your problem,' I told him confidently, 'and I thought the best idea would for me to come into your factory on the pretext of doing a radio programme on your work here. That would give me reason to move around the place and speak to the work-force without undue suspicion.'

Rupert Routledge leaned back in his chair, eased his stomach onto the desk and clasped his hands behind his head. 'I don't know exactly what Ms Lorenzo told you but I must say I find the possibil-ity that one of my staff is passing on information very unlikely.'

'But…'

'The lady came to me originally with a story that somebody here might be stealing secrets from her clients in Spain. I allowed her into my company as a courtesy. She then tells me that our information also is being misappropriated. To be honest, Mr. Ace, I am not con-vinced.'

'Miss Lorenzo told me that someone tried to shoot her.'

She had obviously not passed on this gem of information to Mr. Routledge because he looked quite shaken. But he recovered quick-ly.

'I don't know anything about that. If it's true, which I doubt very much, it need not have been in any way connected with events here. However,' he continued, 'I'm prepared to go along with this charade but for one week only. If you haven't found anything amiss in that time, forget it. I'm not prepared to have our routines disrupt-ed beyond then.'

I didn't argue. It seemed a strange attitude to take. I didn't know too much about the world of pharmaceuticals but I knew enough about patents in general to realise the vast amount of money they could be worth. If details of DRP experiments were going elsewhere then Mr. Routledge's potential financial loss could be very signifi-cant. I'd have expected him to have been pretty concerned at the thought and very grateful that I was there to help him. What did he know that I didn't?

'Tell me a bit about the set-up here,' I said.

'There are three main divisions. The factory is on the ground floor and this is where all the manufacturing takes place. On the first floor are the offices. All the administration is done from there. On this floor is my office, the boardroom and the research laboratories.'

'Which is where the experiments take place to find new drugs?'

'That is so. We have a team of four full-time researchers. You must realise, we are very small fry in this business. The conglomerates hold the lion's share of the market and our research budget is a drop in the ocean to theirs.'

'So why have a research department? Why not concentrate on the manufacturing side, which I presume is profitable?'

'Very. But to people in the drug industry, finding new cures for diseases is like the Holy Grail. It takes a decade to develop a drug and nine out of ten compounds fail.' His eyes lit up as he spoke. 'The challenge is everything and the rewards, the rewards are beyond comprehension.'

'But what chance has a company like yours, that you yourself admit is a minnow in a big pond, what chance have you got of beating the multi-nationals with all their millions?'

'As much chance as James Dyson had of beating Hoover and creating the world's finest vacuum cleaner.'

I took the point. So what if there might have been a thousand others before James Dyson who had failed in the task.

'The secret,' he continued, 'is to concentrate on one specialised area.'

'Which in your case is Alzheimer's Disease.'

'Yes. For years, all the big charity donations have been going to AIDS research. Celebrities involved, you see. They pull in the money. Plus the pink pound. People don't realise the enormous power of the gay lobby, Mr. Ace, and, let's face it, they're the ones most affected by AIDS, the gay community. Ever since Rock Hudson, woofters have been dropping like flies.'

His choice of expression startled me but I merely said I believed they had.

'And now there's CJD, that could be the next big one. CJD thrives on public fear. Apart from strict lifelong vegetarians, any one of us can get it at any time. Indeed, half the country may be incubating it as we speak. I'm talking about millions of people here. Think the Black Death. Now they're saying sheep might have got BSE too so everybody who's ever eaten a lamb chop or a hamburger will be sweating. You see what I'm saying? Public fear.'

'But surely Alzheimer's is a big concern and a growing one?'

'Yes but people associate it with old age and think they can worry about it later by which time, they reckon, they'll probably have dropped dead from a heart attack or cancer anyway, and it won't matter. So they forget about Alzheimer's and it isn't high on their list of priorities when someone shoves a collecting tin under their nose.'

'It's not just old people who get it though, is it?'

'No indeed, but with life expectancy increasing, the hospitals and nursing homes may soon be overflowing with dementia patients, many needing round the clock care and without the money to pay for it. That could just about finish the NHS, the state it's in. So you can see how big the prize is for the company that makes the break-through?'

I could, which made it all the more puzzling why he was so reluctant for me to investigate possible leaks. I asked him how advanced his research was.

'We're very lucky to have the services of one of the world's lead-ing experts on the disease, Dr. Heather Schneider.'

'German?'

'Scottish. She's married to an Austrian Professor of Geriatrics. They met at Edinburgh University. That's why she's here and not abroad. Her husband works at the Royal Liverpool Hospital.'

I wondered if Hilary knew him.

'And the company in Alicante that Ms Lorenzo represents? They're in a similar field?'

'Yes. Many companies are involved in Alzheimer's research but there are just four of us working in this one particular area of study.'

'Where are the other two based?'

'Sydney and Dublin.'

'So it's a case of who gets there first?'

'Something like that.'

'With the winners scooping the global jackpot?'

'Indeed.'

'And I've got a week to find out if there is indeed a leak?' I treated him to one of my reassuring smiles and he agreed.

'I'll come down tomorrow morning and begin with the Research Dept.,' I said. 'That seems the most likely place to start.'

'Suit yourself.' Rupert Routledge seemed resigned but then he sat up sharply. 'I wouldn't hold your hopes too high.'

But I knew Gabrielle Lorenzo had not been fooling when she said someone had tried to kill her. Huge sums of money were at stake here and I could see we were getting involved in a very dangerous game.

The trouble was, knowing who was on whose side.

Given the circumstances, I was at least sure of one thing. It wasn't a game we could afford to lose.

Chapter Seven

I left DRP and drove back to Liverpool in time for a late lunch at Lucy in the Sky in Cavern Walks.

I'd hardly walked in when Margie nodded over to the back of the café. Hilary was sitting in a corner, her head in a magazine. 'You still seeing her, Johnnie?' Margie whispered.

'Sort of.'

'I know what you mean, love,' she said. 'Shame to lose touch isn't it? Maria all right is she? And the little one?'

'Fine,' I said.

I ordered a curried chicken baked potato and Margie said she'd bring it over. I joined Hilary at the table.

'Johnny.' She threw down the magazine. *New Woman*. Hilary always chose the raunchiest magazines in the rack. 'I was going to ring you this afternoon. I've not seen you for nearly a fortnight.'

'It's been a bit difficult, Hil. Jim and I have got a couple of new cases on that have been taking up our time.'

'And how is the irresistible Maria?' She could never keep the sarcasm out of her voice.

'Fine.'

'There's no need to feel guilty, Johnny. You and I, we're old friends, we go back a long way.'

'I know, Hil, but…'

'You're not worried about her baby?' The use of the *her* didn't escape me. As if I'd played no part in the proceedings. 'It's not going to know anything is it?' Her foot stroked my calf under the table. 'It's my day off tomorrow, Johnny. Why don't you come round to mine in the morning and bring me my breakfast to bed just like the old days.'

She looked ravishing. She'd had highlights put in her blonde hair and she wore a pair of embroidered jeans with a lemon top that showed off her suntanned midriff.

'Do you remember the night we went to the Stripes Club?' she went on.' I wonder if it's still going?'

How could I forget? It was during my very first case. We'd been tracking down a suspect and we'd ended up at Liverpool's equivalent of the Hellfire Club. Hilary had got pretty excited by what was going on there. I recalled the time we'd had at my flat afterwards.

'Probably not. It's over four years ago. A lot can happen in four years.' And didn't I know it?

'What do you say then, Johnny? Tomorrow?'

'One curried jacket.' Margie put the plate on the table in front of me. 'Nice to see you two together,' she said. 'Another drink for you, pet?'

Hilary said she'd have another coffee.

'I have to be in Speke in the morning,' I said, 'interviewing people at this drug company about research into Alzheimer's Disease although it's actually tied in with this case we're on.'

But Hilary was not too interested in cases. 'How about Saturday afternoon then, unless you've got a football match on?'

I hadn't. Everton were away at West Ham and, as it happened, the match wasn't being played on Saturday anyway. Thanks to Sky TV, it had been moved to Monday.

I remembered that Maria had told me she was going to her sister's in Formby on Saturday.

'OK, Hil. I'll come round Saturday afternoon.'

'Great.' She leaned forward and kissed me. 'It'll be just like old times.'

Half of me was glad to be spending time with Hilary again, but the other half felt a certain disquiet. Was this fair to Maria? But I already knew the answer and I wondered if Casanova or Peter Stringfellow had ever suffered pangs of conscience.

Jim Burroughs looked pleased about something when I got back to the office.

'You look happy,' I said. 'Solved the case?'

'Which one?'

'Any.'

'We've got a new one now. I've told Mike Bennett we'll look into this Selina Stark business.'

I groaned but hadn't I known it was inevitable? 'I hope he's paying.'

'On results.' Jim looked sheepish. 'It'll get us a few kudos with the Force not to mention the publicity.'

'I think I'd rather have the money. I can take care of publicity myself and I couldn't give a shit about what the Force thinks. What does Bennett want us to do?'

'Look for motives I think.'

'Jim, you said yourself, Scotland Yard and Special Branch have been involved in this and probably the CIA and the SAS for all we know, not to mention Interpol. What can you find out that they couldn't?' Sometimes, I think running the agency has gone to his head. 'We should stick to social misfits in Singles Clubs, that's our forte. Talking of which, anything new on Dorothy Grove?'

'Not a word but I don't expect it. I told you, it's in police hands now.'

Not as far as I was concerned, it wasn't, but I didn't intend arguing about it at the moment.

'Well, it's all systems go on the drug company case.' I gave him a brief resumé of my trip. 'I'm going over to DRP tomorrow morning. There's four people working in the Research Dept and they're the most likely ones to be selling any secret information so I'm starting there.'

I took Roly back to my flat before I did the show and rang Maria to say I'd be staying there for the night. I don't know why I did that but part of it was a reaction to Maria's attitude to my coming in late. The other part, I guess, was guilt about Hilary.

Ken was waiting for me when I got to the radio station. 'Nothing outspoken today, Ricky Creegan's keeping an eye on you after the refugees yesterday.'

'Shouldn't that be an ear? This is radio or is he getting confused?'

'Oh funny.'

'Did many illegal immigrants ring in to complain then? Oh, I forgot, none of them speak English. That'll be a handicap for them getting a job won't it?'

'That's not the point.'

'But it's just the point,' I told him. 'When the Italians and Russians emigrated to America in the last century, they didn't hide themselves in little groups jabbering in a foreign language to one another and forbidding their women to marry the Yanks. They changed their names to Dean Martin and Irving Berlin and Freddy Cannon, learnt English and became all-American boys.'

Before he could think up a reply, I went on.

'Anyway, Ken, I thought we'd have a competition today to guess how many IRA murderers have been set free by the Government since they came to power.' As I said it, I could see the blood rising from Ken's neck until his face resembled a red onion. 'A week in Belfast for the winner, all expenses paid and a free riot shield.'

'Look...'

'Time to get the show on the road.' I pushed past him into the studio and started loading the night's playlist. With the latest technology, I can pretty well put the show together at home and feed it into the station computer. And to think some people said they'd never give up vinyl. Now we don't even need CD's. How long before we all download music from the Internet and the country's record shops turn into Oxfams overnight?

I played Roxy Music's 'Love is a Drug' for Gabrielle Lorenzo, although I think Alicante night have been out of our listening area, and 'Mothers Little Helper' by The Stones which I dedicated to the staff at DRP.

After the show, I walked over to Casa Bella in Dale Street for an Italian. I had the chicken in red wine and saved a slice of the *pollo* for Roly. It seemed odd not to be going home to Blundellsands. When I stopped to work it out, I realised I'd spent only ten nights at my flat all year. Maybe Maria was right, it was time for her and I to get a place together. Yet... I still figured I needed to keep a place of my own too. A bolthole.

It was nine o'clock when I returned to the flat. Roly was waiting patiently for me. He didn't seem too pleased to have been left on his own. He'd got used to having the company of Maria and Victoria. I gave him the contents of the doggy bag from Casa Bella. 'It's Italian,' I told him and he wolfed it down. Being part lurcher and part deerhound, he was always snobbish about his food.

I couldn't settle. TV never holds my attention for more than five minutes. Even football is better on radio than on the box where you can hardly hear the commentary for the background noise of the crowd. Give me Alan Green on Five Live rather than the TV commentary any day.

I switched to the CD player and gave a spin to a newly released Wee Willie Harris CD, full of great rock'n'roll. Hard to believe he never had a chart hit. 'Lollipop Mama' was as good as anything that came out of America in the late fifties. An hour of this and I was revitalised. I put on a jacket and walked down to the Masquerade Club. They were having a *Stars in Your Eyes* Competition. I got in a Scrumpy Jack and stood watching from the bar.

'Most of the regulars could double for Ronnie Kray,' I remarked to Tommy McKale, the owner, who was hovering nearby. 'The trouble is, he never sang anything.'

Tommy grinned. 'Frankie Fraser came in one night and we tried to get him to do 'I'm mad about you'.'

Onstage was an emaciated girl wearing sandals, a beige sarong, frayed at the edges, and a red bandana. Her voice grated like a train running on rusty rails and red veins stood out on her neck as she performed an off key rendition of 'Me and Bobby McGee', waving her arms about her like a demented windmill.

'Janis Joplin,' I guessed. 'Or is it Ally McBeal on speed?'

'That's what I would have said,' said Tommy, 'but she insists she's Doris Day.'

'She looks anorexic.'

'Lollipops they call them I believe. Heads on sticks.' He sipped a drink of fresh orange juice. 'Vince is on next.'

Vince is the barman, camp as they come but hard as nails in an uneven fight and, with Vince, all fights are uneven.

'Who's Vince doing? Boy George? Julian Clary?'

'Bruce Willis. Doesn't bear thinking about does it?'

'It sounds as bad as Dolly doing Marilyn Monroe.' Dolly is Tommy's grandmother and knocking on for ninety. She works on the door.

'You think that's funny? Just you wait. Dolly's threatened to go on later. She says she's doing Geri Halliwell singing 'It's Raining

Men'. Brought her umbrella specially. I told her to stick with Mae West.'

'Or Katie Johnson.'

'You mean that old bird in *The Ladykillers*.

'I'm impressed,' I said. 'How come you've heard of her? I didn't know you were a film buff.'

'Ealing comedy, late fifties. I'm not, but it's a question that keeps coming up in the quizzes.'

'You go to quizzes?'

'Me and Denis play for The Enforcers. We're top of the second division in the Quiz League.'

I said I supposed it was an appropriate name for them.

'Big Alec's in the team and Corkscrew Colin.'

'I don't think I know him.'

'Used to break into motors with a corkscrew but that was in the old days. He's got a Nissan dealership now. He's a member of our Lodge.'

'I thought he might be.' I wondered if they held regular Masonic evenings in Walton or Broadmoor.

'Anyway, Johnny, to change the subject. How's the wives?'

The question threw me for a second. 'Both well,' I answered casually.

'Only your Hilary was in here the other night.'

'Oh yes. Who with?' I tried to sound nonchalant.

'That doctor bloke she sometimes goes with.'

'Oh, him. Yes, she's known him years.'

I'd never been able to decide whether or not the relationship was platonic and, in view of the fact that I had Maria, I could hardly complain if it wasn't. However, I always like to tell myself they're just friends.

Sometimes I wonder if the doctor thinks the same about me.

'Maria all right then? And the baby?'

'Fine.'

'Christ, you get away with murder. How's the detective work going? Have you got no juicy cases on that Denis and I can help you with?'

The McKale Brothers had been very useful to me on several occasions in the past when I'd needed a bit of muscle.

'Nothing exciting. I'm working on an industrial espionage job at the moment.'

'Spies under the factory bench, eh?'

'Something like that.'

'That's where the big money is now, Johnny, the snoop industry. CCTV cameras, bugging devices, computer hacking. Denis and I have just set up a security company and you'd be amazed at the fucking business we're getting.'

Not true. Nothing that Tommy McKale did would have amazed me. If he'd said he'd got planning permission to turn St. Georges Hall into a ten-pin bowling alley I'd have believed him. He wasn't Worshipful Master of his Lodge for nothing.

'I'll know where to come if I get stuck on this case then.'

'No danger, son, but remember, some of these companies are playing for big stakes and they can't afford anyone to wreck their plans so be careful, Johnny.'

It was a warning I should have heeded.

Chapter Eight

I dropped Roly off first thing at the office and turned up at DRP at ten prompt the following day. Rupert Routledge himself took me to meet his team of researchers.

The head of the group, Dr. Heather Schneider, shook my hand and said she welcomed the publicity my programme would bring, before going on to introduce me to her team.

James Scanlan was a tall, distinguished man in his early thirties with jet-black hair and teeth straight from an advert in *Dentists Weekly*.

Leroy Holden hailed from Brixton and was of Caribbean origin. Six foot five and wearing a Hugo Boss suit, as opposed to the white laboratory coats of the others, he looked more like a barrister who played basketball at weekends.

Next to Leroy, Alison Whyte was tiny by comparison, but quite beautiful. She had dark hair, a sallow complexion and the sort of figure that trendy designers used for perfume bottles.

I explained to them that the programme I was making was a broad look at the work of several local manufacturing companies. Consequently, I wanted to get an insight into the various activities within the firm.

I thought it sounded reasonable enough and I just hoped they felt the same.

After the introductions had been made, the other three went into the lab to start their day's work but Dr. Schneider stayed behind.

'What is it exactly you need to know?' she said. She had red hair and freckles, not an easy match for fashion coordination, but I thought the black trousers showing below her uniform looked fine. I put her age at about thirty-five. I could just about understand her broad Scottish accent. Some good had come from watching *Taggart*.

'Just general stuff, really. Mr. Routledge tells me you're searching for a cure for Alzheimer's Disease. It must be an expensive business.

I imagine the chances of success must be affected to a great extent by the amount of funding you can attract.'

'That's right, especially for a small company like this.'

'Does all your money come from donations?'

'Most of it. We do apply for various grants and, of course, there are profits ploughed back from the commercial side of the operation but charities form the main bulk of our income.'

'Mr. Routledge has been telling me about the competition with other companies to find this cure. Might this not mean there's danger of industrial espionage?' I tried to make it sound flippant. 'Sort of James Bond meets Louis Pasteur.'

Dr. Schneider's eyes narrowed. 'Exactly what angle is your programme taking on this, Mr. Ace? Roger Cook meets John Pilger perhaps? Price fixing cartels amongst drugs manufacturers?'

'I was merely interested in this idea of a first to the post situation, Dr. Schneider, that's all. It's a bit like a gold rush, isn't it? Winner takes all. What happens if you make an important breakthrough? That knowledge would be worth something to your competitors.'

'So one of us might sell it on? Is that what you're suggesting?'

'I'm suggesting nothing. I'm just, as you say, looking at angles.'

'We work on this night and day, Mr. Ace. We are professional scientists who are doing a valuable job to help mankind.' Her cheeks reddened as she spoke, matching her hair. No wonder they say fiery redheads. 'We are not in it for the money. If it was money I wanted I'd be working in private medicine. This is my vocation.'

I let it rest at that. No sense in antagonising her. Besides, I believed her. To a point. But everybody is in it for the money to some extent. Nobody works for nothing. The question was, how much money would it take to make Heather Schneider sacrifice her principles? And who might offer it?

'Would you like to look round the laboratory, Mr. Ace?'

I followed her through into a large room, which occupied almost the entire top floor of the building. Amongst the various items of scientific equipment I noticed a bank of cages containing small white rodents.

'My mother used to have a rat,' I said. 'A pink one. When she was eight. She used to take it to school inside her blouse and frighten the teachers with it.'

'These are actually mice,' said Dr. Schneider. 'They're the most suitable animals for this particular branch of neurological research.'

'And how near are you too finding a cure for Alzheimer's?'

'We make advances constantly but they're only small advances. All pieces of the jigsaw though.'

'What about this human genome project that been in the papers?'

'That's another branch of research. There are all sorts of revolutionary experiments taking place these days including gene therapy and work on stem cells. Mostly it's about prevention rather than cure.'

'And what is DRP's particular angle?'

'Oh we're definitely on the side of cure. Finding a drug which we can patent and licence which will either alleviate, slow down or halt the disease.' She stopped beside a desk where Alison Whyte was busy feeding data into a computer. 'Can I leave you with Alison, I have some calls to make.'

Alison told me to pull up a chair and she'd explain the figures on the screen. I fetched the chair but the computations were beyond me.

'How did you get a job like this?' I asked her.

'I did post-grad medical research at university for a few years but I got fed up of the cloistered atmosphere so, when I saw this job advertised, I applied and I've been here ever since.'

'How long's that?'

'Just over three years.'

'You like it?'

'Love it.' She lowered her voice. 'I preferred it when old Mr.Routledge was in charge, mind you.'

'That would be Derek, I take it?'

'That's right. He started the company but he stepped down last year for Rupert to take over.'

'What don't you like about Rupert?'

She made a shivering motion. 'He gives me the creeps. Something about him.'

'But work-wise he's O.K?'

'Mmmm. Sometimes. But I don't think he has Old Mr. Routledge's vision.'

I raised my eyebrows to encourage her to continue.

'Derek Routledge was an idealist. He looked on drugs as a weapon in the fight against disease. Rupert thinks of them as money-makers.'

'Maybe you have to think like that to succeed in business nowadays.' She looked at me sharply. 'I'm only playing Devil's Advocate,' I quickly assured her. It was something I did every day on the show. 'I can see your point, Alison.'

'Yes, well. Money isn't everything.'

'But the company needs to make a profit to finance the research.'

'Oh, I know that. It's just…I don't know.' She shook her head. 'It's just different wavelengths I suppose.'

I stayed a few minutes more with Alison then moved on to Leroy Holden who was dissecting a mouse on the far bench. He carefully slit open its skull and lifted out a portion of brain, which he placed under a microscope.

'We feed them a controlled dose of our latest drug compound and see the effect it has on the nervous system. This mouse has got Alzheimer's Disease.' He arranged the brain tissue on the slide and peered through the lens.

'I bet it didn't before it fell into your clutches,' I thought. He must have read my mind because he informed me the creature had been bred especially for the purpose and had not suffered at all during its short life.

Dr Mengele had doubtless said something similar to anyone expressing concern about the several million Jews he'd experimented on.

'What line of work did you do before you came here?' I asked him. It was a silly question. This was hardly the sort of job you'd find yourself headhunted for if you got fed up of working for the Halifax Building Society.

'Nothing. I went to university to do a degree in Biochemistry then, after I left, I spent five years enjoying the life of a playboy on the Riviera. My parents are very rich, you see. I lived on board their yacht which was moored at St Jean Cap Ferrat.'

'What made you settle down to a mundane life?'

He smiled but not with his eyes. 'I got married. My wife, Sangria, is a doctor. She made me see I should use my knowledge for something worthwhile.'

'Another doctor. Dr. Schneider's husband is a doctor.'

'My wife specialises in Psychiatry. Incidentally, my life is not mundane. I find this work absorbing.'

'I stand corrected.'

'And to succeed would be the ultimate reward.'

'By succeeding, you mean finding a cure for Alzheimer's?'

'Precisely.'

I thanked him and looked around for James Scanlan but he was nowhere to be seen.

'If you're looking for James, I think he's gone to the University for some papers,' said Alison. 'He should be back after lunch.'

'You work in conjunction with the University then?'

'James does some part-time lecturing on one of their science courses. In return, we have access to their information resources.'

I went along to Dr. Schneider's office and thanked her for her time.

'I hope it's been useful for your programme,' she said.

'Very. I'll arrange to bring the recording equipment down in the morning and do a few interviews. It shouldn't take too long. Hopefully, I'll be able to talk to Mr. Scanlan then.'

'Are you going down to see the factory now?'

'Maybe tomorrow,' I said. 'Thanks again.' I told her I could see myself out. I didn't particularly want to bump into Rupert Routledge again. I took the lift down just one floor and made my way through the open plan office. I estimated there were perhaps twenty people sitting in front of monitor screens. A few of them looked up as I passed but nobody took any particular notice of me.

I walked down the last flight of steps at the opposite end and found myself at the far corner of the factory. Perhaps as many people again were working down here amid the clatter of machines.

They all wore white coats and masks. Radio City blasted out on the Tannoy.

I didn't venture in but looked for the door leading to the car park outside and walked round the building to where the RAV4 was parked.

None of the three people I'd spoken to in the laboratory had shown much interest in the financial aspect of their employment. Holden was already mega rich and the other two seemed to regard their work more as a vocation. I didn't know yet about James Scanlan. He, for the moment, was the Unknown Factor. Had he been trying to avoid me?

It did seem to me that if there was a leak at DRP, the Research Dept was where it would stem from. I couldn't see the people who worked in the office or the factory having easy access to the data in the labs and, even if they had, would they be able to interpret it?

I drove back to Dale Street where I found Jim waiting for me at the office. 'Get some lunch in, will you,' he said. 'I'm starving but I can't go out, I'm waiting for a call. And take that thing with you.' He kicked out at Roly who was sleeping peacefully under the desk. 'It's been farting all morning. Place smells like a midden.'

'It's your own fault. I told you not to give him that spicy bean-burger yesterday.'

I walked Roly down to Toffs for a couple of oatmeal bread sand-wiches filled with tuna salad and two bottles of freshly squeezed orange juice and took them back to the office. Tommy McKale's healthy eating habits were obviously rubbing off on me.

'About Dorothy Grove, Jim,' I said when we got back.

He took his sandwich and drink without looking at me. 'That's finished, Johnny.'

'No it's not. I'm not giving up on this one. I want you to do a bit of checking this afternoon, give you a chance to use your contacts.'

Jim looked at me suspiciously. 'What sort of checking?'

'We've got her address on file. See what you can find out about her. Run a credit check. Find out if she was in debt. Where did her income come from? Where did she used to work before she retired? If indeed she was retired? Was she telling the truth about her husbands? They could have both been shot too for all we know. Has she got a criminal record?'

'OK, OK, you don't have to tell me. What are you going to do?'

'I thought I'd go and have a word with her neighbours. I might pick up a bit of gossip.'

'And I say you're wasting your time.' He corrected himself. 'Our time.'

Maybe he was right but it wouldn't stop me. I was determined to find out who had killed Dorothy Grove.

Chapter Nine

I took Roly with me and parked the car outside the pub we'd been at two nights before. I then traced my steps along the road where Ms Grove had walked to her death.

It was tree-lined, the houses were 1930s semis and it was quiet. No other pedestrians were about. I guessed most of the occupants would be at work; it was too early for kids coming out of school and I imagined that any retirees would be tuned into Jerry Springer or one of the innumerable 'celebrity chefs' that proliferate on TV. As most people in these days of ready made meals have never peeled a potato and wouldn't have the faintest idea what to do with a packet of flour, I don't know who watches these programmes.

Dorothy Grove had lived at number 42, towards the far end of the road. I stopped outside number 44. The front room window was bereft of curtains and, with the sun behind me, I was able to see some way into the room. An upright piano with sheet music stood against the opposite wall on which was hung a large Victorian landscape with a gilt frame. The wallpaper was of a floral pattern, predominately brown.

I rang the bell and an elderly man opened the door. Talk about colourfully attired; he wore carpet slippers, a pair of fawn cords, a striped blue shirt and a red and yellow bow tie. All he needed was a straw hat and he could have played Archie Rice. Roly growled and he stepped back nervously.

In the background I could hear Billy Butler's afternoon show on Radio Merseyside. He was introducing Ann Breen's 'Pal of my cradle days', the record that stayed in the charts for a longer time than any other. I wondered what had happened to Wally, his old sidekick. Probably watching the TV chefs with everybody else.

'I called about the lady next door,' I began, pulling at Roly's lead. 'Ms Grove'.

'You'd better come in. She's dead you know.'

He led me into the front room and motioned me to sit on a

dralon-covered settee. He sat at the opposite end. 'Maxie Leather,' he said offering me his hand.

'Johnny Ace. I'm a private investigator. I've been working for Ms Grove.'

'Really?' He perked up at this. 'In what capacity may I ask, if that's not too impertinent?'

'I'm afraid I can't tell you that. Confidential.' I touched my nose conspiratorially. 'Had she lived here long, Maxie?'

'About ten years. Her husband cleared off a few months ago. I don't blame him. She's ferocious.' He corrected himself. 'Was.' He saw me looking at the sheet music open on the piano. '*The Boy Friend*', he volunteered. 'I first saw it in 1959, with Julie Andrews. Wonderful girl, our Julie. Would you like to hear a bit?' Without waiting for an answer, he leapt across the room, perched himself on the mahogany stool and treated me to a rendition of 'Room in Bloomsbury' on the piano.

Roly whined intermittently throughout the number though I suspect he thought he was singing along.

'Very good,' I said, as he returned to his seat. 'Do you play professionally?'

'Used to. I started in the London shows at the end of the War after which it was a long slow decline round the provinces until the work there dried up. Eventually I was reduced to doing amateur productions with the odd hotel or bar gig for pin money. Even Charlie Kunz would find it hard making a living today.'

'Unless he switched to rap,' I thought.

'You're the Johnny Ace that's on the wireless at teatime, aren't you?'

I admitted I was.

'Thought I recognised the voice. I liked that version of 'I Get a Kick Out of You' that you played last night, the one by Dolly Parton.'

'It's on her new album,' I said. '*Little Sparrow*.'

'Of course, I remember Cole himself singing it although he never really had the voice you know, not even for his own songs.'

'Ms Grove,' I persisted. 'What did she do?'

'Good heavens, what didn't she do? She was one of those committee women, always organising something or other.'

'I meant her job.'

'Oh, she didn't have a job. Housewife I suppose you'd call her if that isn't a derogatory term nowadays.'

'It probably is but I wouldn't let it worry you. What committees was she on?'

'Don't ask me. I know she was big in the Neighbourhood Watch and the Residents Association and she led the 1999 Clean Up The Street Campaign against persistent dog poo.' He glanced warily at Roly as he spoke. 'And I believe that she had a position with the Methodists.' He gave a shrill laugh. 'Flat on her back probably, with her legs in the air,' and rubbed his hands together.

'What did her husband do?'

'He was in cement.'

'What?'

'Had some big contracts, I believe, civil engineering jobs and the like. God knows what happened to him. Word is she took him for every penny, poor blighter.'

'He could have started up again. Tell me, have you ever seen Mr. Grove at the house since they parted?'

'Oh, he wasn't Mr. Grove. Grove is her maiden name. She reverted to it soon after the divorce. She was Mrs. Morton when they first came here and, before that, I believe, she was Mrs. Prescott.'

'Interesting. You didn't know Mr. Prescott too by any chance?'

'No. They say he's disappeared to somewhere out Saudi way. The further away from her the better I shouldn't wonder.'

I tried again. 'You were saying, Maxie, did you see Mr. Morton at all after the split?'

'Funny you should ask that. I thought I saw him walking down the road a couple of weeks ago. Looking very furtive. Of course, with the street lights the way they are, I could have been mistaken. I'm used to seeing him in a car.'

'Not a silver Lantra by any chance?'

'No, they had a Mondeo estate, a blue one.'

'Did Ms Grove have any regular visitors that you know of?'

'Only her niece. She came every Sunday to see her.'

'Local is she?'

'Works in Lewis's I believe, in town.'

'What's her name?'

'Elsie. Elsie Wishart. She's in Ladies Casual Trousers.' He chortled. 'All my life I've been trying to get into ladies casual trousers,'

'Boom boom. The old ones are the best, eh Maxie?' I smiled. I'd heard Jackie Hamilton use that line.

'A pleasant woman, Elsie, if rather plain.'

'I might go and see her.' I thanked him for his help.

'You think it was murder then? I thought so,' he added without stopping. 'There have been rumours on the street.' He made the district sound more like Harlem than Stoneycroft. 'You know how it is, how people talk?'

'And what's the general opinion on the street?'

'The husband,' snapped Maxie instantly. 'Morton. Come back to get his revenge on her.'

'Thanks, Maxie. I'll let you know how I get on.'

I walked the few steps past Ms Grove's empty house to No 40 but there was no answer there so I decided to call it a day.

'Any joy with the neighbours?' asked Jim when I returned to the office.

'Could be. I spoke to this old queen called Maxie, next door. He reckons most of the neighbours have the husband down for it.'

'Sounds plausible. The spouse is always the first choice and by all accounts, she took him to the cleaners. He'd have the motive all right.'

'I'm not sure. It seems an unlikely way for him to go about it.'

'Never discount anything, however unlikely,' said Jim. 'First rule of police work.'

'Maxie did say he thought he saw him skulking near the house recently,' I admitted, 'but if he was the stalker, who was driving the Lantra?'

'The hired killer maybe. The husband was merely there to finger her.'

'Mmm. I'm not convinced. What about you? What have you uncovered about our mystery lady?'

'Not much. No debts, no criminal record. She had a private income from investments her late father left her.'

I raised my eyebrows. 'You mean she was loaded?'

'Not really. They brought in enough to keep her but I don't imagine she lived up to the standard she was used to while they were married. Unless the alimony payments were high of course.'

'Don't you know?'

'Give me a bloody chance, Johnny. You've not been gone two hours. Anyway, I thought he ended up with nothing after the divorce?'

'You're right. We'll assume he wasn't sending her anything.'

'Even if he had got back on his feet, he'd make sure she didn't find out, if he had any sense.'

'True. What about children?'

'None.'

'And she didn't have a job?'

'Not a paid one but she belonged to several committees.'

'That ties in with what I heard.'

'So all we've got so far is the husband,' said Jim.

'I don't suppose it was a mistake? They got the wrong target?'

'No. Remember, Johnny, she told us she'd been followed on two previous occasions so they'd had a couple of trial runs.'

'If it was Morton that set it up, he wouldn't have needed the trial runs.'

'I wouldn't rule him out altogether. What did you say he did for a living.'

'According to Maxie, he's in the cement business.'

'Can't be him then,' grinned Jim. 'He'd have put her under the M6, no messing. How about Hubbie Number One?'

'He's hanging out with the Arabs. I have got another lead though. Maxie told me Ms Grove had a niece come to visit her every week. Works at Lewis's.'

'Are you going to see her then?'

'Tomorrow. Right now I need to do some swotting up on those DRP notes before I go back to that factory in the morning.'

I took Roly back to the flat, made myself a pot of tea and spent an hour pouring over the information that Gabrielle Lorenzo had gleaned from the Alicante factory and Derek Routledge's place.

She'd put in a lot of footwork but, in the end, there wasn't much in the way of concrete evidence. The boss of the Alicante operation, Paulo Romero, had suspected that someone was sending out information and he instructed El Greco Detection to investigate.

Their operator obtained a position in the company and set a trap with the result that they were able to identify the culprit as one of the research workers, Guiseppe Roma. Before they could apprehend him, Roma disappeared. They went round to his apartment but he'd left without trace and had never been seen since. A snapshot was enclosed. It showed a small dark haired man with a prolific moustache curling over his lips.

At this point, Gabrielle Lorenzo was called in. She was installed in the research department as a consultant, ostensibly to check over the company's computer network with a view to upgrading it. That was the story. In fact, Gabrielle was actually a top grade computer boffin and, after a few hours tinkering with Roma's P.C., she was able to discover the link he had made with Liverpool.

As one of the other four firms in the world doing this particular research was situated in Liverpool, suspicion naturally fell on them so she followed the trail and took a plane over and assumed a similar role at Derek Routledge Pharmaceuticals.

It was when she delved in to the DRP computers that she found a similar situation to that at Alicante; someone was sending out classified information, but because the computers were linked, she was not able to say whose machine the e-mails were sent from.

I examined the notes she had made on the research team. Beside each name she had inscribed a few brief words. Heather Schneider was "well respected in her field" and "averse to criticism"; Alison Whyte was "idealistic" and Ms Lorenzo had questioned whether she might be "susceptible to overtures from idealists" which could have been interpreted in a number of ways. Leroy Holden she didn't seem too keen on, "single minded, possibly obsessive", yet alongside his name she had written in pencil the word "dishy".

But the most interesting feature was the comment next to James Scanlan's name. There was just one word. "Absent".

James Scanlan had disappeared before I could talk to him too. Somehow, I didn't think this was a coincidence but what could he be hiding?

Chapter Ten

Roly came with me to the radio station though I left him in the car whilst I did the programme. Ken had been adamant about not letting him in the studio ever since he nearly ate a talking parrot that was guesting on the afternoon chat show.

Afterwards, we went straight over to Maria's. Victoria had already been put to bed and my reception was a trifle frosty.

'Did you have a good time last night?' Maria wasn't smiling.

'So so.'

'Where did you go?'

'I had a drink at the Masquerade, then I went home.'

'On your own?'

'No. I took a couple of the strippers home with me.'

'There's no need to be sarcastic.'

'Sorry.'

'You didn't see Hilary there then?'

'No.' Lying by default. I had seen Hilary but not at the Masquerade. And I took care, of course, not to mention meeting her at Margie's. Lying by omission.

Maria gave up and asked instead about the case. 'What's happened about the woman who was shot? I saw the story in the *Echo*. Have they found out who did it yet?'

'No.' I was glad to move the subject on to less controversial ground. 'It could be the husband. Revenge for being dumped.'

Maria smiled and said she knew something about revenge. I didn't like the way she said it and quickly changed the subject.

'I'm more busy with this drugs case at the moment,' I said, and told her about DRP and the research into Alzheimer's. That led on to a discussion on Euthanasia and the cost of nursing home care in Britain which moved along to a general debate on pensioners and how wrong it was for the Government to make them sell their homes to pay for their nursing home care when people who hadn't saved a penny were allowed in free.

By eleven o'clock, an acceptable harmony had been restored between us. We went to bed and ended up making love just like the old days.

'Will you be home tonight?' Maria asked over breakfast. Her black hair was tied up in a bun, she had no make-up on, she was wearing a lilac dressing gown and she looked gorgeous. Victoria was in her high chair smearing her breakfast over her face and, through the open kitchen door, we could hear Roly lapping noisily at his bowl. Happy families. What could really be better than this? I asked myself.

'Soon after the show,' I said.

'What are you doing tomorrow if Everton aren't playing? Do you want to come with me to Kay's? We could have a meal in Formby later.'

I didn't like to think about Saturday afternoon. 'I thought I might go and watch Tranmere Rovers,' I said. At least I'd have a reason for being on the Wirral. 'Tell you what, why don't we go for the roast lunch at the Cheshire Lines on Sunday instead. We haven't been there for ages.'

The Cheshire Lines is an old fashioned little pub in the back streets of Southport, one of the few left that hasn't been bought and given a bland makeover by one of the big breweries. Forget your measured portions of microwaved frozen crap, Marge at the 'Chesh' serves home-cooked meals and food doesn't come any better than that.

'Oh yes, that's a good idea Johnny. Victoria loves the trifles there, don't you darling?'

I kissed them both, said I'd be home for eight and set off for Speke. I was at the DRP factory for nine, armed with my mini disc recorder and microphone.

'I'm afraid James Scanlan isn't in today,' Heather Schneider informed me. 'He's rung in sick but the other two are here.'

'Thanks,' I said. Was this significant? Could James Scanlan be deliberately avoiding me? And, if so, why?

I spent a quarter of an hour recording Dr. Schneider's views on the research of Alzheimer's. It was all good stuff. She spoke authoritatively and I could see why she headed the department. Towards the end, I asked her innocently if they exchanged information with researchers in other countries.

'Certainly not. Every bit of new information we discover is a closely guarded secret.' You wish, I thought.

I interviewed Leroy next. He left his mice long enough to explain to me exactly what his job entailed, which seemed to be mainly vivisection. I challenged him about the moral aspect of this and he said it was justified by the numerous medical advances that had been bestowed on the community over the years. I didn't press the point. I wasn't doing a Jeremy Paxman.

Alison Whyte seemed to be more concerned with the cataloguing and data collection side of things. She wrote up the results of experiments and did the necessary calculations on her computer. Maybe, I thought, the person with the best opportunity to transfer information to another, illegal, source.

After I'd finished the interviews, I sought out Rupert Routledge.

'Well, have you found anything?' he asked.

I had to admit I hadn't and, truth to tell, I couldn't see how further visits to the Lab would achieve anything. Gabrielle Lorenzo was a computer expert who'd had the opportunity and the knowledge to examine the machines in Alicante and trace the leaks. At DRP, she'd been able to discover that there was a leak but no more. And, if she couldn't find out with her technical know-how, then I had no chance.

My best bet, I decided, would be to talk more with the researchers on a casual basis away from the company and see if they dropped any hints. I couldn't believe it wasn't one of the four researchers who was responsible for the leaks.

Routledge seemed relieved. 'You're finished here then?'

'For the time being.'

'Good. Well, thanks for your help anyway. I'm just relieved you were able to confirm my confidence in my workforce.'

This wasn't what I'd said but I let it pass.

On my way out, I stopped by Alison's desk and asked her if she'd care to have some lunch with me.

'I only get an hour.'

'That's OK. Where should we go?'

'We've got a canteen here.'

'No. Too much like work.'

'There's a pub half a mile down the road.'

'That'll do. What time?'

'Half twelve.'

'I'll be outside the staff entrance. I'm driving a black RAV4.'

It was only 11.30am. I took the recording gear to the car and drove across to the airport for a cup of tea and a croissant while I waited. The departure lounge was full of straggling queues. Since Easyjet arrived with their £35 return flights to France and Switzerland, traffic had grown exponentially and major construction work was already underway to enlarge the building.

Alison Whyte was just coming out of the DRP offices as I pulled into the car park, dead on twelve thirty.

'I wish taxis were this punctual,' she said, as she climbed into the passenger seat.

She directed me to the pub and ten minutes later we were seated in the lounge bar with our drinks.

Alison wasted no time in getting to the point. 'So, what did you want to ask me?' she said.

'What makes you think I want to ask you anything? I might have just fancied taking you out for lunch as a prelude to seducing you.'

She had the grace to blush. 'I don't think so.'

'Well, first of all, have a look at the menu and see what you want to eat.'

She glanced at it briefly. 'I'll just have a toasted sandwich if that's all right with you.'

'Whatever. Ham, cheese or tuna?"

'Cheese and onion.'

I went to the bar and ordered two toasted cheese and onion toasties.

'Well?' she demanded when I returned.

For a brief moment, I considered telling her I was running an investigation but I quickly remembered what had happened to

Gabrielle Lorenzo when someone had found out that she was spying. She was shot at. The same thing could happen to me if they realised I was following in her footsteps. And this time, the bullet might not miss. Alison Whyte was still a potential suspect.

'I just wanted to fill in a few gaps in the interview that's all.'

'Like what?'

I felt she was being suspiciously aggressive, always a sign that there was something to hide. I tried to phrase my question to indicate a parochial interest as befitted a local radio station.

'I never asked how you stand in relation to your competitors. Would you say Liverpool was at the forefront of the race to find a cure or are Australia, Ireland or Spain ahead of you?'

Her shoulders dropped and she relaxed somewhat. 'You're turning it into a competition like a medical Olympics or something.'

'Not a bad analogy. After all, you can't deny it is a race and first past the post scoops the jackpot. Tell me, what are the chances of any one of you being headhunted by the other companies?'

'They wouldn't know us.'

'I don't think that's true, Alison. Companies nowadays are very aware of potential recruitment possibilities. What if the Australian company, say, offered to double your salary and give you a company flat overlooking Sydney Harbour, wouldn't you jump at the chance?'

She laughed. 'Maybe, but I don't think it's likely to happen.'

'Leroy wouldn't need it, of course. He owns most of the Caribbean already.' She laughed again. 'And Dr. Schneider seems pretty well set up. Perhaps James would be tempted.'

'I don't think so. He has a fiancée in England, they're getting married next year.'

'She could go with him. Honeymoon in Bali on the way? Sounds good to me. The salary hike would come in useful.'

'I don't think James does too badly,' she said. 'He's just bought himself a new BMW.'

'The 300?'

'No, the 700 series. Likes to pose round town does our James.'

'He lives in Liverpool then?'

67

'Yes, of course. He and his girlfriend have just moved into a new apartment in the Kings Dock.'

I knew it well. Not far from my own place and even more expensive. This was the sort of thing I wanted to hear unless, of course, he was marrying an heiress.

'What does his fiancée do?' I asked.

'Nothing wildly exciting. I think she works in telesales or something like that.'

So she wasn't contributing much to James Scanlan's income.

'I've still not managed to interview your James for the programme. We keep seeming to miss each other.'

'Try the University. That's where he hangs out a lot.'

'I will. Tell me, you said you preferred working with Derek Routledge. What was he like, the old man?'

A wistful look crossed her face. 'Charming. A true gent.'

'When did he start the company?'

'Soon after the War. Built it up from nothing. I think he'd like to have been a doctor but he never got the qualifications.'

'Why did he retire? He owned the company, he didn't have to go.'

'I don't know. I think Rupert was putting pressure on him. Rupert was always more profit-orientated and he wanted a free hand to run the business. Then Derek's wife became ill and I think he wanted to spend more time with her so he decided to let Rupert go ahead and take over.'

'And has it worked? Have the profits gone up?'

'Actually, yes, they have. But Rupert's made a few enemies along the way.'

'What sort of enemies? Jealous competitors?'

'Those too. But he's had… look, I shouldn't be telling you this.'

'Strictly not for broadcasting,' I assured her.

She looked doubtful but carried on. 'He had a couple of anonymous letters a while back.'

'Saying what?'

'Threatening him.'

'How do you know this?'

'I opened one by mistake. It wasn't recently; it was shortly after he took over the company from Derek. Block capitals on a blank sheet of paper. I can remember the exact words. RUPERT ROUTLEDGE YOU WILL DIE. THE COURT HAS DELIVERED ITS VERDICT. I thought it was a joke of some kind and put it back but I saw his face when he opened the envelope himself.'

'Scared?'

'Ashen. He was shaking. I don't think it was the first one he'd had.'

'Why do you say that?'

'I don't know really. I suppose because he didn't look surprised. Just frightened.'

'What did he say?'

'To me? Nothing. He walked away.'

'Has he had any more since?'

'Yes. Or rather, I think so. I took to checking the mail each morning and a similar envelope arrived a few weeks later, but I never saw what was inside.'

'"The Court", you said? Does it mean anything to you?'

'Not a thing.'

'Strange.'

At this point, the toasted sandwiches arrived and we concentrated on the meal. Afterwards, to allay any lingering suspicions she might have had about my real reason for inviting her to lunch, I asked her if she'd like to have dinner with me. 'I told you I wanted to seduce you,' I smiled.

'So you were after my body after all.' She grinned. 'Sorry, Johnny. I'm spoken for.'

His name was Phil, she told me. He was 38, supported Liverpool and he worked in a bank. She said he was worried about his job as more people were switching to Internet banks for the considerably better interest rates. I said I could understand; I'd have been worried in his shoes. Despite Natwest's protestations to the contrary, it seemed to me that more banks than ever were being converted into wine bars or funeral parlours.

'Thanks for the lunch, anyway,' she said. 'Will you be coming back to work?'

'If I can't get hold of James this afternoon, I'll be round again next week to see him.'

I made her take down all my phone numbers in case she ever wanted to get in touch with me. I didn't know what she might be able to tell me but I liked her and I felt a day could come when I could use an ally inside DRP, although she was still on my suspect list.

I dropped Alison off at the factory then drove back into town to Liverpool University. I parked in Abercrombie Square. Back in the Sixties, this was at the heart of the Red Light district but now it's part of the University campus. Probably more sexual transactions are conducted there than ever before but these days it's the students who are at it; enthusiastic amateurs rather than ladies of the night.

'I'm looking for a James Scanlan,' I told the receptionist.

She consulted her book of extension numbers. 'I'm sorry, we have nobody of that name.'

'He lectures in medical science.'

'Scanlan, you say?' She checked again. 'No, sorry. Are you sure he's not at John Moores?'

'Definitely not. University of Liverpool.'

She turned the book round and pointed at the page. 'See for your-self.'

I examined the list. Savage, Robert; Sawyer, Graham; Scafone, Giovanne; Scott, Jim.

Of James Scanlan, there was no mention.

Chapter Eleven

I'd had enough of DRP for one day. Time, I thought, to have another crack at Dorothy Grove's murder. I wanted to talk to her niece in Lewis's.

I left the RAV4 in the Button Street car park by Lime Street Station and crossed over the road in front of the Adelphi Hotel, entering Lewis's under the famous fig leaf statue. Hard to believe it had once created such a stir. Nowadays, you could have a neon-lit giant-size plastic dick hanging outside your shop and people would just walk past it disinterestedly and assume that you sold condoms.

I took the escalator to Ladies Wear and sought out Elsie Wishart. She turned out to be a chubby little woman with Edna Everage spectacles and suspiciously golden hair arranged a la Mrs Thatcher circa 1982. I put her in her late forties. She had a stern expression and I could see the likeness to her late Aunt.

Mrs. Wishart?' I began.

'Miss.'

'Sorry.' I handed her a card. 'Your aunt, Dorothy Grove, was a client of mine. I wonder if I might have a few words with you.'

She looked puzzled. 'What would Aunt Dot want with a private investigator?'

I could see we weren't going to retreat to anywhere secluded to conduct the conversation. Luckily, it was a quiet afternoon and ladies trousers, casual or otherwise, didn't appear to be in much demand.

'She was afraid she was being stalked.'

'Stalked? Aunt Dot? How ridiculous.'

'Why do you say that? You know how she died I take it?'

'Yes. She was murdered.'

'And does that appear ridiculous to you too?'

'Of course not. When I say ridiculous, I mean stalking rather suggests a sexual motive, hardly within Aunt Dot's compass wouldn't you say? Whereas killing someone to steal from them…'

'Is that why you think she was killed, a bungled robbery?'

'Why else?'

'She was shot, Miss Wishart, a single bullet to the head. No struggle, no handbag ripped from her grasp.'

Elsie Wishart looked confused. I pressed on. 'Haven't you read the papers? Seen it on TV? Have the police not contacted you?'

'The police? Oh yes, they had to. I'm her next of kin.'

That stopped my line of questioning. 'What about her divorced husbands?'

'They don't count. I'm blood. My father was Aunt Dot's brother. He's well dead now of course.'

'Has she any other family left?'

'No. Only me. She never had children.'

'So you'll be the one who inherits then?' Could this be the first sign of a motive? I waited for her to protest that there wouldn't be much to inherit but she didn't. Instead she readily agreed with me.

'I expect so. Does that make me a suspect then?' She said it in a matter of fact voice.

'Probably.'

'I have an alibi though for Tuesday evening. I was at a bridge party with friends.'

I smiled at her reassuringly. 'I never thought it for a moment.' I didn't bother to suggest she could have hired someone for the job. 'Like I say, your aunt wasn't robbed so can you think of any other reason why someone should want her killed?'

'Uncle Jake was pretty bitter when she dumped him. His business went bust after the settlement.'

'Where is he now? Have you seen him since they split up?'

'No. He went down South somewhere I believe but I heard he'd started up again in the building trade.'

'You knew him quite well, I presume. Would he be capable of murdering her?'

'He had a temper when he'd had a few, I suppose he might have bashed her one in a drunken rage but not cold blooded murder, no.'

'Do you live near your aunt?'

'No. I've got a flat just off Ullett Road. Why?'

'No reason.' Ullett Road, Liverpool 17, bedsit land. I had a couple of houses myself round there. Miss Wishart was not living in the lap of luxury.

'You say you'll inherit. Have you any idea how much?'

'No. I'm seeing the solicitor next week. Aunt Dot always promised me I'd get the house and anything she had left.'

I didn't suppose Ms Grove's recently divorced husband would feel too happy about most of his money ending up with his niece.

I wondered how much Elsie Wishart liked working in Ladies Casual Bottoms. Standing around a shop floor at her age, for eight hours a day, six days a week, didn't seem like fun to me. It was the sort of job that led to chronic lower back problems and varicose veins in later life. Knowing her aunt's death could open the door for her to enjoy a comfortable early retirement, might not this have been enough temptation for her to arrange Ms Grove's premature demise?'

I pondered this as I drove back to the office to collect Roly. I was beginning to find out a little bit more about Dorothy Grove and already I had two possible suspects for her murder, her ex-husband and her niece. Wasn't it John Cleese who said families were always trouble?

I told Jim about my meeting with Elsie but he was more anxious to hear about my day at DRP.

'That's our bread and butter in case you'd forgotten.'

'It's a funny one to solve, Jim. I think maybe they need to get another computer boffin in rather than us; someone who can recover deleted e-mails and messages from the computer hard drives. I'm just having to rely on gossip.'

'Gossip is often the best policy, Johnny, as our old friend DCI Glass in London would say. If people kept their mouths shut, the police would never solve half the crimes.'

'What do you mean, half? They only solve ten per cent as it is.' I could never resist winding him up, but this time he let it pass.

'So what has the gossip told you?'

'For a start, someone sent threatening letters to Rupert Routledge after he took over the operation from his old man.'

'That's odd. Do you think there's any connection with the case?'

'I don't know. I can't see it yet but…'

'What did the letters say?''

'I only know about one. That said, "You will die, The Court has delivered its verdict". No explanation.'

'Why should anyone want Rupert Routledge dead?'

'Not a clue.'

'And I wonder what "The Court" is?'

'Or who.'

'Where did you find out about this?'

'Alison Whyte, one of the researchers. She opened the letter by mistake and she reckons he's had more.'

'Odd he never mentioned it to you. What about the leaks? Do you think they're coming from the Research Department?'

'It's the most likely place. This James Scanlan has come into money of late and he also seems to be avoiding me.' I told him about the University register. 'They'd never heard of him at the Uni.'

'You obviously need to talk to him. When are you going back there?'

'First thing on Monday but I thought I might go over to Cheshire in the morning and speak to Derek Routledge.'

'That's the old man?'

'Rupert's father; the man who founded the company.'

'I thought he'd retired.'

'He has but, you never know, I might find something useful.' I didn't tell him Cheshire was also handy for my afternoon visit to Hilary's at Heswall.

'Worth a try,' agreed Jim.

'But, right now, I'm going home to get changed. I've got the radio show to do.'

Jim pointed to the brown creature asleep under the desk. 'Don't forget your revolting companion over there. He's been stinking the place out. Have you been feeding him on prunes or something?'

'It's the new organic dog biscuits Maria bought him. They go right through him.'

'I suppose you could mount him on a board and stick him on a wall like that Big Mouth Billy Bass thing. Instead of a singing fish you could have a farting dog.'

'Very funny. Come on Roly.' I called out. 'Time for tea.'

'Maria's tonight is it?'

'Yes,' I replied shortly and quickly changed the subject before he could make any comment. 'Regarding Dorothy Grove, Jim. You might check out this Jake Morton, her last husband. Find out where he is, what he's doing.'

'You still think he could have killed her?'

'Maybe. But Elsie Wishart had an equally strong motive.'

'I'm sure DI Warnett is well aware of both of them so why don't you leave him to it. He'll have it cleared up in no time.'

'And what about the stalker?'

'It will have been the husband.'

'OK. So who was in the Lantra?'

'Maybe the car wasn't involved at all. Just passing, nothing to do with the shooting.'

'But the man had disappeared. He must have been picked up by the car.'

'Not necessarily. He could have shot her and run on out of sight the other way.'

'I'd have seen him. I wasn't that far behind.'

'Then maybe he jumped over a garden wall and ran into one of the houses. Perhaps it wasn't the husband at all, perhaps it was one of the neighbours.' He sounded exasperated. 'Look, concentrate on DRP, Johnny, for Christ's sake. There's sound money in that one. This other's just a waste of our time. Leave it to Warnett. We don't work for nothing.'

'That's not what you told Mike Bennett.' That struck home. Jim had the grace to look embarrassed but I pressed on. 'Has anything happened with that Selina Stark business, by the way?'

'Not so far, no.' He looked embarrassed. 'As a matter of fact, I have to admit you might be right about that one, Johnny. I can't see a way forward there. It's been done to death. Fitting up Fatty Arbuckle was a last resort for CID. They'd drawn blanks everywhere else. I reckon we should just forget it.'

'What about Mike Bennett?'

'I'll sort Mike out, leave it to me.'

As least that was one case less to worry about, I thought, but I could not have been more wrong.

Chapter Twelve

Derek Routledge lived in a large detached eighteenth century farmhouse on six acres of land on the outskirts of Chester, Cheshire hunt country, with a Toyota Land Cruiser and a Range Rover in the drive and a splendid view across to the North Wales mountains.

It was a bright Saturday morning as I came off the M53 and drove through the country lanes towards Waverton.

'Forgive me for calling without an appointment,' I said, after I'd been conducted into a spacious lounge and offered a drink. The wood panelled walls displayed a number of gilt-framed Victorian landscapes interspersed with polished horse brasses and the occasional moose's head. The stone fireplace looked large enough to roast a pig in, whilst a suit of armour in the corner did not dwarf the rest of the room. I'd been in less impressive museums.

Derek Routledge was taller than his son and, although nearly thirty years older, he looked the fitter of the two. He was thin but muscular, had a thick head of silver hair and walked with a straight back. Good shape for seventy. He wore a tweed suit in keeping with his surroundings.

'No problem,' he said. 'Tell the truth, I'm glad of the company. Since my wife passed away, I find I've got too much time on my hands.'

It was the perfect opening for me. 'Do you miss running the business, Mr. Routledge?'

His mouth tightened. 'I certainly do. DRP was my life's work.'

'But your son is carrying it on for you.'

He snorted. 'If that's what you call it.' I raised my eyebrows. 'It's not what I'd call carrying on. More like a U-turn.'

'Why's that?'

His eyes blazed. 'Different philosophies, I suppose. Rupert is only interested in profit,'

'Surely that's the idea of going into business?'

'Not in this game. I was in the business of curing people. He's in

77

the business of printing pound notes. Anyway, you haven't told me why you are here, Mr. Ace.

I handed him a card. 'Officially, I have been interviewing DRP employees for a radio programme on the company but, in reality, I have been hired to investigate a leak of information from DRP.'

'My son hired you?'

'Not exactly but he has been most co-operative.' I explained about the Spanish connection and Ms Lorenzo.

'And have you discovered who has been parting with this information?'

'Not yet,' I admitted. 'I think, though, it must be one of the people in the research department.'

'But surely that's the way it should be, a free exchange of information between companies towards the common goal of finding a cure for the disease.'

His answer came as a surprise to me although, after what Alison Whyte had told me about her former boss, perhaps I should have expected it.

'But how do you proportion the cost of the research?'

'You don't. Each company contributes what it can afford from the profits of other areas of the company.'

'I take it Rupert doesn't share your altruistic ideals?'

'He thinks the profit should go into the directors' pockets and, needless to say, he is the chief beneficiary.'

'What about yourself? I presume you are still a director so you'll benefit as well.'

'I contribute privately to the research,' he said stiffly.

'You surely don't approve of the leaks, Mr. Routledge?'

But he would not be drawn. Instead he asked, 'Are you carrying on with this investigation?'

'Yes, of course. Is there any reason why I shouldn't?'

He seemed displeased. 'I think you'd be wasting your time, that's all.'

'But the leak could cost your company millions in lost profits if someone else beats you to a cure.'

'I doubt it. Anyway, I can tell you nothing. I'm no longer

involved in DRP on a day to day basis, in fact I can't remember the last time I visited the office.'

'How do you spend your days now you've retired?'

'I ride, I have a couple of horses in the stables here and I'm a member of the local hunt.'

'Not a popular occupation these days.'

Derek Routledge grimaced. 'Bloody town people. They've no idea how the country works. They shouldn't interfere. Did you know that if you find a fox in your back garden killing your chickens you're not allowed to shoot it unless you have a certain calibre of gun. Any old shotgun won't do. And, of course, you can't have a gun at all unless you can give the authorities a bloody good reason why they should give you a permit to own one.'

'So you set a trap instead.'

He shook his head. 'No, against the law. Wildlife protection. Poison's out too. And gassing.'

'You chase it and club it to death.

'Try catching it. You'd need to be on horseback. And it would run underground. You'd need to ferret it out.'

'Don't tell me. Hounds.'

He grinned triumphantly. 'Exactly. And they're trying to ban it. Wait till the hunts go and the foxes move into urban areas in a big way. A few cats mutilated. Food stolen. Babies attacked. Then the beggars won't be so keen on Basil Bloody Brush.'

He was really getting into it. I only wished we'd been on air. 'Perhaps we can do a phone-in on the subject on my radio programme one day. It's about time somebody put the other side of the argument.'

'I'd like that very much.'

The conversation came to an abrupt end. I felt he'd been relieved the subject had moved away from DRP but I wasn't finished with that subject yet.

As he conducted me to the door, I stopped to ask him the killer question. Years of watching *Columbo*! Catch them when their guard is down. 'Has Rupert ever mentioned anything to you about any anonymous letters?'

'No.' He looked genuinely surprised by my question. 'Why, has somebody been sending them to him?'

'Apparently so.'

'What about? Surely not blackmail? Not having an affair is he?' Mr. Routledge seemed amused at the idea.

'Nothing like that. These were death threats.'

'But why?'

'I thought you might know.'

Now Rupert's father did look worried. 'Well I don't. Has he been to the police? If not, he should go. You don't mess about with things like that.'

'You're right.'

Before I left, I promised to ring him about the radio interview then took the A540 back road out of Chester towards the Wirral.

I switched on the car radio. The Ivy Three's 'Yogi' was playing so I knew it must be Frankie Connor's sixties show on Radio Merseyside. Who else would dare to play that on British radio on a Saturday morning? Brilliant.

I passed the Mollington Banastre Hotel and felt I was in a time warp. I often used to appear there in the sixties with The Cruzads, mostly for 21st parties and wedding receptions for the Chester jet set.

It was one o'clock as I came into Heswall so I decided to stop at the Dee View Inn, overlooking the Lower Village, for some lunch. Hilary was not expecting me till two. Over a bowl of ham broth and a steak sandwich, I tried to make some sense out of the DRP case.

Derek Routledge disliked the way his son was running the business and originally I'd had a wild notion he might have sent the letters but, having seen his reaction, I knew that was out of the question. So, could it be one of the research team who didn't like the way the operation was going? Favourite had to be James Scanlan, the mystery man who seemed to be avoiding me. He was top of my agenda for Monday morning.

But Alison Whyte, too, disagreed with Rupert Routledge's ideas and, if it wasn't either of them, who else inside or outside the team had a grudge against the current head of DRP?

There was something else. Someone had tried to kill Gabrielle Lorenzo, or at least frighten her off, and she could be said to be on Rupert Routledge's side. Was that the reason he'd appeared so strangely reluctant about encouraging the whole investigation? Because he was afraid of being killed himself?

And the person who was most likely to harm him was the person who was passing on the information.

The sooner I could find out who that was, the better chance I had of preventing a tragedy.

Chapter Thirteen

I lay naked in the bed. A tortoiseshell cat sat on the windowsill across the room, keeping a watch for any stray birds that might encroach into her garden. A Skyliners CD played quietly in the background.

'Oh Johnny, it's just like old times.'

Hilary lay beside me, her hand resting affectionately across my thighs under the yellow cotton sheets, her full warm boobs pressing against my chest.

'Isn't it?'

We were in Hilary's cottage in Heswall and the possible execution of Rupert Routledge was the last thing on my mind. Here was a place where I'd spent so many happy nights in the past, although not so many of late.

I stroked her long blonde hair and kissed her and we started all over again. Sex had always been wonderful with Hilary.

'Where shall we go tonight?' she asked me afterwards. The question hit me like a metaphorical bucket of cold water. My expression must have said it all. 'Don't tell me. You're seeing *her* aren't you?'

'What do you expect? Anyway, you were out with your doctor friend the other night.'

'If I sat in waiting for you to take me out I'd grow barnacles.'

Stalemate. It was an opportunity for me to finish it once and for all but I couldn't say the words that would end a relationship that had lasted for most of our lifetimes and she knew I couldn't. But, then, neither could she and we both knew that too.

So I smiled and I said, 'They'd probably suit you,' and I squeezed her hand. We were back from the brink but the brink was where we were doomed to stay. It was that or nothing. There was no going back to the carefree pre-Maria days and to go forward would mean our parting, probably forever.

'I'll make us a drink,' she said at last.

I looked at the clock. 'Is is five already? '

'You mean you have to get back to wifey'.

'No, I mean the full time scores will be on. Pass the remote while you're up. I can check them on Ceefax.'

We drank tea, made conversation, mostly about things we'd done together in the past, and at six o'clock, I said I'd have to go.

'I'll ring you,' I said, at the door. I didn't say when.

'Right,' she said and she didn't ask. But we both knew I would. Sometime. We kissed. How many times had I stood in this doorway? I wondered if I would ever come here again and the thought that I might not made me indescribably sad.

Traffic was busy as I took the Birkenhead Tunnel into Liverpool and branched off along the Dock Road to my flat. I needed a shower and a change of clothes before I went to Maria's. Roly would already be there. She'd taken him to Formby with her for a walk in the Pinewoods before she went to her sister's.

There were no messages on my answerphone. I stood in the shower, turning the water piping hot to wash away the guilt of the afternoon. My flat had become a halfway house between two worlds. Maybe that was the only world I really belonged in. Yet now I had responsibilities I couldn't ignore.

I tried to put my mind to our other case. Dorothy Grove's death could turn out to be no more than a domestic gone wrong. A niece who wanted to bring forward her inheritance or a husband seeking revenge. Two powerful motives for murder and ones that could turn ordinary, everyday, mundane people into killers. I shuddered. Would Hilary or Maria kill for revenge? And, if so, would it be each other or me?

I forced my mind back to Ms Grove. The whole business of the stalker made me think it was more than just a family thing. Families didn't need to stalk. I sensed an outsider somewhere in the picture but how could I trace him? I had the feeling that motive would be the key. Who else besides her family might have benefited from her death?

I towelled myself down and put on a charcoal suit with a blue shirt and tie for dinner with Maria. She didn't like us sitting down to eat in trainers and jeans. Before I left, I logged on to *www.sports.com*

on the Internet for the report on the Tranmere match, just in case Maria should ask about it.

In the event, she didn't. We had a pleasant meal and followed it by watching a couple of DVDs, which took us to midnight. Maria had been into Global Video at Formby and taken out *Gladiator* and *The Royle Family*.

'I think I'd have enjoyed *Gladiator* more with Ricky Tomlinson in the Coliseum,' said Maria. 'Imagine him as Jim Royle in the arena facing the lions.'

'The lions would have been gassed,' I said.

Next day we drove across to Southport for lunch at the Cheshire Lines and Marge brought out her usual high chair for Victoria. 'She's growing fast, isn't she?' she said.

Maria laughed. 'Don't I know it. She grows out of things quicker than I can wash them.'

'Is she walking yet?'

'Oh yes. Like nobody's business. I've taken her with me to keep-fit a couple of times and she can't wait to get on the treadmill.'

The place was packed as always. Word had got around about the food and punters were queuing up at the door most weekends. Some people from a nearby local drama group were practising their lines on each other in a corner. At the bar, a couple of men were reading the papers and casting occasional glances at the Sky Soccer Sunday match on the TV in the snug.

After we'd eaten, we collected Roly from the car and walked him across the bridge over the Marine Lake to the seafront. I took Roly's lead and Maria pushed Victoria in her buggy. The golden sands pictured in earlier guidebooks of Southport were nowadays covered with parked cars.

'Good job the tide's out,' commented Maria.

I said, 'It's bad enough they charge you for parking your car in town on a Sunday but to charge you to park on the beach as well is unbelievable. I do believe Sefton Council would charge people to walk on the pavements if they thought they could get away with it.'

Maria agreed. 'Give them time, I'm sure they'll come up with something.'

We walked past the Pier round the ruins of the latest collapsed building scheme, indicative of the plight of English resorts. What had been planned as a seaside development with a water park, leisure centre and bowling alley now looked like ending up, after numerous stop-starts, as the sort of downmarket retail shopping park that you find near run-down inner city housing estates. Either that or it was going to be grassed over. I think I preferred the grass option though I knew that would be a non-starter. Grass wouldn't bring in any business rates.

We stopped off at Ladygreen Nurseries in Ince Blundell on the way home. Victoria liked looking at the ducks swimming in the pond and we enjoyed the homemade cakes in the café.

'How did you get on in Cheshire yesterday?' Maria asked as she poured out the tea.

'Not much to tell, I'm afraid. I'm still no nearer finding out who's sending out information from the Routledge factory.'

'The question you should be asking,' said Maria, 'is who is likely to be paying to receive it.'

'Someone from one of the other research companies, I suppose,'

'Not necessarily. After all, the Alicante one was losing information the same as Liverpool. Maybe the other two are losing stuff as well.'

'But who else would want that information?'

'Anyone with the right connections could sell the formula on. There'd be no shortage of buyers.'

'That's what Gabrielle Lorenzo said. And she also said she thought it was someone in Liverpool.'

'There you are then, all you have to do is find them. Easy.'

I told her about the anonymous letters. 'I could see why someone might want to kill Gabrielle Lorenzo but what had Rupert Routledge done to merit death threats?'

'They probably found out he hired her to investigate the company so they're warning him off.'

'No, these people do their warnings with guns not the Royal Mail. Anyway, the death threats were sent well before then.'

The letters puzzled me. Maybe they had nothing to do with the case after all. Perhaps they were connected with his personal life. Maybe he had been having an affair after all, in which case the threats could have come from his mistress's husband (if she had one). Or his own wife, or any members of either of their families and even friends who didn't approve. The list was endless. Nothing like illicit liaisons for making enemies.

So could Rupert Routledge have had a mystery lover? It wouldn't help solve the espionage problem but it would at least rule out the death threats from the enquiry.

I decided I would have to tackle Rupert again.

Chapter Fourteen

Before anything else, next morning, I had a house purchase to attend to. Geoffrey Molloy looks after my property business from an office in Aigburth Road. He's been with me for over ten years and it's his life. As the detective agency these days takes up more and more of my time, Geoffrey is virtually running the operation, and running it efficiently too, but occasionally there are things I need to attend to. Geoffrey may be good at letting flats, collecting rents and organising repairs but I like to do the buying and selling myself.

A fortnight ago, an old Victorian house converted to bedsits had come up for auction. It was pretty tatty and hadn't reached its reserve price but it was near Sefton Park, an area that I reckoned could well be on the upturn in the not too distant future.

I'd subsequently made a bid that had been accepted. My idea was to turn it back into a single dwelling house. So many new purpose-built flats were being built everywhere that I figured the market for family sized houses was being neglected. It was worth a gamble anyway.

I took Roly in the car and drove over to Aigburth.

'Alistair Crawford sent the contract across yesterday,' Geoffrey said. 'Are we applying for planning permission?'

'Have to, I'm afraid.'

'The council won't like losing council tax from ten tenants when they're only getting one lot back in return.'

'Don't worry, Geoff, they'll just up the ante. Council's don't lose out, you should know that.'

'I bet they've been hoping some developer would come along and knock the whole lot down and put twenty purpose built flats there.'

'Let them hope. Nobody has done yet. They're all too busy turning the city centre into suburbia.'

I sorted out all the paperwork then, as I was already in Aigburth, I decided to drive the extra few miles to Speke to question Rupert Routledge.

His greeting, when I was shown in, was abrupt. 'I thought you'd finished here now.' He was in the middle of dictating notes to a secretary who looked like an extra from *Dracula*, white face, crimson lipstick and heavily mascarared eyes. She was quickly dismissed with a curt nod.

I came straight to the point. 'Something new has come up. I believe you've been receiving death threats, Mr. Routledge.'

'Who told you that?' The reddening of his cheeks confirmed Alison Whyte's story.

'It's true then?'

He thought for a minute before replying. 'It was a long while ago.'

'How long?'

'For God's sake, I don't know. Well over a year and they stopped ages ago.'

Through the office window, I could see the four researchers working away, including James Scanlan. It looked like I'd finally be able to talk to him but first I needed to find out more about Rupert Routledge's letters.

'How many of them were there?'

'Two or three, I don't remember.'

'All by post or did you get telephone calls as well?'

'No. Just letters.'

'And you never found out who sent them?'

'No.'

I didn't believe him. 'What did you do about them?'

'Threw them in the bin where they belonged.'

'Why didn't you go to the police?'

'What could they do? Anyway, as I said, the letters stopped.'

'Why do you think that was?'

'How do I know? Perhaps the sender died.'

He said it facetiously but could it possibly have been the truth? If so, it was unlikely he'd died from natural causes, which begged the question, was Rupert Routledge capable of murder?

'Did you part with any money?'

'Why should I? They never asked for any. Anyway, I wouldn't have been able to if they had.'

'Why's that?'

I knew the answer but I wanted him to tell me. 'Because I didn't know who they were, did I?'

'You wouldn't need to know *who* they were. People pay ransoms without knowing the identity of their blackmailer.'

'Well I wasn't being blackmailed.'

'Are you sure?' I looked him in the eye. 'Were you having an affair and somebody found out? Threatened to tell your wife?'

He stood up. With his puffed cheeks and pompous air he could have played the lead in *Dad's Army*. Perspiration had broken out on his forehead. My questions were starting to irritate him.

'Absolute rubbish. Look, once and for all, let me tell you. I'm a businessman. I'm interested in doing deals and making profits. I leave all that other stuff to younger men. How can I make it plain to you that I've never done anything that I could remotely be blackmailed for.' He paused for breath. 'What puzzles me is how can this have anything to do with the information leaks from my company?'

It puzzled me as well. 'That's what I'm trying to find out. Remember, somebody tried to kill Gabrielle Lorenzo.'

'And did she get prior notification by post?'

'No.'

'Then I don't see how the two things are connected and, as I told you, these letters stopped long before the woman came here.'

He could have been lying but it was obvious I was not going to learn any more.

'Well, if you think of anything, please get in touch with me. In the meantime, I'd like a quick word with James out there before I go.'

'Help yourself.' Routledge was only too relieved to be rid of me. I walked through into the research area. Alison Whyte, who was nearest the door, looked up from her computer.

'Hello again. I thought we'd seen the last of you,' she smiled, 'in the nicest possible way.'

'I never got to talk to James the other day so I thought, while I was here…'

'Oh, what a pity. He's just gone for his lunch.'

'I looked at my watch. 'Half past eleven. A bit early isn't it?'

'He had some things to pick up from the Uni on the way. He'll be back at two, if you want to call back then.'

'It's all right, I'll catch him another time.'

It couldn't be coincidence, I thought, as I left the building. Scanlan had obviously seen me in Routledge's office and disappeared before I could speak to him. Why?

On the way back into town, I stopped off beside the disused Garden Festival site for a bite to eat at the Britannia. I took a seat by the window, looking across the Mersey towards the Wirral.

I couldn't fathom the situation at DRP at all, mainly because I couldn't understand Routledge's reactions to events. He was reluctant to allow an investigation into something that could cost his company huge sums of money and he, reputedly, a man who was very money orientated. And when someone threatened his life he reckoned to do nothing about it.

What was going on?

I drove back to the office past the Marina and Albert Dock. As more businesses have relocated to the area and more flats have been built, traffic seems to have increased tenfold. I wondered which flat James Scanlan owned in Kings Dock. I was more determined than ever to talk to him after today's disappearance.

My mobile rang as I was passing the Pier Head. 'Elsie Wishart's been on,' Jim said. 'Wants to see you urgently. Can you pop into Lewis's sometime?'

'I'll go now.'

I left the RAV4 at my flat in Waterloo Dock and walked across to the store. Elsie was still at the Casual Trousers counter.

'I'm glad you came,' she said. She looked careworn. The Mrs Thatcher coiffure was in disarray, giving it the look of an ill-fitting wig, and her cheeks below her glasses were puffy and red. 'I've heard from the solicitor this morning about Aunt Dot's will.'

'Oh yes.'

'I told you she was leaving me the house, didn't I?'

'That' right.'

'Well she didn't. And she left me no money either.'

'Then who…?'

'Who inherited? I'll tell you who inherited. Some bloody,' she spat the word out, 'charity.'

This revelation threw me. I'd thought she'd been going to say Ms Grove's dumped husband.

'Charity?'

'I've written the name down.' She took a piece of paper from the pocket of her beige suit. 'Here it is. The Society for Humane Animal Treatment.'

'I've never heard of them.'

'Neither have I but my solicitor tells me they are one of these extreme animal welfare groups one reads about in the newspapers that cause disturbances.'

'Like the Animal Liberation Front you mean?'

'Probably.'

'Why would she leave money to them? Was she a member?'

'Not as far as I know but, then,' she said bitterly, 'it seems there's a lot I don't know about Aunt Dot.'

'Were there no other bequests?'

'None at all.'

'Somebody must have done a good brainwash job on her.'

'The will was dated last year.'

'And she never told you she'd changed her mind about leaving you the house.'

'Never, the old hag.' Elsie Wishart sounded venomous.

I left her to a lifetime of selling ladies bottoms and returned to the office.

'Society for Humane Animal Treatment,' mused Jim. 'An unfortunate acronym. Appropriate though. Your Miss Wishart was well and truly shat on by the sound of it.'

'It doesn't take away her motive though. She was expecting to inherit. She hadn't known the will had been changed.'

Was this why she was so annoyed, because she'd paid to have

her aunt killed in expectation of a windfall and instead she was left out of pocket?

'I wonder how her ex will feel when he hears all the hard earned money from his business has ended up at a charity?'

'Much the same, I imagine. Very pissed off.'

But in this case, I was wrong.

Chapter Fifteen

Jake Morton's new business was listed in Directory Enquires on the Internet. Jake Morton (Cement) Ltd, the entry read. The number was local, it was in the building trade, I figured it had to be him so I rang the number and I was right.

He'd set up again in Preston, less than forty miles away, not down South, as Elsie Wishart had said, at all. He probably put out that rumour about so his ex-wife wouldn't be chasing him for money. I asked if I could drive over and talk to him. He said that would be fine but not until the evening. In the daytime he grafted.

Jim wasn't optimistic about my trip. 'You don't really think he had her murdered do you?'

'No, but he's the only person we know so far who's connected with her, apart from the niece, so I may as well give it a go. He could have been the one who hired the hit man remember.'

I motored over to Preston at seven o'clock after I'd finished on the radio. Jake Morton (Cement) Ltd was housed in a builders yard off the Blackpool road. The proprietor lived in a newly built detached house adjoining it.

Jake himself answered the door and led me into the front room, which served as an office.

'Living on the job,' he grinned. 'The price you pay for being your own boss.' He was a large, jovial man, dressed in a leather jacket, blue check shirt and jeans. His hands bore the calluses of a manual worker and traces of cement dust covered his boots. I couldn't imagine him married to Dorothy Grove.

'Will you have a beer with me?' He produced a fourpack of Boddingtons from a cupboard on the wall.

I took a can, opened it and took a swig. 'Thanks.' I explained to him why I was there. 'Your ex-wife, Dorothy, hired me just before she died. She was convinced she had a stalker.'

'He must have been a brave man stalking my ex-missus.' He laughed. 'I've still got the scars.'

'Why did the two of you part?'

'She got bored with me. I wasn't clever enough for her.'

'Didn't she know that before she married you? Not,' I added hastily, 'that it was true.'

He laughed again, a raucous belly laugh. 'Of course it was true. Dorothy was an academic; I'm just a simple working man. But I'll tell you what though, I'm not short of common sense and I know how to make money, two things my late ex-wife was not particularly noted for.'

I didn't argue with him although it seemed to me that Dorothy Grove had found a much easier way than Jake Morton of making money, namely through the divorce courts.

As if reading my mind, he continued, 'I wonder what poor sod got lumbered with her after me. She liked a regular income did Dorothy.'

'You didn't pay her alimony then?'

'Not a penny. I saw what was coming in time and I quickly wrapped up the old firm and got most of the money out before she could get her hands on it.'

'I heard she'd bankrupted you.'

'Good. That's what I want them to think. Her solicitors, that is. Not that it matters now. So did she manage to find a replacement for me then?'

I remembered the moustached midget she'd dragged round the dance floor at the singles club. 'As far as I know, she was still looking.' I gave Jake an account of the evening at Simply Single. It tickled him.

'I always thought they got some rum buggers at those places. Well, Dorothy for one, though I shouldn't speak ill of the dead. I might be dead myself one day.'

'It could happen,' I agreed. 'If you're not careful. And talking of the dead, I don't suppose you've heard who she left her money to?'

'No, but I can hardly expect it was me. Probably that spinster niece of hers.'

'Elsie Wishart, you mean?'

He nodded.

'She was certainly expecting it but I saw her today and she told me she got nothing.'

'No?' He didn't seem surprised or even too interested.

'Your ex-wife left everything to charity.'

'Typical.'

'Did you know she was involved in charity work?'

'She was on a lot of committees for various things though I couldn't name you one of them. I never had that much to do with her.'

'This one was an animal charity, Society for Humane Animal Treatment.'

'Whatever that means. She was worth a few bob, you know. Did all right out of her first husband. I wonder how much was left.'

'I don't know the details but the house must have been worth a hundred grand for starters. How come you didn't automatically get half of it?'

'It was her house. I moved in when we got married. She always kept her finances apart from mine. Had her own bank account. He laughed hollowly. 'She just allowed me to pay a standing order into it every month.'

'What grounds did she divorce you on?'

'She found out I'd been having it off with Gemma, my secretary. Gave her the excuse she was looking for.'

'Are you still with Gemma?'

'God, no. She was just light relief from Dorothy and boy, did I need it.'

Before I could broach the subject of her murder, Jake Morton himself brought it up. 'Who do you think did for her then?' He didn't look too grief stricken about her demise.

'Well, you and Elsie Wishart must be the bookies' favourites, the ones who might have hoped to inherit.'

'Except neither of us got a bean.'

'But neither of you were to know that before she died.'

'I think I had a good idea. But assuming it wasn't me or the niece, who do you reckon could have done for her?'

'Strange as it may seem,' I said, slowly, 'it had all the hallmarks of a contract killing but for what motive, I've no idea.'

'Perhaps the animal people arranged it, after all they're the ones who copped for the cash.'

'Not the normal way charities arrange their bequests.'

'Funny if someone like the RSPCA turned out to have a special department specifically set up to do away with any old biddies who were likely to name them in their wills. They'd probably get away with it too. Nobody would ever believe it.' He smiled happily at the thought.

'What made you marry Dorothy, Mr. Morton?' I was curious. Having met the woman myself, I couldn't see any obvious attraction.

'Jake, please. I was on the rebound. My first wife ran off with a sodding librarian. I met Dorothy at a Christmas party. She fancied a legover and so did I and that was it. Aggressive and ugly she may have become but, in those days, she had a certain glamour and between the sheets she was dynamite.'

It wasn't something I cared to contemplate. 'How long ago did you meet her?'

'Fifteen years. We'd been married twelve but we'd grown apart long before that.'

I drained the last drop of Boddy's from the can and tossed it into the wastepaper basket under the desk. I'd heard all I wanted to hear. I couldn't see Jake Morton as his late wife's killer.

'Thanks for your time, Mr. Morton - Jake. I'm glad Mrs. Morton didn't manage to clean you out after all.' It seemed odd to refer to Ms Grove as Mrs Morton. 'Incidentally, I take it the police have been round to interview you?'

'Twice. Fellow called Warnett. Dour sort of chap. Nothing I could tell him I haven't told you. He hadn't a clue about what happened to Dorothy. Scratching in the dark he was.'

'Aren't we all?'

'And if that's it, I've got a date at ten. Got to keep the old testosterone pumping.' He winked and escorted me to the door. 'If you find out anything, let me know. You've got me wondering now. The old bat didn't deserve that.'

I pondered on the conversation as I drove back through

Ormskirk to Blundellsands and Maria's. I'd found Morton to be a likeable bloke although his brusque acceptance of his ex-wife's death was slightly disquieting. Nonetheless, that didn't make him a murderer and, indeed, I could see no reason why he would have wanted Dorothy Grove dead.

Yet, if he and Elsie Wishart didn't kill her, who did?

I was thinking about that when I realised I'd forgotten Everton were playing at West Ham. I switched on the car radio just in time to hear the result – two-nil to The Blues. That would silence some of the 'When Skies Are Grey' critics for another five days at least. Maybe more, as next week we had Manchester City at home and they were on their way down.

'How did you get on?' Maria enquired over supper.

'He was quite a pleasant bloke. He'd been clever enough to hang onto most of his money when he split up with Ms Grove, or should I say Mrs. Morton.'

'So you don't think he killed her then?'

'No way, no.'

'If you ask me,' she said, 'you've done all you can. You'd be best concentrating on the DRP case.'

'Maybe but that isn't exactly progressing brilliantly either.'

'Let's change the subject then,' said Maria. She put down her knife and fork and looked across at me. 'I've been thinking about selling my flat.'

It caught me by surprise even though she'd mentioned us moving in together before.

'This flat? Selling? Whatever for?'

'You may not have noticed, Johnny, but this place is a bit small for three of us and Victoria really needs her own room. She can't sleep in ours forever.'

'Where were you thinking of? My flat's hardly any bigger.'

'Not a flat, my love, a house. One with a garden for Vikki to play in and there's Roly to consider too, don't forget. It's no fun for a dog living in a flat, especially one his size.' Roly wagged his stump at the sound of his name and she patted him affectionately.

'Where did you have in mind?'

97

'Somewhere nearer town than this. After all, both of us work in the centre.' Maria is in the local history department at the Picton Library, although she has only been going in part-time since she became a mother.

'How big a place do we need?'

'Depends if we sell both our flats. What were you thinking of?'

'Funnily enough, I'm just buying a place in Sefton Park that I'm thinking of converting back from bedsits into a single dwelling house. It's on three floors with six bedrooms, three entertaining rooms and cellars not to mention a double garage.'

'You could put your recording studio in the cellar. Is it a big garden?'

'Big enough for Roly to wear himself out.' I did some mental calculations. 'I could turn the first floor into three bedrooms. Two of them en-suite, one for us and one for guests. The third could be the nursery for Victoria. And I could have the attic for an office, it's huge.'

'Big enough for two offices maybe? Only, we could have a craft room for me.' Maria has taken to making jewellery. She started out doing her own Christmas cards and did quite well selling them to local shops. Now she's moved on to bracelets, brooches and earrings.

'Good idea. At this rate, you'll be opening your own shop.'

'Do you know, Johnny I'd quite like that. I think I've been a librarian long enough. Maybe I'll give it serious thought in the future. But you don't think the house is a bad idea then?'

'No, I don't.'

'So can I come and see it?'

At that moment, Maria looked as radiantly happy as I'd ever seen her but at the back of my mind I wondered how Hilary would react to me moving in permanently with Maria. And would I want to give up my own flat? I wasn't at all sure.

'I'll take you in the morning,' I told Maria.

But we never got there because Jim Burroughs rang first thing next day in a state of some excitement.

'Get down here, Johnny, pronto.'

'Why, what's happened?'

'Startling new development in the Dorothy Grove case. You'll never guess.'

'Jim, you're sounding like a fucking headline writer. Just tell me.'

'Mike Bennett's just been on. Apparently, Forensic have been doing tests on the bullet they extracted from Dorothy Grove's skull and guess what?

'Surprise me.'

And surprise me he certainly did.

'They've found it matches up with the bullet that killed Selina Stark.'

'What? You're kidding me?'

'I'm not. The gun that was used to kill Selina Stark was the same one that was used to kill Dorothy Grove.'

Chapter Sixteen

The reaction at Police HQ, when the news broke, could not have been greater if the Chief Constable had been found in a public lavatory with George Michael.

According to ex-D.I. Bennett, the horrific discovery had opened up a whole new can of worms as the police were forced to consider publicly the possibility that Wayne Paladin, currently enjoying the hospitality of Her Majesty's Prison, could be innocent after all. As, indeed, he had always claimed. As, indeed, the police already knew. Heads were going to roll.

'Obviously, he couldn't have shot Ms Grove because he's been in the nick for months,' pointed out Jim unnecessarily.

'Obviously.'

'No gun was ever found after Stark's death.'

'Didn't Paladin's defence lawyer point that out at his trial?'

'Yes but the prosecution maintained that he'd simply disposed of it and that was that. They steamrollered the case through and Paladin went down.'

'He won't be down for long when this gets out. It'll be The Birmingham Six all over again.'

'I'm afraid you're right,' said Jim.

'Paladin's solicitor will be on to it like a rat up a drainpipe. Wrongful arrest for a start, probably a fair bit of alleged police brutality followed by a hefty compensation claim.'

Jim winced at the thought.

'You can't blame him, either,' I said. 'Paladin was framed good and proper.'

'There'll be a few early retirements after this, I shouldn't wonder.'

'On full pension, of course.'

Jim ignored the barb. 'And, meanwhile, the real killer is still on the loose.'

'As he always has been as we know only too well.'

'Yes, well,' murmured Jim uncomfortably. He didn't like to be reminded that his former employers were capable of using tactics more suited to the KGB.

'Hang on a minute, though,' I said carefully. 'There's a catch to this. Just because the same gun was used, it doesn't follow the same person was using it. Whoever shot Selina Stark could have passed on the gun to a third party who subsequently shot Dorothy Grove.'

'Very possible, of course, and something the police will be aware of but will they be able to use that argument? The thing is, they know Paladin didn't shoot Selina Stark but they can't come out and say it publicly. Really, they're in an invidious position because once Paladin's defence team get hold of this, who knows what unpleasant disclosures might crawl out of the woodwork? The easiest thing for them would be to admit they might have made a mistake and hold their hands up now rather than wait to see what shit hits the fan.'

'You mean they know what an outcry there'd be if it ever got out that Paladin was fitted up?'

'Maybe so,' admitted Jim.

'So what is the latest police take on it all? Did Mike say?'

'Now that the weapon has been used again, the suggestion is that whoever killed Selina Stark is likely to be the same person who dispatched Dorothy Grove to her maker.'

'A reasonable assumption, I suppose.'

'I tend to go along with it, especially when the method of killing was the same in both cases.'

'The single shot. But what connection could there possibly be between those two women?' I glanced across at Roly who was lying on his blanket under the desk. 'Has he had anything to eat today?'

'Not from me he hasn't. He's too fat as it is.'

'Nonsense.' I went into the kitchen and fetched him a marrow-bone to chew. He gnawed at it appreciatively and I returned to the matter in hand.

'Yes, that's the big question. What have a T.V. superstar and a sad middle-aged woman from a singles club got in common?'

'Simple. They were both shot by the same person.'

'But why? Who did Dorothy Grove know who would be likely to be friendly with Selina Stark?'

'You tell me. Happily, like you said yourself, it's not our concern.'

'So you've told Mike Bennett you're not taking the Selina Stark case on then?'

'Didn't need to. It's back in police hands, isn't it? Case reopened.'

'All the same, aren't you curious, Jim, because I certainly am? Ms Grove knew someone was following her but I can't believe she genuinely thought her actual life could be in danger. I feel responsible, Jim. We didn't take her seriously enough.'

'Come on, Johnny. On the information she gave us we acted with full professionalism. We thought we were dealing with a harmless stalker.'

'Maybe not harmless.' Were any stalkers harmless?

'OK, maybe not harmless but certainly not life threatening. We spent the whole evening with her, never let her out of our sight and you followed her home.

'And allowed her to be murdered along the way. Yes, I see what you mean, very professional of us.'

'Nobody could have prevented that. Look at President Reagan that time he was shot. He had a crowd of armed security men around him. You can't legislate for that type of action. It was a highly organised, pre-arranged job carried out by a trained hit man.'

'That's what you reckon? Not a lone stalker or a psycho?'

'No. My bet is on the contract killing and the fact that Selina Stark was killed in the same way confirms it in my book. Mike Bennett himself said the police thought at the time it was one or the other, a gangland hit or a nutter.'

'And they plumped for the nutter as an easy option.'

'Yes, well. We've already been over that. Remember, Johnny, experienced assassins are the hardest of all criminals to catch. The victim doesn't know them, they're probably from another town, even another country and they have no personal motive…'

'Whoa there. Somebody has a motive, Jim. The person who hires them has a motive. The person who wants them dead. And that is what we need to find out.'

'Why would anyone want to take out a contract on Dorothy Grove? Christ, Johnny, she was a nomark.'

'Maybe. But she was shot, all the same and it wasn't a mistake.'

'At least this puts the nail in the coffin that it was someone in the family.'

'I'd say the ex was in the clear, he obviously didn't expect to inherit.'

'And, according to you, the niece is a middle-aged spinster shop assistant. I take it you're not suggesting she moonlights as a hired gun on her afternoon off?'

'No, I tend to agree with you, Jim. I can't really see either of them being involved.'

'What about Dorothy Grove's first husband?'

'Nah. He's well gone and, anyway, he's out in Saudi Arabia.'

'Let's look at it from the other way, then,' said Jim. 'Who stood to gain from Selina Stark's murder?'

'I've no idea but thinking about it, Jim, listen to this. A bit of lateral thinking for you. Touch of the Edward de Bono's.'

'Go on.'

'Isn't it possible that the two cases are not actually connected?'

'It was the same gun, they must be.'

'Hear me out. It could be just a coincidence that two people looking for someone to do their dirty work for them happened to hire the same organisation.'

'Hang on. You're saying this is the work of the same contract killer who was hired by two different people to do two different jobs at two different times but using the same gun?'

'It's possible isn't it?' I laughed. 'They probably both got him from an ad in the Yellow Pages.'

'Many a true word, Johnny. It's certainly easier these days to hire a hit man. At one time, of course, you'd have a job to find someone to commit murder on demand and even if you did, the price would be way above what the average man in the street could afford.'

'True.'

'But nowadays, there's any amount of smackheads and yobbos

willing to kill anyone for the price of their next score. I don't know what's happened to the world.'

'Its called the Moral Breakdown of Society,' I told him, 'A bit like the Roman Empire. You can read all about it in Samuel Huntingdon's *Clash of Civilisations*. But I don't think the people who did this were smackheads or yobbos. It was too well organised, and I don't believe it was a one-man operation either. Don't forget the car involved, the Lantra. That's two people minimum who were involved for a start. No, this was definitely a job for a firm.'

'Well, however many there were, it's not our pigeon anymore, whatever Mike Bennett might have hoped. We might as well forget it.'

'I don't think so, Jim. Not entirely. Certainly not Dorothy Grove at any rate. She was still our client. Besides, I expect DI Warnett will be back with more questions.'

I spoke prophetically. Warnett arrived at noon, this time accompanied by a girl hardly out of police training school. 'This is WPC Hagen,' he indicated briefly before getting straight to the point. 'We need to talk to you some more about Ms Dorothy Grove.'

'Have there been developments?' I asked innocently. I wondered if Warnett had ever considered taking a course at Charm School but thought better of suggesting it.

'We think she may have been involved in some criminal activity which led indirectly to her murder.'

'What sort of activity exactly?'

'I was hoping you might tell me that.'

'It's an interesting theory, Inspector,' I said, 'but I can't imagine anyone less likely than Ms Grove to emerge as a secret safebreaker or ram-raider. In fact I'd have put money on it that she didn't even own a balaclava.'

'I wasn't implying that she herself was in breach of the law,' he muttered through clenched teeth, 'merely that she'd perhaps inadvertently got mixed up with some dubious characters.'

'Or fell foul of someone who employed the dubious characters.'

He glared at me suspiciously. 'What do you know you haven't told me?'

'Nothing. I've told you everything I can concerning our association with Ms Grove. I know absolutely nothing else about her.'

I could see he was clutching at straws. They obviously had nothing on the woman. I knew Warnett must be aware of the connection between the two victims, Dorothy Grove and Selina Stark, but he wasn't willing to share that information with us. Not yet. But suggesting Ms Grove's death could have been a gangland grudge killing was the surely the stuff of desperation.

Warnett glared at us. 'This may be more than a one-off street mugging'.

'I'm sure you're right,' I said, 'but we can't help you any further.'

'If money wasn't the motive, then somewhere in Dorothy Grove's life there must be somebody who had a grudge against her,' said Jim after Warnett and his colleague had left.

'I'll go along with that, but who? The only ones we know of are the two ex-husbands and we've as good as ruled them out. Maybe we should start looking at Selina Stark's life for the answer.'

'We know nothing about her.'

'She was a celebrity, Jim. There's nothing in her personal life that hasn't been published in intimate detail in every paper from *Hello!* to *The Police Gazette*. The life she's led, there's bound to be jilted lovers or jealous wives somewhere along the way.'

'I'm sure every person who ever spoke to Selina Stark has been interviewed already, Johnny, and doubtless will be again. Let's face it, this is a police job. We'd do best forgetting it and concentrating on the Routledge case.'

I couldn't really argue with him. 'Maybe you're right.'

And the man I really wanted to see at DRP was James Scanlan. Maybe, I thought, I should try ringing him and making a definite appointment to see him.

'Derek Routledge Pharmaceuticals,' the secretary's voice answered.

'I'd like to speak with James Scanlan, please.'

'I'm sorry sir, James Scanlan is no longer with the company.'

Chapter Seventeen

'I don't understand it,' I said, 'had you any idea he was leaving?'

I was in Rupert Routledge's office, anxious to find out the reason for James Scanlan's defection. The MD was pacing up and down.

'None at all. He said nothing about this yesterday. He was on a five year contract and was supposed to give three months notice if he wished to leave.' I noticed his eyes were puffy and his hand trembled slightly as he stopped to pour himself a drink from a water jug on his desk.

'Is that usual?'

'I don't know if it's usual or not,' he snapped, 'but it's what we do here and there have been no complaints before.'

'What excuse did he give you for leaving?'

'None. He was working late last night on his own. He said he had a couple of projects he wanted to finish. When we arrived this morning, his desk was cleared and he'd left a typewritten note.'

He handed it to me. *Regret forced to resign post. Will contact you later regarding paperwork. James.*

'Short and sweet,' I said. 'By paperwork I presume he means his P45 and any salary he's owed?'

'I imagine so but he'll be lucky to get anything from me, jumping ship like this.'

'Have you tried to contact him at all?'

'I sent somebody round to his flat but there was no reply and he isn't answering his telephone.'

'Can you let me have his address?'

'What for?'

'I think he may be the one responsible for the leaks.'

'Oh those.' His mind seemed to be elsewhere.

'I'd say he was favourite at the moment, yes.'

'He lives in the Kings Dock. I'll get my secretary to fetch it for you.' He gave the command on the telephone.

'No more death threats?' I asked conversationally as we waited.

106

'Why do you go on about those?' he snapped impatiently. 'I told you, they finished a long time ago.'

'Will you find it hard to replace Scanlan?'

'In the short term, yes, but there are any number of qualified people out there who'd give their eye teeth to do a job like his so I don't think we'll have a problem getting anyone. It's the time wasted in between that's annoying.'

The secretary came in and handed her boss a piece of paper, which he passed across to me. 'If you find him, I want to know immediately, right?' he ordered.

'Of course.'

I took the paper with Scanlan's address and left him to it. I was puzzled by Routledge's reaction to Scanlan's disappearance because his Mr Angry act hadn't deceived me for a moment.

Far from being annoyed, Rupert Routledge looked like a man who had had the fright of his life.

* * *

The flat was on the first floor with a balcony overlooking the Mersey. I buzzed the Entryphone but got no reply. I pressed the bell of a couple more flats until someone answered.

'Parcel for Mr. Scanlan,' I mumbled. The buzzer sounded to release the lock and I pushed open the door.

As always, it amazed me how people who spend a fortune on security can be so easily conned. But then, I can't believe people who waste money on expensive car alarms when it takes just 20 seconds to put a brick through the window and then run off with anything on show. The only way is to leave nothing worth stealing in the car and buy a tracker system so at least you'll get the vehicle back if someone nicks it.

I walked up to the first floor and found the front door of Scanlan's flat. It was slightly ajar. I pushed it open and walked inside.

The lounge was tidy, the furniture in position. No sign of a break-in or a struggle that might have indicated abduction, two of the three things I'd most feared. The third was murder but I checked out all the rooms and didn't find a body.

The kitchen led off the lounge. All the dishes had been put away. I felt the electric kettle. It was cold. Nobody had had coffee this morning. I looked inside the dishwasher. It was empty but the fridge was full of food, including two pints of milk. I peeled off the silver top of one of the bottles and sniffed. It was fresh.

I moved across to the bathroom. The bath and shower were both dry as were the towels on the radiator.

In the bedroom, the duvet cover was neat and tidy on the double bed. If anyone had slept in it the night before, they'd been careful to make it before they left.

I remembered Scanlan was supposed to be living with his girlfriend. I opened the door of the fitted double wardrobe and, sure enough, it contained two sets of clothes, men's on the left, ladies' on the right.

I went back into the lounge. On a coffee table were a couple of magazines. The top one was the latest *Sunday Times Culture* giving the week's TV programmes. It was open at Monday evening, which suggested they'd been in the night before. Or perhaps they'd turned the page in readiness when they retired to bed on Sunday night.

In the corner of the room was a large Victorian reproduction mahogany desk. I opened the drawers one by one but they were all empty.

I realised I knew nothing at all about Scanlan's partner. Perhaps the neighbours could tell me. I knocked on the door on both sides without success then a man appeared at the end of the corridor.

'Looking for someone, pal?' He was a ringer for Dudley Moore, small with black curly hair, suntanned and wearing a granny vest and a pair of faded denims. All that was missing was the gold medallion although he did have a gold tooth. I noticed strands of white in the hair. He was older than he dressed. Maybe around fifty.

'The couple in here,' I said, indicating the Scanlan flat. 'Don't know them by any chance do you?'

'Not their names I don't but the bird's a bit tasty.' He licked his lips for emphasis. 'Friends of yours are they?'

'No. I was asked to bring them a message but they appear to be out. You don't happen to know where they work?'

'I think the girl is with the *Echo*. Don't know about him.'

I realised that Alison Whyte might be able to tell me more. I thanked him and went back to the flat to close the front door behind me when I noticed a telephone on the hall table. Out of curiosity, I dialled 1471. The computerised operator gave me an 0151 236 number. City centre.

I dialled 141 then the number. No sense in giving away my location. The ringing tone came up but there was no reply. I allowed it twelve rings before putting down the receiver and wrote down the number in my notebook to try again later.

There was nothing more I could do there. I made sure the door was still slightly ajar as I left and drove back into town.

'Do you think he's done a runner?' asked Jim.

We were in the Grapes in Mathew Street having a late lunch. I'd drunk there with Bob Wooler in the Sixties when he was DJ at the Cavern and The Cruzads thought they could be the next Beatles. Doubtless Jim had thought the same about The Chocolate Lavatory. We all have our dreams.

'Hard to tell,' I replied. 'His clothes were still there, along with hers. If he was snatched, I'd say it must have been from DRP. Routledge said he was working late there on his own.'

'Sounds familiar,' said Jim. 'The Spanish bloke that went missing from the drug company in Alicante. He disappeared and has never been seen since.'

'Which points to Scanlan being the spy too. Unless, of course, he was kidnapped but who would kidnap him and why?'

'Perhaps he found out something he shouldn't have and had to be silenced.'

'You mean you think he could be dead?' It wasn't a possibility I wanted to consider. 'But his desk was empty like he'd taken all his stuff with him.'

'The best thing would be to find his partner. She'd probably be able to tell us something.'

I never like that word partner. It sounds like a business

arrangement not a romantic liaison but it's crept into the language along with other misnomers like "referee's assistant" and "gay".

'One of the neighbours told me she works at the *Echo*.'

'But we don't know her name?'

'Alison Whyte might know it. I'll give her a ring at DRP when we get back to the office. Drink up.'

'It's Lisa something,' said Alison, when I phoned. 'I'm not sure of her second name. What do you want her for?'

'I'm still trying to get hold of James for my radio programme and I thought she might know where he is.'

Alison seemed satisfied with the explanation. 'You won't have heard,' she said breathlessly. 'James has left.'

I pretended I didn't know. 'Left DRP? When?'

'Last night. He left a note for Rupert. Everyone's talking about it.'

'Now I'll never get my interview. Did he give a reason?'

'Apparently not.'

'What's the general opinion in the office?'

'Nobody really knows but we decided he must have had a row with Rupert.'

I knew that not to be the case but I saw no point in enlightening her. 'Do none of the others know this Lisa's second name?'

'Hang on.' I heard her calling out to her colleagues and there followed a muffled discussion before she said, 'we think it's an Irish name. O'Brien, O'Bong, something like that.' I heard a voice in the background shout something to her. 'Leroy reckons it's O'Donoghue.'

'O'Donoghue. I'll try that. I believe she works for the *Echo*?'

'Does she? I thought James once said she sold advertising. Maybe I'm wrong. If you find out what's happened to James, you will let us know won't you?'

I promised I would and proceeded to dial the *Daily Post & Echo*. 'Lisa O'Donoghue, please, in Advertising.'

'Putting you through.' The voice was metallic. These days I'm never sure whether I'm speaking to a computer or a human being. One day we'll all get DNA chips implanted in us and nobody will be able to tell the difference. Frightening.

'Advertising.'

'Could I speak to Lisa O'Donoghue, please?'

'I'm sorry. Lisa no longer works here.'

Chapter Eighteen

Lisa O'Donoghue had given her notice in the week before and had left the previous Friday. The girl at the *Echo* either didn't know, or was not prepared to tell me, where she had gone and, no, she didn't have, or wouldn't give me, a forwarding address.

'Back to square one,' said Jim.

It certainly looked like it. It seemed we could do nothing until Scanlan showed up. Alive or dead.

I decided I might as well take Maria to look at the house after all so I rang her to say I'd pick up her and Victoria in half an hour.

'What's all this about buying a house then?' asked Jim, eavesdropping unashamedly. 'You've said nothing to me about it.'

I filled him in with the details and he looked suitably astonished. 'You mean, you're moving in together at last.'

'What do you mean, at last?'

'Well. It's about time. The kid is nearly bloody two.'

'Fifteen months if you don't mind.' But I knew he was right. The fact was, we were now a family and, as such, should be together all the time.

'What does Hilary think about it?' he asked, but my expression told him everything. 'She doesn't know, does she? You're not thinking of still keeping her on are you?'

'Of course not,' I said and murmured something about when the time comes.

'Bloody two thousand and thirty if I know you. When you're both in your wheelchairs.'

I drove back to Blundellsands to pick up Maria, Victoria and Roly. They were all very excited to see their new home, which they'd already decided on before they even saw it. Geoffrey met us down there with the keys.

Roly bounded round the garden like a gazelle on speed. 'I know you said it was big,' cried Maria, 'but you didn't say it was big enough for a pony. I've seen smaller paddocks. Maybe when Vikki's older…'

'What have I let myself in for?' I whispered to Geoffrey.

He laughed. 'My Uncle Peter had a horse once,' he said. 'Zebedee it was called. He reckoned it cost him three grand a year what with food, vets fees, new shoes and everything. If I were you, boss, I'd get her to make do with a gerbil.'

'I think we'll settle for a greenhouse,' I told Maria. 'Grow our own tomatoes.'

She didn't seem keen. 'There wouldn't be enough room, not once we'd built the swimming pool.'

'What?'

'And maybe a swing and a slide in that far corner.'

We did the tour of the house and went over the plans together. Maria made one or two suggestions that I duly added to the drawings. I felt I was beginning to lose control of the project.

'When can we move in?' she asked.

I looked at Geoffrey.

'Once we get planning permission then another three months to do the conversion, that is providing we don't meet any snags.'

'So we can be in by December.' Maria squealed with delight and kissed me. 'A proper family Christmas in our new home.'

It sounded idyllic but part of me felt uneasy about the loss of freedom and, also, what would I do about Hilary?

I had to drop Maria off at home before I did the show. On the way, we discussed the progress, or lack of it, in the cases.

'If James Scanlan is the person passing on information, why would he disappear at this point?' she asked.

'Someone was on to him perhaps?'

'But who? Think about it, Johnny. You're the one who's doing the investigating and you've done nothing to make him think he's in imminent danger of discovery.'

'He might have thought he can't keep out of my way much longer.'

'He's managed it so far. The Spanish woman is well gone, and Routledge would have told you if he'd suspected anything so why did he decide to disappear at this particular time? No, I think

113

there's something else with this Scanlan, something you don't know about.'

She lapsed into silence and I pondered her argument as I drove past the Liver Buildings. Coming up along the dock road was my flat in the Waterloo Dock. How would Maria feel about it if I kept it on after we moved to Sefton Park?

'What about your other case?' Maria broke the silence. 'Dorothy Grove. I was wondering, who she would have left her money to if this charity hadn't come along.'

'Does it matter?'

'It might. And there's her ex-husband too…'

'Jake Morton you mean? What about him?'

'I wonder if he really did manage to keep his money like he said. He may have told you that so you wouldn't think he had a motive for killing her.'

'I'm not sure about that, Maria. He is back in business don't forget.'

'That could be on borrowed money.'

'I suppose so.'

'Or even if he did hold on to his money, he might still have hoped she hadn't got round to changing her will since they split up.'

'All supposing she was leaving it to him anyway.'

'He was her husband, Johnny. It would have been a reasonable assumption. But maybe you should go and see her solicitor. You might find out something.'

'Maybe so.' Maria had often been right in the past about such things.

* * *

I was in the office bright and early but Jim had beaten me to it. 'Have you seen this?' and he handed me the *Daily Post*.

'*Selina Killer Doubt*' screamed the front page headline, accompanied by a picture of the late singer alongside one of Wayne Paladin. I noticed they hadn't used the usual one of Paladin, the one that made him look like a cross between Charles Manson and Jack the Ripper.

This was an earlier photo, in which he appeared young, fresh-faced and innocent.

'I wonder where they dug that up from?' commented Jim.

'Probably his old choirmaster sent it in. They're obviously preparing him for martyrdom. I see there isn't one of Ms Grove.'

'There is, on page two.'

'Obviously they didn't think she was pin-up material.'

I glanced through the article. Nothing there we didn't know already from Mike Bennett. An enquiry was to be held and the Stark case re-examined. Paladin's brief was demanding a pardon. The argument of lone psychopath versus professional assassin still raged but the latter was now favourite, probably because of the method of execution used. Unfortunately, no connection between the two victims or motive for the killings was forthcoming.

'Read the tabloids.' Jim pushed more papers into my hand. The *Sun* and the *Mirror* both came up with the possibility of a deranged serial killer taking the lives of innocent people at will for personal gratification. *'Who will be next?'* they cried.

The *Daily Mail* blamed the Government for a breakdown in law and order and called for a policy of zero tolerance and the immediate recruitment of five thousand more police officers to patrol the streets.

I threw the papers onto the desk. 'I need to speak to Ms Grove's solicitors, Jim. Can you get their name and address from D.I. Warnett? You could say you need it in order to send in our account to Ms Grove's executors for services rendered to his late client.'

'Warnett'll like that. He'll think we've come off the case.'

Jim was right. The pretext worked.

'A firm called Stanley, Stevenson and Stanley, Johnny. He gave it me without any trouble.'

The offices were situated on the first floor, above a bathroom showroom, in Penny Lane but The Beatles never mentioned them in their song. Down the road was the Rose of Mossley pub where John Lennon's mother used to party during the wartime years, in preference to the air-raid shelters.

I managed to park the car a few doors from the office and made my way up a set of uneven wooden stairs where a pleasant black receptionist took my name and within a minute ushered me into a dark room with a small Victorian fireplace, beige painted walls and a low wattage lamp.

Behind an oak desk sat a bald man, obviously on the threshold of retirement, who had compensated for his smooth-skinned head by growing a prolific grey beard and matching sideburns.

He stood up to greet me in a wavering voice. 'Donald Stanley. Won't you take a seat?' He indicated a bentwood chair in front of the desk and leaned back with his thumbs in his waistcoat. I'd not seen anybody do that since Fat Bill Marsden, my old history teacher, back in the 1960s. Stanley even had the silver watch chain. It was like a scene from *Pickwick Papers*. 'And what can I do for you, Mr. Ace?'

'I have been acting for a client of yours, the late Dorothy Morton nee Grove.' I explained the circumstances. He was not slow to catch on.

'So basically, you want to know details of the lady's previous will, information which is, of course, client confidential.'

'But as your client is dead…'

'Nonetheless…' His voice trailed off.

'I know she altered her will in favour of a charity and that could have been enough motive for the previous beneficiary to murder her.'

'Knowing of her intentions and hoping he was in time to prevent the change, you mean?'

'Possibly. Or because he'd already found out that she'd changed it and it made him angry.'

'Angry.' The solicitor gave a reedy giggle. 'Angry. I like that. He'd have had to have been very angry to kill the poor lady, wouldn't he?'

A silence ensued. I tried a different approach.

'My other question concerns the settlement with her husband, Mr. Morton. Is it true Mrs. Grove came out of the marriage with a sizeable amount of money, which ultimately bankrupted Mr. Morton?'

Mr. Stanley laughed again, which this time ended up as a

wheeze. He coughed into a large white handkerchief. 'Is that what he told you?'

'It's what I've heard from other sources.'

'Again, I cannot divulge figures but I can tell you that Mr. Morton was astute enough to hold on to the bulk of his undisclosed fortune to the chagrin of my client. Not, of course, that it made a tremendous difference to her wealth.'

'No?'

'She had already received a substantial settlement from her earlier divorce, the interest on which provided her with a more than adequate income, even for a woman with her taste for conspicuous consumption.'

Conspicuous consumption? This was puzzling. The Simply Single Club in Queens Drive was hardly a venue for lovers of the high life. Dorothy Grove had no car and lived in a pretty ordinary semi. What did she spend her money on?

'All right, so Mr Morton managed to keep hold of his business and his money. At the same time, he might have hoped, on hearing of her death, that she'd not got round to changing her will immediately after the divorce, so he could still inherit a sizeable fortune?'

'One salient point here, Mr. Ace. What makes you think Mr. Morton was the previous named beneficiary?' He peered at me over his small wire-framed spectacles.

'Well naturally, I'm assuming she'd leave everything to her husband.'

'Never assume anything in this life, my friend.'

I waited. I knew he wouldn't be able to resist surprising me and I was right.

'Mrs Morton changed her will a long time before their separation, cutting out Mr Morton altogether, but she didn't leave everything to the charity on that occasion. That came quite a while afterwards in her last will. In the will we are talking about, the penultimate will, she left her entire fortune to a Mr. Graham Lessiter, her gentleman companion.'

Chapter Nineteen

If Mr. Stanley had indeed hoped to surprise me, he was not disappointed. I was astonished. This was indeed a revelation. There had been no hint or suggestion that Ms Grove had enjoyed an extra-marital liaison.

'You mean, she had a lover?'

Mr. Stanley coughed nervously. 'Let us say I got the impression from my client that he was a friend in inverted commas.'

'Did you really?

I supposed that was a polite way of putting it. I wondered if Jake Morton had known about his wife's infidelity. Another motive for killing her perhaps, although, as he was already having an affair with his secretary, he might have been glad for someone to take Dorothy off his hands.

Yet it didn't always work out like that. Jealously did strange things to people.

'You don't happen to have his address by any chance?' I asked.

All reticence gone, he reached into a drawer, pulled out a bulging file and started leafing through a sheaf of papers. 'Here we are. Mr. Graham Lessiter. He lives in Manchester. I'll write it down for you.'

He scribbled it onto a letterhead and handed it to me across the desk.

'I can't see any harm in you knowing it,' he said.

'So when did she change her will for the second time?'

'Only a few weeks before she died.'

'And was she still seeing Mr. Lessiter?'

'I've no idea but I would hazard a guess that she would have ter-minated the relationship. Otherwise why else would she suddenly decide to drop him altogether and leave everything to charity?'

Why indeed? It was something I needed to find out.

'Was Mrs Morton's niece never mentioned in any of these wills?' I asked him. 'A Miss Wishart?'

'Mrs. Morton did mention a niece to me once or twice but she didn't like her. No, she was never a beneficiary.'

So much for all Elsie's weekly visits to her aunt. Whether they'd been made for altruistic motives or in the hope of copping for the jackpot when the old lady snuffed it, they hadn't done her much good. Happy families indeed. I supposed she'd get her reward in Heaven, as they say, but it wouldn't help her varicose veins.

Jim Burroughs was as surprised as I when I told him about Ms Grove's paramour.

'How she could pull all these blokes looking like she did.'

'I think the attraction was her bank account rather than her feminine mystique.'

'I can't see a connection though with this bloke and Selina Stark.'

'Neither can I and I don't think there is one. I told you, Jim, I'm treating these as two separate cases. One hit man, two contracts but if we find who killed Ms Grove, he might tell us about who did for Selina Stark.'

'It'll be interesting to see what this Lessiter fellow's like.'

I didn't intend to wait long to find out. Half an hour later, I was on the M62 heading for Manchester. Even with the usual everlasting roadworks, I did the trip in under an hour. Lessiter lived in Withington so I got onto Oxford Road and drove out of the city centre past the University. Only a few weeks before, I'd been to the Academy there to see Hank Williams III who was advertised to perform there as part of his British tour, but he didn't turn up. Like grandfather like grandson.

Soon afterwards, the road becomes the famous Curry Mile as it passes through Rusholme. A few blocks further on, when I reached Withington Library, I turned right and headed into a maze of small pre-war houses.

I found Lessiter's place without much trouble and parked right outside his gate. I was banking on him being retired and at home in the daytime.

All the curtains to the front windows were drawn as if somebody had died. I hoped I wasn't too late. I rang the bell and after a long delay, I saw a tall figure approaching through the frosted glass. He opened the door and peered down at me. Not too many people do that.

He must have been six foot seven. He had thick jet black hair brushed back from his forehead and his aquiline nose and hooded eyes gave him a sinister appearance. He was dressed in a white shirt, black velvet jacket and black trousers. The hair must have been dyed as his face looked as if it had been around for a good seventy years.

Think Christopher Lee as a waiter about to plunge a carving knife into his next victim.

'Can I help you?' He had a deep voice and spoke with a cultured accent.

'Mr Lessiter?'

'I am he.'

'I'm acting on behalf of Dorothy Morton.' I figured that was the name he would know her by. I showed him my card.

'You better come in.'

He led the way through a dark hallway into the front room. A single bare bulb dangling from a white cord illuminated the middle of the room, which was occupied by a huge table piled high with books, most of them covered in dust.

Mr. Lessiter seated himself in an old leather armchair beside a tiled fireplace in which burned a gas fire and gesticulated to me to sit in the matching chair opposite.

'How is Dorothy?' he asked. 'I haven't seen her in a while.'

It sounded convincing but her murder had reached the national press and television. It was hard to believe he hadn't been aware of it.

'She was shot dead a week ago.' He looked shocked. 'Surely you saw it on TV or read it in the papers?'

'I never read the papers. I am a historian, my work is in the past.'

I looked at some of the titles on the desk. *Mein Kampf*; David Britton's *Lord Horror*, the first British book to be banned since *Lady Chatterley's Lover*; *Last Exit to Brooklyn* by Hubert Selby jr., another one for the "restricted stock" shelves of the country's libraries; Colin Wilson's *Rasputin and the Fall of the Romanovs* and an impressive volume of David Lindsay's *A Voyage to Arcturus*. Lessiter was certainly not your average Jeffrey Archer or Dick Francis reader.

'Who killed her?' he asked.

'I was hoping you might tell me.'

'I? Why should I know?'

'What exactly was your relationship with Mrs. Morton?'

'We were both involved in the study of treatment of prisoners in concentration camps during the Second World War. Mrs. Morton was preparing a dissertation on the subject.'

It wasn't what I'd expected to hear.

'When did you last see her?'

'A good many months ago. We had a disagreement over some minor matter connected with her studies. She took umbrage and I never heard from her again.'

'So this was not a physical relationship?'

'Certainly not.' He seemed genuinely appalled at the suggestion. So much for Mr. Stanley's suspicions, although I wouldn't have put it past Ms Grove to have allowed her solicitor to believe she had a secret lover. Women like to be thought desirable.

'But you had become quite close to her?'

'That's a strange supposition.'

'Not so strange in view of the fact that you were the main beneficiary of her will.'

'How ridiculous. I don't believe you. The woman had a husband.'

'Mr. Morton wasn't in the will.'

For the first time, he showed interest in the conversation. 'How curious. All right, I believe you. How much am I to get?'

'Nothing.'

'I thought you said...'

'She changed her will after she stopped seeing you.'

'Back to the husband.'

'No, as it happens she left everything to charity. Tell me, Mr. Lessiter, how did you come to meet her in the first place?'

'An evening class in Politics at the University. She became interested in my work. I am in charge of a foundation concerned with the rights of war criminals. We have a worldwide organisation thanks to the Internet.'

'How is the foundation funded?'

'Subscriptions and donations from members.'

'And Mrs. Morton was a fellow member?'

'For a while, yes.'

'And did she donate as well as subscribe?'

'I can't see that is any business of yours, Mr. Ace. Let us say she was an active member of the foundation.'

Something he'd said about a minute earlier suddenly struck me. The *rights* of war criminals. They had rights! 'Whose side were you on in the War, Mr. Lessiter?'

'I am Austrian by birth if that answers your question, sir.'

It did, all too clearly.

'And did that fact have some bearing on your contretemps with Mrs. Morton by any chance?'

'It may have had.' He didn't have to spell it out. Once they'd got down to serious discussions about the treatment of POW's, Dorothy Grove must have become aware she'd got mixed up with a fanatic who'd been batting for Adolf. I wondered how much money she'd put in before realisation dawned on her.

Lessiter stood up. 'I don't think I have anything more to say to you.'

I didn't have too much to say to him either. I took my leave and drove back to Wilmslow Road to get something to eat. I parked round the back and walked through an entry onto the main road which was full of thriving small shops selling everything under the sun. Just like High Streets used to be before Top Shop and Macdonalds took over.

Within a couple of blocks, I came across a pub called the Victoria that seemed to have survived the dreaded brewery makeover that had turned so many genuine old pubs into faceless restaurants.

They didn't have Scrumpy Jack on draught, just the ubiquitous Strongbow, so I settled for a pint of the local cask ale brewed in Hyde to go with my chicken and chips.

I couldn't see that Ms Grove leaving Lessiter's foundation

would give him reason to kill her. He must have had many defections over a period of time. Not everyone was in the Third Reich Fan Club.

I was curious about her financial dealings though. And the best place to find out more details would be her accountant.

I rang Donald Stanley for his name and he informed me it was a Raymond Wellsby who had an office in Southport.

I finished my meal and made it back to the coast by four o'clock, despite the usual bottleneck at Ormskirk. Several schemes to extend the M57 and the M58 to Southport have been proposed, some even appearing optimistically on street plans and road atlases. But they never get built which is why major companies are reluctant to invest in the town.

Wellsby worked out of a first floor room in a three storey converted office building on Hoghton Street. He was a one-man band, with his wife acting as both his bookkeeper and receptionist.

His wife was very attractive, late thirties with long dark hair, a suntan she didn't get on English soil and an enticing smile. She remembered Dorothy Grove quite clearly.

'She was an old bag.' She giggled. 'I shouldn't say that, should I? Not very professional of me, but she was. Ray found her a pain, always querying things and her books were very involved. But she was a good payer and that's what counts, isn't it?'

Raymond Wellsby was more circumspect about discussing his late client and started by quoting me the familiar tale of client confidentiality.

I was surprised to find he was a good deal older than his wife. He had a thick mop of carefully groomed silver hair, which contrasted nicely with his suntan, and he looked very fit. I noticed too that he dressed better than his surroundings indicated. Not many people in the adjoining offices would be wearing an Armani suit and Gucci footwear. I figured he must be a good accountant. Either that or he sent his wife out lap dancing.

'As she hired me to protect her,' I pointed out to him, 'I naturally want to find the people who killed her so we are really both working to the same end.'

I waited for a moment, knowing it could go either way, but happily, Wellsby accepted this.

'Dorothy Morton had several profitable investments which brought her a regular income. This she supplemented by some clever dealing on the Stock Exchange.'

'The initial money for the investments coming from her first divorce settlement, I take it?'

He bowed acknowledgement.

'What about her outgoings?' I asked.

'Ah, now here she was rather erratic. She seemed to get involved in a lot of crackpot schemes and then, after a few weeks, give them up and go into something else.'

'I know all about the War Crimes Foundation.'

'Oh that wasn't the first. Before that there were the Donkey Rescue people then the Jehovah's Witnesses and, after that, a fringe Socialist group that almost bordered on Communism.'

'She was studying politics at night school in Manchester when she got involved with the War Crimes people.'

'I believe so but her association with them was all over a while ago. The latest thing was this Animal Cruelty organisation.'

'The Society for Humane Animal Treatment?'

'That's them.'

'How did she get involved with them?'

'I've no idea but charities are an aggressive breed these days. They search out potential donors and Ms Grove was the perfect, I was going to say sucker, but that sounds unkind.'

But probably true, I thought. 'She left them all her money. Was that out of character?'

'No. Her donations to the donkey sanctuaries and the Socialists were what I, as her accountant, would describe as over generous. And she gave a even bigger amount to the War Crimes Foundation.'

I remembered what Graham Lessiter had told me about his funding. 'Was that a donation or a subscription?'

'Both. An initial large joining fee followed by regular monthly membership payments.'

'And, of course, she'd named them in her will at one time.'

'You know about that?' Mr. Wellsby looked surprised.

'Her solicitor told me.'

'Then you'll know that she changed her will and this animal charity is now the sole beneficiary of her estate.'

'Had she given them any money previously?'

'She was making regular monthly donations from the day she joined, shortly after she left the War Crimes lot, right up until the time she died. I told her she couldn't afford it, she wasn't doing too well with the shares, but she was hoping for a lump sum from her divorce from Mr. Morton.'

'But she didn't get it.'

'No. Mr Morton was too clever. That confounded her.'

It also explained why she'd been desperate to find a replacement husband to give her an extra source of income.

'I'm interested to know who might have got her money had this animal charity not come along. I assume it wouldn't be her husband but had she been making donations to any other organisations?'

'No. She'd only recently jettisoned the War Crimes Foundation when the animal people came along and hadn't yet revoked her will. They got lucky that they were the ones who happened to be the beneficiaries at the time she died.'

Remembering Jake Morton's jocular remark, was it luck or had they had prior knowledge of her intended bequest? The accountant couldn't tell me.

'All I know is what went out of the account and that was the rather excessive monthly standing order.'

'To whom was it made? Have you any names?'

He buzzed for his wife to fetch him the file. She asked me if I'd like a cup of tea but I said I was fine, I'd soon be leaving. There weren't many more questions for me to ask.

Wellsby looked up from the file. 'No, no names. Not even the name of the organisation, just the initials. SHAT.' He smiled. ' Not the best name for a charity.'

'I take it you've never come across them before?'

'No, but there are so many charities of one kind and another these days, it's hard to keep track of them.'

'That's true.'

'They thrive on women like Dorothy Morton but they need to in order to afford the inflated salaries they pay their staff.'

I said, 'I prefer to give my money to buskers. At least you know who the money goes to and you get to hear the song as well.'

Wellsby smiled and wished me luck in my quest to find his late client's killer although he didn't feel he'd been able to contribute anything of value.

Neither did I but I didn't think about it too much as I had to race back to Liverpool to do the show.

It was seven thirty when I finally returned to the office to pick up Roly and found Jim was hanging on for me. 'I don't suppose you'll have heard,' was his greeting, 'seeing as how you've got your mobile turned off.'

'The battery's run down. Why? What's happened.'

He said, 'Lisa O'Donoghue's been found outside a house in Toxteth. Dead.'

Chapter Twenty

It was headlines in the late night edition of the *Echo*. The body had been discovered in the early hours of the morning in the front garden of a bricked up property in Jermyn Street near Princes Park in Toxteth.

She was identified by a diary in her pocket. Police said robbery was not the motive and neither had she been sexually assaulted. The inference being that the killer was somebody known to her.

No mention was made of James Scanlan but I knew the police would not take long to find out they'd been living together. So where was Scanlan now?

'I'm getting off home,' Jim said. 'Rosemary's keeping the dinner hot. We'll discuss it tomorrow.'

The next morning brought no further information. The *Daily Post* had it as their lead story but the content was much the same as in the *Echo*, apart from a brief hint that it might possibly be drugs related. I figured that was because it was Toxteth.

I was surprised to find, when I reached the office, that Rupert Routledge had called me. Jim said he sounded agitated.

'Perhaps he's had another anonymous letter,' I said and rang him to see if that was the case.

I was put through to his office immediately. I guessed he had been waiting for my call.

'I need to see you,' he said brusquely. 'Now.'

'Give me half an hour,' I said. What was he going to tell me? But, when I got there, it turned out he was as much in the dark as I was.

Without preamble he asked, 'Have you found James?' Jim was right. This was a worried, even a frightened, man.

'No. I went round to his flat yesterday but he'd left.'

'Have you seen the headlines in today's paper? The dead woman?'

'Yes.' I decided to let him tell me. 'What about her?'

'She was James's girlfriend.'

'Lisa O'Donoghue? And you think this may have some bearing on why he left the company?'

'I don't know what to think.'

'You don't think James killed her?'

'No, no, of course not.' He sounded very sure of that.

'Then what?'

'You've no idea where James might be?'

'Not the slightest. I know he's always managed to miss me whenever I've come to here which, in my book has made him number one suspect for your spy.'

But Routledge seemed strangely disinterested in matters of industrial espionage.

'Forget about that for the moment.' I noticed the beads of sweat again on his forehead. 'I need to know what's happened to James. Have you no leads at all you can follow?'

'I'm afraid not. Every time I look for him I hit a blank wall. I'm told he lectures at the University but when I asked for Mr. Scanlan they'd told me they'd never heard of him.'

He looked at me surprised. 'Well of course not. That's understandable. His name is Kanlan not Scanlan.'

'But everyone I've met has called him Scanlan.'

'No. The two names run into one another, that's why. It's James,' he paused, 'Kanlan. I made the same mistake when he first came here. If you tell them to look under K instead of S they'll find him.'

That explained a lot. 'OK, you could be right but that doesn't explain why he's been avoiding me.'

'He probably hasn't. Just coincidence.' By now he'd stood up and was pacing the room behind his desk. 'Look, I want to know as soon as you find him, do you hear?'

'You think something's happened to him, don't you?'

'Of course not.' He gave a hollow laugh like a man on the Titanic who's spotted the iceberg. 'Why should anything happen to him?'

'His girlfriend's been strangled so something is going on.'

'Ring me,' said Rupert Routledge, in a dismissive tone. 'Find out and ring me.'

I went back to the office. There'd been no further news. 'Routledge is scared of something,' I said to Jim. 'But I don't know what.'

'Even if Scanlan…'

'Kanlan.' I put Jim right about his name. 'That's what caused all the confusion.'

'Even if he is the spy, why kill his girlfriend?'

'I don't know but I'd say James Kanlan disappeared for a reason. I think the two of them were on the run from something.'

'Or someone.'

'It's bound to be connected to this information leak.'

'It would appear so. And whoever was after them caught them up and killed her. But why didn't they kill him too?'

'Perhaps they did,' I said, 'but nobody has yet found his body.'

We were pondering this when the phone rang. It was Hilary.

'I fancy going to the Grand National on Saturday, Johnny. Would you like to take me?'

I had to hand it to her. Her timing was good. Maria was taking Victoria to Bakewell for the weekend. Her son, Robin, from her previous marriage had recently started a new job there. Did Hilary have sixth sense?

'O.K.' I said. 'Why not?' It was a public event. No chance of a repeat of the previous week at her house. I was still feeling guilty about that. 'Can you meet me at the Dale Street office at eleven?'

Hilary said she would. Neither of us mentioned what we'd do in the evening.

'So what about Kanlan then,' asked Jim when she'd gone.

'I'll go to the Uni and see if they've seen him.'

This time I had better luck. The receptionist instantly found a Mr. James Kanlan in her directory and rang his extension.

'He doesn't appear to be in at the moment,' she said.

'Which room does he have? I'll put a note under his door.'

By this time, a couple of students had formed a queue behind me and she was anxious to move me on. She told me the room number and warned me that he shared with two other people.

One of the other people answered the door when I knocked. He

129

was a black man, around thirty with thinning hair. His blue polo shirt was unfashionably tucked into his jeans.

He didn't look like a University lecturer but who did nowadays? I wandered if anyone was left wearing the old cap and gown, outside of graduation photographs. Even vicars are deserting the dog collar for T-shirt and jeans. He introduced himself as Simon Churchill and said he lectured on Biochemistry.

'I only see him from time to time,' he said in reply to my query. 'We really just use this room to keep our stuff in. James's cupboard is over there.'

I crossed the room to inspect it. The door was unlocked. All the shelves were filled haphazardly with textbooks. I glanced through a few of them, all medical and all beyond me.

I asked Simon Churchill when he had last seen James. It was over a week ago, he said, and, no, he didn't look unduly worried.

It was only when I got back to the office that I remembered the telephone number I'd scribbled in my notebook, the 0151 number when I dialled 1471 on the phone in James Kanlan's flat.

'This is our only clue,' I said to Jim, as I dialled the number, not forgetting the 141 prefix. 'These were the last people to phone Kanlan although we don't know if they actually got through.'

'Certainly worth a try.'

'Let's hope they're in this time.'

They were. The phone was picked up on the first ring, hardly giving me time to be surprised when a gruff Scouse voice answered, 'Society for the Humane Treatment of Animals.'

I did a double take. These were the people who had inherited Dorothy Grove's money. Whatever did they have to do with James Kanlan?

Chapter Twenty-One

'Hello. Can I help you?'

'I'm sorry. Who did you say you were?'

He repeated it.

I was thinking on my feet. 'Yes, I wanted to join the Society.' I was about to say James Kanlan had recommended me but thought better of it.

'OK mate, we'll send you a form. What's your address?'

'I'm in town at the moment, I can drop in at your office.'

'Suit yourself.'

'Whereabouts are you?'

'Newington Street off Renshaw St.' I knew it. It was opposite the Renshaw pub, just up the road from Lewiss's, and it ran through to Bold Street. He gave me the number and said they were on the second floor.

'What's up?' asked Jim as I replaced the receiver and when I told him he said, 'it might be just a coincidence.'

'How many times have I told you, Jim? I don't believe in coincidences.'

'Well I can't see any connection at all. I mean, they are a charity and people must be giving them money all the time. Ms Grove probably saw an advert for them in a paper.'

'And Kanlan?'

'I don't know. Maybe he's friendly with someone who works there.'

'We'll soon see. I'm going over there now.'

I walked across town to Newington Street and found the SHAT HQ building without much trouble. There was no mention of them outside the building but the front door was open. The entrance was shabby and the stairwell ill-lit. I climbed up the uncarpeted wooden stairs to the second floor.

A small visiting card with the initials SHAT was stuck on one of the doors facing me. I walked in without knocking. A man sat with his back to me at a table. He turned round when he heard me.

'Can I help you?' I recognised his Liverpool accent from the phone call.

'I rang a few minutes ago about joining.'

'Oh yeah.' He rummaged in a desk drawer and handed me a form. 'Here yerrare. Do yer wanna fill it in now?'

'I'll take it with me if I may. Have you got any literature about the society as well?'

He sighed and rose clumsily to his feet. He was a big man, probably in his late thirties and looking more like a football hooligan than a charity worker. He had a ring in his right ear, a shaven head, designer stubble and he wore combat trousers and a black T-shirt bearing, in blood red, the inscription BAN HOUNDS printed over a picture of a Beagle skewered to a tree.

I recalled what Elsie Wishart had said about SHAT. Her solicitor had described them as 'one of those extreme groups'. It wasn't hard to believe him looking at their representative in front of me.

As he rummaged through different drawers, dragging out various leaflets and brochures, I glanced at some of the posters displayed on the walls. They were pretty unpleasant, most of them showing pictures of animal experiments in laboratories. Dogs, cats and monkeys being subjected to what looked like medieval torture. There was a long cloth banner protesting against the Waterloo Cup, the hare-coursing event held at nearby Altcar, and another complaining about the savagery of the Grand National fences.

'Here you are, these'll give yez something to think about.' He thrust a pile of papers into my hand. 'Here, don't I know you, pal?'

'Johnny Ace,' I said. 'I have a programme on the radio.'

'That's right. Thought I recognised yer. How about getting us some publicity then? It's the Grand National on Saturday and a crowd of us are going to Aintree to demonstrate. You could have us on yer show and we can tell people how fucking cruel it is.'

I didn't bother to argue the point. Instead, I asked him his name.

'Garth Greer.'

'So who runs this charity of yours, Garth? Is it a national outfit or local or what?'

'Three of us run it; me, Kevin Mason and Jake Leech but we've got people in cells all over the country. Listen, we could do with a plug on the radio.'

'It must take a lot of money to run. Have you got a sponsor? Do you run money-making events or what?'

'No, we rely on donations mainly, like. People do give us money, we charge a membership fee to join and we get left money too. I tell you, mate, there's a lot of people not happy about the way animals are treated in this country or anywhere for that matter.'

'I think it's worse in Korea,' I said. 'They eat dogs there. And the Spanish aren't too kind to bulls and donkeys.'

'Yeah, well, you can't do everything. We just work on this country.'

'Are there other offices besides this?'

'We've got virtual offices. On the Web. Listen, do we get on your programme or not?'

'Leave it with me,' I promised. 'I'll have a word with the station bosses and see what I can fix up for you.'

He seemed appeased. 'All right. Thanks, mate.'

The meeting gave me plenty to think about. A few doors down, on the top floor of another old building, was The Egg Café, little known to your average Liverpool shopper but a favourite haunt of students, vegans and street people.

I went up and ordered a bean salad and tea and took a seat on an unmatching, paint-spattered folding chair. The food in The Egg is good but you'd never mistake the surroundings for The Ritz.

Posters and pamphlets adorned the painted walls, advertising, among other things, clubs, bands, food supplements and political meetings. I noticed one for SHAT, stuck up behind a Muslim girl eating a bowl of thick soup.

I needed to do some serious research into this outfit. There was obviously a connection with James Kanlan, otherwise why would they ring him? However, whether it had anything to do with his disappearance I couldn't be sure.

Dorothy Grove had left them a sizeable fortune yet they certainly didn't seem to be her kind of people. How had she come across them?

However, before I went back there and started asking questions, I wanted to gen up on them, read their literature, check out their website.

I finished the meal and walked back to the office.

'Well?' Jim looked at me inquiringly.

'Very dodgy. Fellow called Garth Greer running it with two of his pals. He looked a right hard case.' I tried to remember the names. 'Mason and Leech I think the others were called.'

Jim shook his head. 'I know Greer, he's a professional enforcer, and I once pulled in a guy for GBH called Leech, Jake Leech. Lived out towards Clubmoor.'

'Jake, that's him. I bet it's the same man.'

'You're right. Very suspect then, Johnny, if he's involved. They may call themselves a charity organisation but I don't think we're talking Children In Need quality here.'

'So you think it could be a scam, a front for making money?'

'That, or a bunch of fanatics hell bent on destroying property like the anti-hunt people.'

'Or the ones who attacked the Huntingdon research lab not so long ago.'

'Not to mention the idiots that released all those minks into the wild?'

'Or, Jim, it could be a combination of both. A large scale fraud putting the money in the pockets of the organisers as well as co-ordinating a nationwide gang of protesting anarchists.'

'Who are happy to use violence to achieve their aims.'

'The violence is part of the attraction I'd say.'

'The question we must ask, Johnny, is what has any of this got to do with a respectable middle-aged lady like Dorothy Grove?'

'You said she probably read about them in the paper. All I can say is, they must have a good advertising agency.'

'And how does James Kanlan fit into the puzzle?'

This puzzled me too because in Kanlan's case there was a connection in that Kanlan worked for a medical research company. I'd seen Leroy Holden dissecting his mice at DRP. Did mice qualify under the SHAT campaign or were they too small to count? Fair game, like rats, for the vivisectionists.

'I'd have thought that if they were gunning for DRP, they'd have gone for Routledge. Kanlan's just one of the workers.'

'Yet he's the one that's gone missing,' said Jim, grimly. 'And his girlfriend's been murdered.'

'I'm off to do the show,' I said. I needed time to assimilate the rush of recent events and work out some plan of action.

Ken hadn't heard of SHAT when I asked him but Ken had never been too *au fait* with current affairs.

'They're mounting a protest at Aintree on Saturday,' I said, 'I thought we might do a phone-in tomorrow.'

'If you like.' He was hardly enthusiastic. 'Isn't it a bit old hat? The Grand National fences aren't what they were. That dog of yours could jump Bechers these days.'

'We'll see.' Before I invited Garth Greer on the show, I thought I might ask Tommy McKale what he knew about him, which meant a late night so I rang Maria to tell her I'd be stopping at the flat.

'It's to do with the strangled girl.' I gave her a brief resume of my day and the meeting with Garth Greer. 'I'm going down to the Masquerade to see if Tommy McKale knows him.'

It was eleven o'clock when I made it to the Masquerade and the place was already packed.

'We're having a Drag Queen Night,' Dolly explained. She was dressed in a waistcoat, bow tie and shirt and a pair of black trousers with a top hat on her head. 'We couldn't get a bowler,' she explained. 'I'm meant to be Ella Shields, you know, *Burlington Bertie from Bow*.'

Tommy McKale came over, having escorted a group of Russian

seamen into the club, depriving them of several twenty pound notes each on the way.

'This Euro's going to be a problem for you, isn't it Tommy? You won't be able to bamboozle them with all the different currencies anymore.'

'Maybe not, but short term we'll make a killing while they get used to them. Mind you, most of the gormless buggers are so pissed by the time they come in here it wouldn't matter if we just told them to empty their pockets and then fucked them off down the road.'

If The McKale Brothers had been put in charge of The Millennium Dome, Tony Blair would have been quids in.

'I've let Vince do the DJ-ing tonight. He's in his element. Come and have a look.'

'Before I do,' I said, 'I want to ask you about a bloke called Garth Greer. Have you come across him.'

Tommy's brow furrowed. 'Very nasty piece of work, Johnny. Steer clear.'

'He's running a charity called the Society for Humane Animal Treatment.'

'He is an animal, no doubt about that, but humane? No way.'

'A Jake Leech and a Kevin Mason are in it with him.'

'Leech is a GBH merchant.'

'Yes, Jim Burroughs said he put him away for that.'

'I thought Greer had got life for murder. Mind you, life means nothing these days but they're a bad crowd to cross. Mason's the one with the brains. Greer's a sadist. What's the anti? Subscription blag? Squeezing old ladies consciences along with their bank balances?'

'Plus a fair amount of violent protest stuff.'

'You can find any amount of rent-a-mobbers amongst the liberal fraternity. Makes you want to puke. They've no principles, they just like a good punch up. One week they're burning holiday homes in Wales, the next week it's down with fox-hunting.'

'All organised on the Internet.'

'Be careful, Johnny.' He gave me a serious look. 'Not the best people to cross.'

With that, he led me into the club and bought me a drink.

'All the waiters tonight are transvestites. We've imported them specially.' I looked around. At a nearby table, an attractive brunette wearing a mini skirt, off-the-shoulder blouse and red lipstick was repeating a drinks order in a deep gruff Scots voice.

'They're not all shirtlifters,' pointed out Tommy. 'Some of them just like dressing up as women, especially when they're shagging them.'

No different than David Mellor dressing in his football strip, I supposed, although I hadn't heard that he ever took his pleasure of the Chelsea team.

Vince was on the DJ's podium dressed in a skintight red sheath dress, black fishnet stockings and a blonde wig. I noticed his silicone implants were coming along nicely.

'I get an orgasm every time I sneeze,' he announced cheekily. 'Someone asked me what I was taking for it.' He paused for effect then delivered the punch line. 'I said, pepper.' The audience whooped with delight.

'He'll be going out as a comedian next,' I said to Tommy, 'Mickey Finn and Jackie Hamilton'll have to watch out.'

'If you've come here thinking you were having a respectable night out, you've fucked up good style,' cried Vince, now well into his stride, and he played a disco version of 'I Feel Pretty' which he dedicated to all the girls who "like to party in Pussy Parlour". Looking around, I thought there were plenty of those in the audience.

'I always said P.J. Proby should have recorded that,' said a voice beside me. It was Spencer Leigh.

'Hello Spen, what are you doing here?'

I'd been meaning to ring him for days to compliment him on a really good interview he'd done recently on Radio Merseyside with Dion, one of my favourite rock'n'roll singers.

Spencer said he was with a group of insurance people celebrating someone's birthday.

Funny how everyone feels they have to apologise or have a reason for being in the Masquerade. Why can't they just say they like a wild drunken night out occasionally listening to ear-splitting music in the company of whores, queers and gangsters? No harm in it.

'I've got Gene Pitney coming up on my programme soon,' Spencer added.

And I'd got Garth Greer on my show if I wanted him. Something wrong there.

But, on the other hand, maybe somehow Garth Greer could lead me to the killer of Dorothy Grove.

Chapter Twenty-Two

I woke at eight o'clock on Friday morning at my flat. My mouth was dry and my head felt like a hundred drums were playing inside it. Too many Scrumpy Jacks.

I lingered for half an hour in a steaming hot bath then jumped under an ice-cold shower which jolted me into life. I put on a leather jacket and a blue shirt over a pair of Pierre Cardin jeans, £20 at a designer reject stall on Birkenhead Market, and set off for breakfast in the Royal Liver Building.

On the way in, I picked up a *Daily Post* from the shop and read the headlines over my tea and toast.

Nothing new had happened in the Lisa O'Donoghue murder except police had now revealed that they were anxious to find her partner, 33 year old James Kanlan, who was missing from their home in the Kings Dock.

Kanlan, of course, would be the number one suspect. Spouses always were. I, of course, knew different. I was sure Kanlan hadn't killed her – he was more likely to be dead himself – but I was a million miles away from finding out who had murdered Lisa.

Selina Stark and Ms Grove had been relegated to the inside pages, just a brief paragraph about the search still going on for the gun and the killer.

'Anything happened?' I asked Jim when I finally crawled up Dale Street to the office, still not feeling a hundred per cent.

'Mike Bennett's been on.'

'Oh yes? What did he want?'

'Nothing special. Just wondered how we were getting on with everything.'

'I think he's missing the job.'

'I'm not sure. He said he's thinking of starting up a security company.'

'Not another one. He'll be in competition with Tommy McKale.'

'I think Mike's operation will be a little different than McKale's,' said Jim drily.

I didn't pursue the matter. 'Does he know if the police have caught Selina Stark's killer yet or have they decided to stick to the Wayne Paladin story?'

At least Lisa O'Donoghue hadn't been shot so we didn't have to worry about any connection with hired gunmen there.

'No. The sentence is up for review I believe but, according to Mike, they've still drawn a blank with the gun and there have been no new leads on Ms Grove's murder.'

'He's on the wrong track, Jim. I've always said it, they're two totally different things.'

He scratched his head. 'I'm not sure about that. There's a chain linking all this lot together, I'm sure of it. The trouble is, it's so bloody confusing I hardly know where to start. Have you found out any more about these SHAT people?'

'Tommy McKale says they're hard men and they're trouble.' I repeated what Tommy had told me about them.

'Well he should know if anyone should. He reckoned Greer had been in for murder did he? It's possible. I'll get Mike Bennett to check them out. He still knows enough people in the Force does Mike, not like me. I'm the forgotten man.'

'It's over two years since you left, Jim. People move on, things change.'

And Jim wasn't one for change. Christ, even The Chocolate Lavatory were playing at some of the very same venues they'd appeared at in the Sixties. Probably half the audience at Crosby Comrades Club, or The Jive Hive as it used to be known, had seen them there the first time round. Forty years was a long time to wait for a triumphant "return visit by popular demand".

'Don't I know it?'

'Maybe we should have another look at Selina Stark's history. Can Mike get hold of her file do you think?'

'I'll ask him. He's still quite pally with his old sergeant, Eric Edwards.'

'I remember DS Edwards. A strange looking bloke. He had a

very hairy chest right up to his neck. The hairs used to curl over his collar like a ring of ferns.'

'He's put in for Inspector now Mike's turned his badge in.'

'He'll probably get it, won't he?'

'I should think so. He wasn't a bad copper.'

'Just a hairy one.'

'I think hirsute is the word you're looking for.'

We were making conversation and I knew why. We had nothing definite we could do. I'd interviewed everyone remotely connected with Ms Grove and not found a motive for her murder between the lot of them.

DRP's industrial spy was as much a mystery as ever. My one suspect, James Kanlan, had disappeared without trace. And although the killing of Lisa O'Donoghue was really not part of our remit, I wouldn't have had any idea where to look if it had have been.

We knew little, too, about the Selina Stark case but then, neither did the police. Despite the thorough investigation that the murder of such a well-known public figure demanded, all they'd come up with was an innocent fall-guy.

Which left SHAT. Yet it was hardly likely that they'd killed Ms Grove. Apart from the obvious fact that charities didn't as a rule pursue a policy of involuntary euthanasia of subscribers, they wouldn't have known that she'd named them in her will. In fact, as she was providing them with a regular monthly payment, it would actually have been in their interest to want her to live to a ripe old age.

'Perhaps we should stick to finding lost budgerigars and catching errant husbands with their lovers,' I said ruefully.

Jim shuddered. 'Never get mixed up in domestics. Some of these jealous spouses are more violent than Mike Tyson and I speak from years of experience.'

'Maybe you're right.'

'We'll have to work out what do we should do next.'

'Have a cup of tea,' I said, 'that's what we'll do,' and, whilst I was making it, the phone rang and decided it for us.

The caller was Gabrielle Lorenzo over in Alicante.

'I have good news for you, Johnny. We've at last got the name of a contact in England.'

'Great. Who is it?'

'A man called Justin Pellowe.'

'Name doesn't ring a bell. Who is he?'

'He's probably the man in Liverpool to whom all the information from the Alicante and Speke companies was going, and possibly from the Sydney and Dublin operations too. He was a scientist who used to work for one of the multi-national drug companies in Germany but he left because he felt the profit motive was overriding the medical side.'

'Sounds like the sort of man we're looking for.' In fact, very much like the workers at DRP. 'So what is he doing now? Setting up a clearing house for secrets?'

'Something like that.'

'How will I find him?'

'Easy. I can give you an address for him. He lives in a place called Hightown outside Liverpool.'

'Know it well,' I said. 'It's on the coast between Liverpool and Southport. Nothing much there except houses, a pub and a few shops.'

'Shouldn't be difficult for you then.'

'Does this mean you've managed to locate that worker in Alicante who went missing, the one who was leaking the secrets? What was his name?'

'Guiseppe Roma. No, but we believe that he's somewhere in England and possibly he's joined up with Pellowe. We know he left Spain by train from Valencia, through Barcelona and Marseilles and on to Nice where he caught a plane to Liverpool.'

So he hadn't been killed after all.

'How did you come by Pellowe's address if you never found Roma?'

'It was hidden in his lodgings.'

'But you must have looked there ages ago. Why didn't you find it before?'

'Because,' she said impatiently, 'in addition to his apartment, Roma was renting a room in a downtown boarding house. We only learnt about it this week. As you can imagine, we searched the place pretty thoroughly and we eventually found an address book hidden inside one of his pillows. Pellowe's was the only name with a Liverpool address so two and two make four.'

'You hope.'

'I think it's a reasonable assumption.'

I asked her if they'd been able to identify any culprits at the Irish and Australian drug companies yet but they hadn't.

'How is the investigation going over there?' she asked.

I had to admit we'd made little progress regarding the leaking of information from DRP. 'My chief suspect was one of the researchers called James Kanlan, but he's disappeared.' I told her about the murder of Kanlan's girlfriend but she didn't seem convinced we were on the right track.

'Forget them for the time being. I want you to go over to Hightown and talk to Pellowe. I feel we could be on the verge of cracking this thing. If you think Pellowe's the man we want, I'll fly over. Meanwhile, you must try to obtain from him the names of the people he's working with.'

How we were to achieve this she didn't say but I am sure that Jim Burroughs' years in the police had taught him plenty about the art of "persuasion".

'With a bit of luck, Roma may be with him so you can apprehend them both,' she continued. She didn't say on what charge.

'This is the job we're being paid to do,' said Jim when I put down the phone. 'I think we should forget everything else, at least for the time being, and concentrate on boxing this off.'

'I agree.' We weren't getting anywhere with the rest anyway. 'I'll get down to Hightown straight away,' I said.

Justin Pellowe lived in a semi-detached cottage in the old part of the village. On the other side of the railway track, streets of new houses had risen in what were, until quite recently, sand-hills.

The last three decades had seen places like Hightown and

Formby double their population as the migration from the city centre continued, though now, with all the new luxury apartments going up in town, people were starting to come back.

There was no answer to my knock. I tried going round the back but the side gate was locked.

Mid morning in full daylight was not the best time to break in and, besides, I'd noticed the burglar alarm outside the first floor window. I gave another knock, louder and more sustained, but to no avail.

I peered through the front window and found myself looking into an office lined with bookcases and filing cabinets. Next to the window was a desk on which stood a PC and printer surrounded by piles of papers which suggested that Justin Pellowe worked from home.

So, it seemed, did the person next door. I rang the bell to inquire about Pellowe's movements and it was answered by a young man in a navy tracksuit, holding a cordless phone to his ear.

'Just a second,' he said into the phone and, to me, 'can I help you?'

'Sorry to disturb you. I just wondered if you knew what time the man next door is usually in.'

'When he's home, he's in most of the day, but he travels out of the country a lot so he's not often about.'

'You don't know if he's away at the moment?'

He thought for a second. 'No, he's here because he had some people round last night. One of their cars was blocking our drive.'

'Only I've been knocking and there's no answer.'

'Perhaps he's asleep, either that or he's gone out already. Is there a Nissan Almera in the drive?'

'No.'

'There you are then, and now you must excuse me,' and he returned to his call.

I took the country route back through Little Crosby and stopped off at Blundellsands to pick up Roly.

144

'How did last night go at the Masquerade?' Maria asked. It was her morning off from the Library and she was seated at the kitchen table assembling a pile of glistening beads into a necklace.

Victoria was in her playpen arranging a number of assorted furry animals in a line, a pastime her mother referred to as "playing zoos". Roly was in there with her, contentedly chewing on a threadbare woollen kangaroo. Probably playing "celebrity chefs".

I said, 'The place was full of woofters dressed as Judy Garland or Marilyn Monroe and lipstick lesbians snogging in corners.'

'Just the usual then,' she smiled, 'but I meant the case. Did you get anywhere with it?'

'Not really. Tommy McKale said the men running that animal charity are gangsters and we've no idea who killed Kanlan's girlfriend. But we do have a lead on the drug company leak. That's where I've been just now, to Hightown.' I told her about Gabrielle Lorenzo's call.

'They still don't know who the person was who was supplying the information out of the Speke factory though?'

'Not yet. I think the idea is that Pellowe will tell us.'

'Mmmm.' Maria looked doubtful. 'Why should he?'

I couldn't think of a reason.

'I came to pick up Roly,' I said.

'Oh. I was going to take him down to the beach later with Vikki.'

'In that case, go ahead. He'll prefer that to lying in the office all afternoon with Jim glaring at him.'

I stayed for a cup of tea and was just helping my daughter align her giant panda next to a small white teddy bear when my mobile rang. Victoria tried to grab it but wasn't quick enough.

'Johnny Ace.'

'It's me,' said Jim Burroughs. Why does everybody say 'it's me' when they ring up? I'm not marvellous on voice recognition.

'Which you is that?' I was tempted to say, but I accepted I should be able to recognise Jim's voice after all this time and settled for 'What is it?'

'James Kanlan has just rung.'

'What!'

'I've just put the phone down from him. He says he's in danger and he wants to meet you.'

'When? Where?'

'He was ringing from Bootle, in the New Strand Shopping Centre. Said he's keeping to crowded places, they're safer.'

The New Strand was where Jamie Bulger had been abducted in arguably the city's most horrific murder case. Didn't seem the safest place on Earth to me.

'I've got to meet him there?'

'No. The lounge of The Merton Hotel on Stanley Road at twelve thirty.'

It was just gone noon.

'OK Jim. I'll be there. Did he leave a contact number?'

'No. He was in a call box. Did you see Pellowe?'

'No, he was out. The neighbour says he travels around but he is in the country at the moment so I'll give him another try later.'

I said goodbye to Maria and Victoria and it was twelve twenty five when I pulled into the car park outside the Merton.

The lounge was quite busy, mainly with office workers from the Inland Revenue and Council offices nearby. I walked around but I couldn't spot James Kanlan.

The barman came over and I ordered a half of Caffreys, all the time keeping one eye on the door.

By one thirty, I'd drunk a pint of ale, eaten a tuna jacket potato and read the back pages of a *Daily Mirror* left at the bar.

And there was still no sign of the DRP research worker. He had told Jim Burroughs he was in danger. His girlfriend had been strangled.

What had happened to James Kanlan?

Chapter Twenty-Three

'I waited an hour but he never showed up. Have you heard anything? Has he rung back?' I was back at the office.

'Not a thing,' said Jim.

'Something must have happened to him.'

'We don't even know who his enemies are.'

'What about Routledge? If he'd found some proof that Kanlan was the spy in the camp.' Yet I didn't really believe that. Routledge had never seemed concerned enough.

'Or how about, If he *was* the spy at DRP, perhaps he'd had enough and was going to blow the whistle on the whole ring so this Guiseppe Roma had come over to shut him up.'

'No, Jim. If Kanlan wanted out he wouldn't tell them. He'd just go.'

'Unless they found out his intention without him telling them.'

'No. I can't buy that. Think of something else.'

But neither of us could.

'Let's hope he rings again,' said Jim.

'We could have a long wait.' If he had been in danger, maybe we were already too late to save him.

And I didn't intend to just sit around waiting.

'I'm going to look up a few things on the Internet,' I said. 'Starting with Selina Stark. Who knows what we might find?'

I typed her name into the Google search engine and, as I might have expected, there were innumerable sites dedicated to the late singer ranging from tributes and potted biographies to detailed accounts of the police investigation and the trial leading to the subsequent imprisonment of Wayne Paladin.

Not surprisingly, there were several conspiracy theories put forward for the murder, most, but not all, of them posted before Paladin's arrest.

Some suggested the assassination was the work of Islamic

fundamentalists. I found this hard to believe but Stark had apparently signed up to an Alpha course before her death, which, in the opinion of the writer, made her a target for anti-Christian groups.

Others thought her well-publicised anti-drug stance in the press had incurred the wrath of the drug barons who had therefore paid for her to be silenced.

Someone with a twisted mind – you get a lot of those in cyberspace – maintained Selina Stark was secretly working for a foreign intelligence and had been eliminated by our own MI6. About on a par with the Princess Diana theories.

I switched back to Google and tried the entries for Wayne Paladin. Again, I found a substantial number of hits with accounts of his life, his previous offences and discussions on the likelihood that he was the killer.

Despite his conviction by jury, surprisingly few people thought Paladin really was guilty which told me a lot about how the police have come to be viewed in this country over recent years.

More than one person declared Wayne Paladin had been fitted up for political reasons, possibly to avert confrontation with a foreign power, whilst others thought the police needed to arrest someone and a lonely weirdo of limited intelligence with a criminal record was the ideal scapegoat.

How right they were, but now it was all going to rebound on the authorities big style.

'Any joy?' asked Jim, peering over my shoulder.

'All heavy stuff but nothing new.' I switched to the *When Skies Are Grey* website to read the latest news from Goodison Park, though I wasn't sure that reading about Everton qualified as light relief. 'It would be funny if, all the time, she'd been shot by a jealous lover.'

'Funny but highly unlikely, Johnny. Every possible avenue regarding her personal relationships will have been thoroughly explored.'

'I suppose so. Yet somebody hired the hitman. Hey, I've just thought. Ms Grove's first husband went to Saudi Arabia, didn't he? Could there be a connection there?'

Jim looked scathing. 'I hardly think so. We're getting into the realms of fantasyland. Anyway, I thought you believed they were two separate incidents.'

'I do really.'

'So nothing new with Selina then?'

I had to admit there wasn't but a thought struck me. 'Did we ever find out who inherited all her money? I mean, she'd be pretty well off with all the hit records and the TV stuff.'

'You're right although I'm sure the police will have gone into that. It's an obvious line of enquiry. Mike Bennett will know. He said he might drop in later so we can ask him then.'

I switched back to Google and typed in "Society for the Humane Treatment of Animals".

Again, I was astonished at how many sites it offered up. I clicked on to the first one which was the official SHAT website.

Beneath a logo of a tiny monkey with a shaven head, a tear in its eye and a needle through its brain, it offered information on the organisation: the date the organisation was formed (1998), the names of the people running it (Leech, Greer and Mason), the address (a P.O. Box number) and a list of campaigns they had fought.

I read them all with disbelief at the scope of their activities. They had organised demos against hunts countrywide; any companies using products tested on animals; laboratories practising vivisection; racehorse trainers and racecourses; cattle and sheep farmers abattoirs; transport companies carrying livestock for slaughter; mink farms, furriers, even people in the public eye wearing fur garments.

It was obvious that they had considerable resources and a large number of members. Either that or they were able to mobilise a huge army of followers at short notice.

Which led to the question, what sort of people got involved in demos like these?

Jim had the answer. 'Special Branch has been keeping an eye

on outfits like this for years. They have a dossier of everyone who contributes to their funds. Probably they'll have your name if you log on to their website more than a couple of times. You'd be surprised how much information people can get on you just through you using a P.C. in the comfort and privacy of your own home.'

I wouldn't and neither, I imagined, would Gary Glitter. Even George Orwell couldn't have foreseen how massive the intrusion of the Government into people's lives would be, nearly twenty years down the line from 1984. CCTV cameras were only the start of it.

Jim came behind me and studied some of the venues on the screen. 'There was big trouble at some of these places, Johnny. I can remember. Violence, people injured, threatening letters, fires started, even small bombs on a couple of occasions.'

'Were they never done for it?'

'People in the front line were but it was hard to pin down the people orchestrating events behind the scenes.. And if we did trace them, they would merely argue that any element of law-breaking was caused by outsiders turning up, outside their control.'

'I want to see if there's any mention of Derek Routledge Pharmaceuticals on here. We know they use mice in their experiments and the last phone call James Kanlan received was from the SHAT office. It's possible they were on the SHAT hit list.'

I trawled through the list of activities but found no mention of DRP despite going back to the start of the list.

'According to this, they started up in 1998,' I said, 'but there's no record here of anything that happened before January 1st 2000. The first two years are missing. I wonder why they were trying to contact Kanlan?'

'More to the point, did it have any bearing on his disappearance?'

'Well, there's no mention of DRP anywhere here. I think I might go and have another word with Rupert's father on Monday. See if he's had any run-ins with them.'

I switched back to the SHAT home page where I noticed a link that enabled people to make online donations. I clicked on to it. It invited people to e-mail their credit card details in order to adopt a rescued animal or just make an outright cash gift.

There were also options for members to become regular monthly subscribers and set up covenants and inheritance trusts for tax-free bequests after their death.

So this was how Ms Grove had come to alter her will.

Membership was pitched at various levels based pretty much on Tommy McKale's philosophy of "screw the bastards for what they can afford". I guessed Ms Grove must have been a pretty senior member.

'Look up some of the unofficial sites,' said Jim, 'and see if there's a message board. That's where the heavy stuff will be if it's anywhere.'

He was right. No end of badly spelt, crude exhortations to cause trouble at mass demos, to illegally picket companies, to start riots at meetings.

'I don't know how they get away with it,' I said. 'Look at all this under "Methods of causing damage and disruption". It gives detailed instructions on how to make petrol bombs, the best way to start fires, glue up locks, and disable security cameras.'

'That's nothing,' said Jim. 'Try looking under bomb making. You can get the full works on how to assemble a Semtex explosive device, where to buy the parts and where to plant it for maximum impact.'

I found Animal Rights Militia and The Justice Department websites which recommended violence against humans who were active in what they considered to be anti-animal activities, including directors and workers in companies and even the personnel of banks that lent money to such firms. Letter bombs, razors in post and contaminated drugs seemed to be part of their weaponry.

And they say the Internet is a tool for improving global relations.

I still couldn't find any mention of DRP though and I was

about to look up their own site when Mike Bennett turned up so I shut down the computer so that we could all sit down and discuss the latest events.

I needed to ask Mike a few questions but, unfortunately, none of his answers took us any further in the investigation.

He'd followed up our enquiry about Selina Stark's will but had drawn another blank. The majority of her fortune had gone to her parents and siblings. There were no unusual bequests.

As for Greer, he had indeed been tried for murder but the sentence was reduced to manslaughter and he'd been released from prison several years ago.

'When I pulled Leech in,' said Jim. 'I thought at the time he should have been locked up for good.'

'Nothing on Mason?' I asked.

'Teflon man,' said Mike Bennett. 'Nothing sticks.'

'Tommy McKale says Greer's a sadist.'

'McKale's hardly bloody Mother Teresa.' The ex-policeman spoke with feeling.

'But he reckons Mason's the one pulling the strings.'

'Certainly Leech and Greer aren't up for Brain of Britain so I guess Mason must be Mr Big in the operation.

'I wonder how much money they're making out of this?' mused Jim. 'Might be worthwhile looking into. It won't be kosher with that lot running it, that's for sure.'

'Not your job anymore I'm afraid,' said Mike Bennett. 'Nor mine. Makes me wish I hadn't retired after all.'

'I believe you're starting up a security business,' I said.

'Not so much security as surveillance, Johnny. You know, cameras, bugging devises, that sort of thing. The word security smacks of night club bouncers.'

'Like McKale's lot you mean,' snorted Jim.

It sounded remarkably similar to Tommy McKale's operation to me. 'What do they say, Jim, set a thief to catch a thief?'

'All I can say is, I wouldn't want him guarding my property.'

Mike handed me a small box. 'Here, take a look at this, this is the sort of thing I mean.'

He handed me a small box to open.

'What is it?'

'A miniature recording device. Picks up any conversation around you when you're wearing it and it's so tiny, nobody would suspect you had it on. Take it, it might come in useful.'

I examined it then put it back in the box. 'Thanks. I'll put it in the car.'

I could see Mike was taking his new career seriously.

'I've decided, I'm going to have Garth Greer on my show tonight,' I announced. 'He wants to protest about the Grand National so I'll see what I can get out of him about how SHAT operates.'

'Worth trying,' said Jim.

I rang the office in Newington Street. Greer himself answered. 'Johnny Ace,' I said. 'Do you still want to come on my programme tonight?'

Garth Greer certainly did. I told him to be at the studio for five thirty, which would give me time to brief him.

'I'll be tuning in to that,' said Mike. 'Make sure you play some decent records in between.'

'How about' The Laughing Policeman' for Colin Warnett?'

Jim glanced down at the phone. 'Still no word from Kanlan.'

'What's this?' Mike hadn't heard about the missing researcher so Jim filled him in.

'You think there's a link between him and the SHAT mob?'

'Could be,' I said. 'Maybe I'll find that out tonight.'

'Watch yourself with Greer,' warned Jim. 'Remember what McKale told you.'

'He's hardly going to attack me on air is he?'

But, with Garth Greer's reputation, I couldn't be a hundred per cent sure.

Chapter Twenty-Four

Garth Greer was already at the studio when I arrived. Ken had imprisoned him in a small waiting room and left him alone with a copy of the previous evening's *Echo*.

'I don't want any rowdyism,' were Ken's first words to me. 'I know what these animal liberationists can be like.'

'Don't worry, just a friendly discussion about a horse race,' I assured him.

A small item at the end of the six o'clock news concerning a possible confrontation between animal rights protestors and Grand National officials set the tone nicely.

I played a couple of records then introduced Garth Greer as a member of the Society for Humane Animal Treatment, a nation-wide organisation whose headquarters were in Liverpool.

'Garth,' I began. Rule One of Broadcasting: Always address your interviewee by his Christian name if you want to lower his status. 'Garth, what exactly have you got against the Grand National?'

His answer came sharply. He may not have been bright but he was well briefed. He informed me that 18 horses had been killed in the race since 1979 and a total of 56 had died at the Aintree meeting in the last 20 years. He wasn't able to tell me which fences had caused the most casualties.

'Statistics can be made to prove anything,' I said. 'Probably, just as many horses have been injured at Cheltenham or Uttoxeter. Have you studied comparable figures for other race-courses?'

He answered immediately. '247 horses died in National Hunt racing last year, that's 1 in 31 of all runners. We want to invoke the 1911 Protection of Animals Act to shut the place down.'

I did a quick mental calculation. 'Taking that as an average year then, nearly 5000 horses would have died in the last 20 years, right?'

He puckered his face as he tried to work it out but in the end admitted he supposed it was "about right".

I continued. 'And sticking to the same average, as only 56 died at Aintree that would mean roughly only 1 in 90 of horses killed died at Aintree. When you consider that there are only about 40 racetracks in Britain that feature jumps, that means each one can expect to have 125 deaths which means Aintree is actually safer than the average racecourse. 28% less horses are killed there than on the average British jump course.'

Rule Two of Broadcasting: Know your subject before you start.

Greer snarled nastily. 'Hah. You can make your fancy figures say what you want.'

'My point exactly, so let's forget about them and talk instead about what has been done to make the course safer. The Aintree fences have been considerably modified in recent years as to be almost unrecognisable today from what they were twenty years ago.'

'Even so,' he said and started to churn out "evidence" that horses were distressed at the height and content of the obstacles but by now he was floundering.

'What about the even more difficult obstacles that horses encounter in show jumping?' I asked him. This threw him off on a tangent and I quickly took the opportunity to switch him over to the aims of SHAT.

'What is your stand on vivisection?' I asked.

By this time, he was almost shouting. 'We oppose all experiments on animals for whatever reason.'

Behind the glass partition of the control room I could see that Ken was starting to look nervous.

'I can understand in the case of cosmetics,' I said, 'but what about life-saving medical experiments.'

'They should practice on humans.'

'They don't reproduce quickly enough to give the constant supply necessary and the waiting time for results would be too long, even supposing there were enough volunteers. Tell me,' I said, before he had time to think up a response, 'have you had any contact with a local drug company called Derek Routledge Pharmaceuticals?'

He hesitated, looked alarmed for a second then said he'd never heard of them. But his cheeks turned purple and I knew without any doubt that he was lying.

'But you telephoned one of their research workers at his home only three days ago, a Mr. James Kanlan. You must remember.'

'What is this?' Greer tore off his headphones and threw them down. 'I'm not staying to listen to this fucking crap.'

Luckily, Ken had faded the guest microphone and all the listeners heard was me thanking Mr. Greer for his time and valued contribution to the debate before introducing Selina Stark's last hit 'before her sad untimely demise'.

Greer stopped at the door of the studio. 'I don't know what your game is, mate, but you'll be hearing from us sooner than you think.'

He was halfway down the corridor as Ken came rushing through the door. 'What the hell's going on, Johnny?'

'Call it a melting pot, Ken. I've thrown in a few ingredients, now I'll wait and see what comes out.'

I wondered if Shady Spencer was listening. He might have thought there'd be a chance of getting his old job back.

I finished the programme with a tip for the big race, Red Marauder, the first name that caught my eye when I looked down the list of runners.

When I got back to Blundellsands, Maria was finishing her packing for her trip to Bakewell.

'It'll be the first time I've seen their house but it looks nice on the photos they sent.'

Her son, who was in his early twenties, had met his girlfriend at Reading University. They'd been going out on and off ever since and the decision to move in together was, I felt, precipitated by his move to Bakewell where he had got himself a well paid job with an IT company.

I'd only met Robin once and that was at Victoria's christening.

He was already at University when I started seeing Maria so I didn't have the problems of a jealous stepchild. All the same, I had been curious to know how he felt about a baby sister coming along at this stage in his life.

We had a light supper and went to bed early after watching an episode of *Morse* on TV. Roly curled up in his usual spot at the end of the bed. Victoria slept in the nursery next door.

I wondered where I'd be sleeping tomorrow.

'I heard the show today,' Maria said. 'I didn't like the sound of that man you were interviewing.'

'The whole SHAT outfit is suspect. Somehow they're involved in James Kanlan's disappearance, I'm sure of it. And there's a link to Dorothy Grove as well.'

'You think they had her killed so they could collect the money she left them? But that presupposes she told them they would inherit.'

'They have a form on the Internet that you fill in to set up a trust or a covenant. It's a tax avoidance scheme similar to ones that lots of charities have. If she filled in one of those...'

'She needn't necessarily have told them how much she was leaving them, need she?'

'Perhaps she let a few clues slip. Who knows? But it must be a possibility.'

The talk turned to other things. She asked me what I was doing over the weekend.

'I thought I might go to the Grand National tomorrow. A few people from the radio station will be there.' Which was true although I didn't expect to be spending much time with them. As for the rest of the weekend, I told myself I was leaving that in the air. I'd see what came up. But I knew very well what that was likely to be.

She said they'd be back on Sunday evening and I told her I'd have a meal ready for them.

They left in Maria's new lilac BMW after breakfast and I took Roly a walk round the block before driving over to the office.

'Cold day to go racing,' Jim said. 'The wind can be biting on that course. Have you had any repercussions after yesterday's programme?'

'Not yet, touch wood. Jim, I was thinking about those people on the Net calling themselves The Justice Dept.'

'The violent animal rights outfit, you mean?'

'That's them. Only, Rupert Routledge's anonymous letters were signed "The Court". Could be significant do you think?'

'I can't see it being The Justice Dept, Johnny. For one thing, surely they'd be only too keen to tell him who they were? Besides, nothing happened to Routledge. I'd say it was more likely a copycat thing.'

'Nothing happened to him *that we know of*, Jim. It would be nice to find out why the letters stopped. And I wonder if his old man ever received any. I might go back and see Derek Routledge on Monday.'

Jim had something else he wanted to say, irrespective of whether I wanted to hear it. 'How come you're taking Hilary to the National then?'

'She wanted to go and Maria's away for the weekend.'

'This can't go on, Johnny, you know.'

'Do you think I'm not aware of that?'

'So when are you going to tell her?'

'Who?'

'Whoever'.

Whoever indeed. That was the big question. Luckily, I was saved from having to answer him by the arrival of Hilary looking a little dishevelled but still glamorous and full of energy. People were always glad to see Hilary, she had that invigorating effect on them.

'This wind,' she gasped. 'I caught the bus over because I knew I'd never find anywhere to park. I tell you what, I'm glad I brought my coat.'

'You'll need it,' said Jim. 'The wind can be pretty sharp on that racecourse.'

'So where's the lovely Maria today?' asked Hilary as I walked with her to the car.

158

'Gone to Bakewell for the weekend with Victoria.'

As soon as the words left my mouth, I knew I'd said the wrong thing.

'Oh, so you can stay the night then, Johnny, that's wonderful. Or would you rather we go to your flat? It's ages since we were there.' She giggled happily. 'It'll be almost like a honeymoon.'

I didn't reply. So much for keeping my options open. Or was this what I'd been expecting, even hoping for, all along?

And, if so, what did that make me? Life, I thought, never used to be this complicated.

As it happened though, I never got to sleep with Hilary that night whether I wanted to or not. The choice was taken out of my hands.

Chapter Twenty-Five

It was Garth Greer I saw first. We had just walked into the Main Enclosure when I caught sight of him moving towards one of the bars. He appeared to be looking for somebody. I steered Hilary towards the paddock. I didn't want to risk any altercation.

We watched the horses parade round for the first race and were about to go and place a bet with one of the course bookies when I noticed another man staring at us. He was in his late forties, tall and built like a concrete shithouse, with dark greasy hair that hung over his forehead. He wore a brown suit that was having trouble encompassing his expanding waistline and carried a thick walking stick.

'Do you know that man?' asked Hilary, 'because he's staring right at you.'

'Never seen him before but I'd know him again,'

We turned and mingled with the crowd but when I glanced back, I saw him pushing his way through a group of people a hundred yards or so behind us.

I said nothing to Hilary. We placed our bets for the afternoon, I looked round. The man kept his distance but was still watching us. We made our way to the rails to watch the race and he kept us in view.

I felt uneasy but carried on as if nothing untoward was happening although I was sure trouble was in the offing.

The National itself turned out to be an incredible race. Due to the extremely heavy going after days of downpours, only four horses finished the course and two of them had been remounted. On the other hand there were no serious injuries to either jockeys or horses, which made me wonder if the Animal Rights protesters, who had been demonstrating throughout the meeting, would be upset or pleased about this.

Red Marauder romped home at 33-1.

'How come you've suddenly started picking winners?' asked Hilary.

'It's not unknown. I tipped Little Owl to win the Cheltenham Gold Cup when nobody else did and I won a packet.'

'When was that?'

'1981.'

'But nothing since?'

I admitted that consistency had been a problem. Hilary put her arm through mine and kissed me.

The horses were coming into the parade ring so we went over and joined the crowds as Richard Guest dismounted from his winning ride, watched by millions on TV all over the world.

'A good result for the bookies,' I said to Hilary, as the jockey went off to be weighed in and we walked back to the rails to collect my winnings. I was right; there wasn't a big queue of lucky punters.

'Time to celebrate,' I said. 'I think champagne is called for.'

We fought our way through the crowds to the main bar. I exchanged a few words with a couple of people from the radio station and spotted Neville Mountbatten, a tenant in my Livingstone Drive house, at the other end of the bar. He was with an attractive, fashionably dressed black girl who was taller than he and looked like a model. He was filling two glasses with champagne. He must have been on the winner too. He waved his glass in salute and I waved back.

Behind him stood the man in the brown suit. Watching us.

I was tempted to go over and confront him but I had Hilary with me. I found it unnerving but I said nothing to her. We drank our champagne and stayed for the next race then I suggested we got away before the end to beat the traffic.

As I pulled out of the car park onto the main road, I saw the man climbing into an old blue Volvo estate. There were seven or eight cars between us. I quickly accelerated and joined the line of vehicles moving along the A59 towards the city centre.

When we came to the junction with Aintree Road, I turned right past Walton Prison and headed down to Stanley Road where the traffic was a bit lighter, just a few late shoppers leaving the New Strand Centre. I wondered what had happened to James Kanlan.

161

'Where do you fancy eating?' I asked Hilary.

'How about going to Chester and then you could come back to mine for the night?'

'Fine.' Probably a good idea because Garth Greer and his associates might know about my Waterloo Dock flat and I didn't want any trouble while Hilary was around.

I took the Wallasey Tunnel and kept on the M53. As we approached Ellesmere Port, Hilary said, 'I tell you where we could go, Johnny. TGI Friday's in Cheshire Oaks. I just fancy something American style. Then we could go and see a film at the multiplex next door.'

'If you say so.'

I pulled off the motorway at the turning for the retail park and turned into the TGI Friday car park. The restaurant was nearly full. After a ten-minute wait for a table, we were shown to a dark corner by a waitress in some sort of fancy dress costume and left to study the menu.

Most of the tables were taken up by families with small children. It was that time of day, people on their way home from the outlet village. As the night went on, the teenage crowd would come in, on their way for a night on the town or for a late meal after the movie.

I tried to weigh up the events of the afternoon but with the general clatter of service, the screams of tired infants, the babble of conversation and loud rock music booming out from every corner, contemplative reflection was not on the agenda. I felt about a hundred years old but I could see Hilary was loving it.

'I'll have the Chicken Monteray,' she decided and I said I'd have the same.

As it turned out, the meal was good and the wine acceptable and by the time we'd finished, my mood had mellowed. Some of the noisier diners had left so we drank our last glasses of wine in something approaching tranquillity.

'What film shall we go to?' asked Hilary. As she spoke, she ran her foot slowly along my leg under the table.

'How about *Billy Elliot?*

'Do you remember when we went to that little cinema in Anglesey back in the Seventies? What was it we saw?'

'*The Pink Panther*, wasn't it?'

'And then we parked out in the middle of nowhere and did it in the Mini with Snowdon in the distance through the back window.'

Twenty years later, despite the larger legroom in the RAV4, I wasn't sure my back would stand up to a repeat performance.

She looked across at me and I saw her eyes filling up with tears. 'We've had some good times, Johnny. I hope they're not going to stop. Not after twenty-five years. Do you realise, we've had each other for a quarter of a century.'

I said nothing and she went on. 'And there was the night we got stranded in Holyhead, do you remember? When you had that French car with the reclining seats?'

I laughed. 'The Simca Aronde. It must have been the only one in England.'

'Wales,' she corrected me. 'Probably not many more in France.'

'Come on,' I said, 'we'd better be going or we'll miss the start of the film.'

We sat on the back row and ate popcorn like teenagers. Hilary thought *Billy Elliot* was a bit slow but I enjoyed it.

'Let's go straight home,' she said as we came out of the cinema. As we got into the car, she threw her coat on to the back seat, which reminded me of a night some years back in the car outside Lime Street station.

Hilary and I play this game of charades where one of us does a mime and from it the other has to guess the title of a song. On that occasion, she'd taken off her coat to reveal herself naked underneath save for a red lace garter. I got the right answer on the second attempt.

'Is there going to be a song here?' I asked.

She grinned mischievously. 'How about Phil Collins' *Take me Home* and make it quick. I can't wait for you.' She slid her hand across my thigh and slowly unzipped my jeans. 'Drive on.'

The journey took under half an hour and we were in bed five minutes later.

'Hey, I'm doing well at the moment aren't I?' grinned Hilary, unclipping her lacy red bra. She wore a matching red thong. 'Getting you back to my bed two Saturday's running. I've got some raspberries in the fridge, Johnny, where would you like to eat them from?' She knelt over me and covered my face with her boobs. 'I wonder what Maria would say if she knew you were here with me? I bet you don't tell her anymore, do you?'

She may have been only teasing but mentioning Maria at that moment wasn't a good idea. I had often asked myself from time to time if the 'forbidden' element that had entered the equation since I moved in with Maria had added a certain frisson to our relationship. Sometimes, I had to admit, it had but this was not one of those times.

From the beginning, sex with Hilary had always been great but when confronted, in the middle of lovemaking, with the image of Maria and Victoria, the awful reality of the situation hit me.

'What do you think?' I replied. My mood had changed but Hilary hadn't noticed.

'Can't upset Maria can we?' she giggled and tried to guide a nipple into my mouth but I pulled away.

'Look, Hilary…'

I knew that the time had come for me to say something but before I could speak, there was smashing of glass and a loud explosion downstairs.

'What the hell!' I leapt out of bed and ran downstairs to find the hall was on fire. 'Christ!' I raced into the kitchen, filled a bucket with cold water and rushed back into the hall. Hilary appeared on the landing, struggling with her dressing gown.

'My God, what's happened?'

'A petrol bomb through the front door.' I threw the water over the flames. 'Fetch some more water. Quickly.'

She rushed to help and five minutes later, the fire was out. I trampled on the ashes to make sure. The hall carpet was ruined;

soaked and burnt through and the walls and ceiling were blackened by the smoke.

'The whole place will need redecorating.' Hilary started to cry. 'Who could have done this and why?'

'I think it's to do with me and this case I'm working on.'

'I might have known it.'

'We need to board up that glass in the front door in case they try to force their way in.'

'You think they will? Who are they?'

'Animal rights people. I had one of them on my programme and I asked him too many questions.'

'For God's sake, Johnny. Why don't you give up this detective business. Look what fun we used to have before ...' She left unspoken the obvious follow up – 'and before you met Maria'.

I went into the front room, being careful to leave the light off, and peered out of the window. Outside in the lane, I could see the dark shape of a car that could have been a Volvo estate.

'They're still outside,' I said. 'We might need some help here.'

'Ring the police, quickly.' Hilary picked up the phone herself but the line was dead. 'It's out of order.'

'They must have cut the line. Good job I've got my mobile.'

I dialled a number.

'Who are you ringing?' said Hilary. 'That wasn't 999.'

A woman's voice answered. 'Masquerade Club.'

'Is that you, Dolly? It's Johnny Ace. Can you get Tommy for me, it's urgent.'

'He's right here, luv.'

Tommy's voice came on the line. 'What's up?'

'Trouble.' I explained the situation and told him where we were.

'I'll have some boys there in 20 minutes,' said Tommy McKale. 'When we get there, stay in the house with the girl. No heroics, OK? Can you hang on?'

'I hope so.' The alternative wasn't an option. At least, I thought ironically, if I was killed, I hadn't left all my money to SHAT. But there had already been too many corpses. I didn't want to add to the list.

165

Chapter Twenty-Six

'What are they doing out there?' Hilary held on to my arm tightly. 'I'm frightened, Johnny.'

'I think they're waiting to see if the law turns up.'

'I don't understand. They surely must know we'll send for the police?'

'They might think there's a chance we've no mobiles or we can't pick up a signal. They're probably tuned into the police radio frequencies so, as soon as they hear a squad car directed here, they'll scarper.'

'How many of them are out there?'

'I don't know.' Greer and Leech certainly, I thought, and the heavy in the brown suit. Mason I wasn't sure about. Did he like to get involved with the day to day violence? I could only see one car. How many did a Volvo Estate hold? At a pinch, probably thirteen men and a couple of Rottweilers. 'Tommy's men are on the way.'

'What will they do to us if they get in?'

'Well I don't think they're here for a Scrabble competition, that's for sure. Have you any weapons in the house, Hil, just in case?'

She thought for a moment. 'Only a carving knife.'

This from a girl living on her own. Mind you, if she did use a weapon she'd probably be the one arrested, as we knew only too well.

'Better have it ready.'

But we didn't need it. In only fifteen minutes, a Cherokee Jeep came roaring down the lane and smashed into the back of the Volvo.

In the glare of the 4x4's headlights, I saw the large man in the brown suit jump out of the estate and fire a gun at the windscreen. Glass splintered everywhere.

He didn't have time for a second shot. A figure I recognised as

Big Alec, Tommy's chief henchman, stormed out of the Jeep and smashed him in the Adams Apple with the side of his hand, knocking him to the road where he booted him in the testicles for good measure and then relieved him of his firearm.

With a cry of fury, Garth Greer emerged from the passenger seat and hurled himself on Big Alec. Greer raised his arm and I saw a glint of metal in his hand but before he could plunge it into Alec's body, Tommy McKale came up behind him, grabbed his arm and, in one quick movement, bent Greer's arm backwards, dislocating his shoulder and going on to break the bone before throwing him to the ground.

Suddenly, Jake Leech appeared at the other side of the car, holding a machete. He ran at Tommy McKale, swinging the weapon at neck height, threatening to slice his head off.

'Don't move.' Alec snapped the words out sharply and Leech stopped dead in his tracks. Alec was pointing the gun straight at him. 'Drop that. NOW!' Leech gave Alec an evil glare and, for a second, it seemed touch and go, then he dropped the machete.

For a second, all was quiet and then the Volvo engine roared into life.

I opened the front door, told Hilary to hide, and went down the path.

'Shit, there's another one in there,' cried Tommy but, at that moment, his brother came racing from the Jeep, ripped open the driver's door of the Volvo and dragged a figure by the collar into the road.

'Any more of the bastards?' shouted Tommy.

Denis peered inside the estate. 'No. This is the last one.' And he pushed the man against the side of the car and hit him just the once.

'Nice one, Den,' approved his brother as the man slumped unconscious to the ground.

Leech made to move but Big Alec covered him with the gun. 'One move and I'll shoot both your kneecaps off.'

Nobody present doubted that he meant it. Leech backed off.

Garth Greer slowly got to his feet, clutching his shoulder. 'I'll get you for this,' he promised.

'One more word from you, fucker,' said Tommy McKale, 'and I'll break your other arm. Now get into your car.'

Greer glanced across at Alec, still holding the gun, and slunk to the Volvo. The driver, who had come round, rose unsteadily to his feet and followed him.

'I think your friend needs urgent medical attention,' smiled Alec. 'You'd better take him with you. An ambulance might not make the hospital in time.' Being careful to cover him, Alec watched as Leech manoeuvred the brown-suited man to the car where Greer helped lift him in.

'If you come anywhere near here again, you're dead,' was Tommy McKale's parting shot.

'Any one hurt in your car?' I asked.

'No but look at that fucking mess.' Tommy pointed to the windscreen. 'The bastards'll pay for that.'

I didn't doubt it, one way or another, but I told Tommy to send me the bill.

'I owe you,' I said. 'I don't know what we'd have done without you.'

'Nonsense. You're doing me the favour, Johnny lad. I enjoy the excitement. Takes me back to the old days. Just buy me a mineral water at the Leisure Club sometime.'

'Don't worry, I'll make sure you get your usual plug on the show.' Over the years, I'd given The Masquerade Club numerous mentions that would have cost Tommy thousands in advertising fees on Radio City. 'You did well to get here so quick.'

'Yes, but I could only bring the three of us,' said Tommy. 'It's a busy night down the club. A load of Irishmen over for the race meeting. We've sold more Guinness in two hours than we normally get through in a month.'

Hilary stepped out nervously to join us. 'Good job I've no close neighbours with all this noise.'

'I think you'd better stay at my flat tonight, Hil, just in case they decide to come back.'

Tommy had other ideas. 'You two stay where you are. I'm leaving Denis here to stop with you. He's got a Uzi in the car and six Molotov cocktails. If they come back, he'll blow up the lot of them.'

We didn't argue.

'Will he get back all right without a windscreen?' I asked Denis, as Tommy and Big Alec drove away.

Tommy's brother smiled. 'He'll maybe have a cold nose but I wouldn't let it worry you. It's never bothered our Alsatian and he's had one since he was born.'

We all went back in the house where Hilary poured some drinks and we sat and talked for an hour, letting the pressure die down. Round about one o'clock, she made up a bed for Denis on the blue futon in her living room and we went up to bed.

'Not much of a honeymoon,' commented Hilary accusingly, as she wrapped the sheets tightly round her.

'It's hardly my fault,' I protested.

'Maybe not but your cases have a habit of getting in the way of everything, Johnny.'

Neither of us felt much like making love. It had been a night we wouldn't forget and for all the wrong reasons. We'd be lucky to manage five hours sleep.

As it was, we overslept and Hilary was on duty at the hospital at eleven.

'Forget breakfast,' she snapped. 'Just get me there.'

We threw on our clothes, locked up the cottage and leapt into the car, along with Denis who needed a lift back into town.

'When will I see you again?' Hilary asked, as I drew up outside the Royal. She didn't look madly enthusiastic about it but this was no time to discuss the situation.

'I don't know, Hil,' I said. 'I'll ring you. Promise.'

After I'd dropped her off, I carried on down Prescot Road to Jim Burroughs' house.

'Surely he can have one day of rest,' groaned Rosemary when she opened the front door.

'Just a social visit, Rosie.'

'I wish you wouldn't call me that,' she said. 'It's Rosemary.'

'Rosemary then.' She came from West Kirby where they don't breed Rosies. 'Any chance of a brew, love?'

I treated her to my best smile and she tripped off dutifully to the kitchen whilst I joined Jim in the lounge where he was reclining in a well worn armchair, immersed in the *News of the World.*'

'It'll rot your brain reading that rubbish.'

He looked up. 'What are you doing here? Haven't you heard about the day of rest.' The he caught my expression. 'Not trouble is it?'

'Not unless you call gunfights, stabbings and petrol bombs in the middle of the night trouble, no. I just came to tell you I won over four hundred quid on the big race yesterday.'

'What are you talking about, petrol bombs?'

He put his paper down and listened as I gave him a full account of the previous night's happenings.

'Christ, Johnny. Why didn't you call the police?'

There was no answer to that. I could have said I hadn't too much faith in them or they'd take too long, or that Tommy McKale might frighten off the villains more than the law would but Jim, being an ex-DI, could have taken it personally.

In the end I diplomatically agreed with him that, in view of the carnage that took place, the police might have been a better option.

'I wouldn't mention any of this to Rosemary,' said Jim. 'She gets nervous enough about this job. Worse than she ever was when I was in the Force. Anyway, to get back to the case, where does all this lead us?' he asked. 'Why do you think they attacked you?'

'I'm sure it's all tied in with Kanlan. When I mentioned his name to Garth Greer in my radio interview, I knew I'd struck a chord. He's obviously warning me off.'

'Maybe more than that if they came tooled up with shooters. Do you think they're holding Kanlan?'

'Don't know, but that must be the optimistic view. More likely he's brown bread.'

'Why would they want to kill him, if he was the one leaking the secrets? In fact, what have leaked secrets got to do with SHAT anyway?'

'No idea but there's definitely a connection between SHAT and DRP. I'm going to go over to Cheshire to see old man Routledge again tomorrow. I'm sure he must know something.'

'What's wrong with today seeing as how you're such a workaholic?'

'Today I'm going back to Hightown to see Justin Pellowe for Ms Lorenzo.'

'Right.'

'After all, Jim, as you have always said, these are the people who are paying our fee.'

He couldn't argue with that and then Rosemary came in with the tea and we changed the conversation to other things.

'How's Victoria?' she asked. 'And Maria.'

Jim coughed into his cup.

'They're in Bakewell at the moment, visiting Victoria's big brother.'

'You'll have to bring them round sometime,' Rosemary said. 'I've not seen Vikki since she was a tiny thing.'

'Do you want me to come to Hightown with you?' said Jim with little conviction. He looked set for a day's slobbing.

'You're all right. It's on my way home. I'll ring you when I get back.'

Half an hour later, I was driving up to Justin Pellowe's house in Hightown. Apart from a couple of people washing their cars, there was little sign of life in Sunday Suburbia.

I walked up to the front door, knocked hard and waited. No reply. I knocked again then tried the side gate. Still locked. So was the garage and there was no way to see inside the up and over doors.

I looked through the front room window and noticed the P.C. monitor was facing a different direction to when I had last called.

Somebody had been in the house since yesterday.

I knocked once more but still nobody came. I opened the letterbox and was treated to a view of a deserted staircase. The house was silent.

I wondered who had been there, and where they were now? I considered waiting for them to return but decided against it. They might be gone for days.

I went back to the RAV4, started the engine and drove off up the road. A few hundred yards after the next bend, I did a U-turn and came slowly back on the other side of the road. As I passed the house, I looked up and saw a face, half hidden by a curtain, looking out from the upstairs window.

It was Alison Whyte.

Chapter Twenty-Seven

There is only one driveable road out of Hightown, a country lane that splits into two half a mile or so from the village, one half going to Little Crosby and Blundellsands, the other to the Liverpool-Southport by-pass. I parked the car just outside the village and waited.

Quite what I was waiting for, I wasn't sure. I'd no idea what vehicle Alison would be driving but, whatever it was, it would have to pass me. When that might be was another matter. I could be there all day and night. Following her without her clocking me wouldn't be easy either. She knew my vehicle from when I took her to lunch.

A couple of cars passed me heading out of the village, both occupied by lone male drivers. Could one of them have been Pellowe? How many other people were in the house with Alison?

And, of course, the big question was, what was Alison Whyte doing inside Justin Pellowe's house anyway? Did this mean she was the person responsible for the leaks from DRP and, if so, what part did James Kanlan play in it all? And where was Kanlan now?

Perhaps he had nothing to do with any of this after all and was missing because he was on the run after killing his girlfriend. In the end, nothing more than a domestic. They had a row, he strangled her, perhaps without meaning to, dumped the body, panicked and ran. End of mystery.

But Lisa O'Donoghue's body was found in Toxteth near Princes Park. What was Kanlan doing there? And why did he telephone Jim to say he was in danger?

Another car passed me, a Micra with a small grey-haired lady driving who looked old enough to have taken lessons in a T-model Ford. She dawdled along the empty road at twenty miles an hour, gripping the wheel almost desperately. Why do they allow these people on the roads? A compulsory minimum speed limit would get rid of a lot of them.

I glanced at the clock on the dash. One thirty. I realised I'd not eaten all day and I was starting to feel hungry.

That was what decided me. I switched on the engine, turned the car round and drove back into Hightown. I pulled up outside Pellowe's house, walked up to the front door, hammered on it and shouted loudly through the letter-box, 'Alison, it's Johnny Ace. Open the door.'

I stood back and looked up at the bedroom window. No sign of life at first but then I thought I saw a curtain move.

I went back to the letterbox. 'Alison! Open the door. I know you're there. Otherwise, I'll have to break in.' I gave the door a hefty kick to emphasise my point.

Suddenly, I heard footsteps clattering down the stairs, bolts were drawn back and the door was pulled open to reveal a stocky man, about five eight tall, with blond hair. I put his age around thirty-five. He wore light coloured slacks, a polo-neck sweater and a pair of designer rimless glasses.

He said, 'You'd better come in.'

He led me into a large back room, which had French windows leading to a long back garden with a lawn and a collection of fruit trees at the bottom.

Sitting on a beige and pink chintzy sofa was Alison Whyte and, next to her, a man of Italian origin who, had he been younger, could have passed as a member of any one of the hundreds of doo-wop groups that sang on the streets of New York in the 1950s.

'I'd better introduce myself, I'm Justin Pellowe,' said the blond man. He spoke with a slight foreign accent, possibly German. 'Alison you already know and this is our good friend Guiseppe Roma.'

Roma had shaved off his moustache since the photograph. It took years off his age. He stood up and shook my hand enthusiastically. He came up to my shoulders.

Alison remained seated. 'First of all Johnny,' she said quietly, 'won't you tell us what your real involvement is with DRP?'

Pellowe sat down and indicated to me to do the same.

I said, 'Shouldn't I be the one asking the questions?'

Pellowe answered. 'Not until we know on whose behalf you are asking them. Not if you want answers, that is.'

'OK. I was hired by a firm called El Greco Detection in Alicante to investigate a case of industrial espionage in a drug manufacturing company there. Secrets were being leaked to somebody in Liverpool. Mr Roma there was a suspect.'

Guiseppe Roma hung his head. 'I knew they were on to me. They planted one of their people in the company. That's why I had to get out quickly.'

'They then sent another of their people to DRP,' I continued, 'a lady called Gabrielle Lorenzo. She was an IT genius who could supposedly work computers better than Bill Gates.'

Alison gasped. 'Gabrielle! So she was really a spy?'

'No Alison,' I said. 'You were the spy, she was the one trying to catch you.'

'But she didn't catch her, did she?' broke in Pellowe.

'No, so they brought me in instead, to find the person at DRP passing on similar information.'

'Right.' Pellowe breathed heavily. 'This is what we suspected. Now we know where we stand.'

'How did you find us?' asked Alison.

'I didn't. Gabrielle did.' I explained about the search of Guiseppe Roma's secret apartment and Pellowe gave him a filthy look.

'You fool,' he snarled. 'I told you to burn everything.'

'Forget all that,' I said. 'The fact is, you are all here now and I want to know exactly what's going on.'

'It's simple,' Alison declared. 'Justin here is a biochemist who was working in Munich for one of the multi-national drug companies. He didn't like the way the profit motive was over-riding the research side of the business....'

'Just like yourself, you mean?'

'Yes. And Guiseppe here, too. So Justin left his job, came to England and set up on his own to co-ordinate advances in his

175

pet project, which was to find a cure for Alzheimer's Disease. He visited companies in different countries that were working in that field and, over a period of time, recruited people.'

'Why England and why Liverpool?'

Alison answered briskly and efficiently. 'England because it was well away from Germany where people knew him, Liverpool because he liked it when he visited DRP and Hightown because it's out of the way. Most of Justin's work is done on the Web.'

'So these people send their information of the latest trials to him and he uses it to try to find a cure before the companies. What happens if he finds it?'

'Once it's out in the open, available to everyone, it can't be patented so it can be prescribed cheaply like a generic medicine.'

'But the morality of it is wrong. If the drug companies spend thousands on research, shouldn't they be entitled to the fruits of their labours as it were?'

Pellowe broke in here. 'To some degree, maybe, but they are greedy. Are you aware, Mr. Ace, of the incredible mark-ups on drugs?'

I remembered reading John Le Carre's novel *The Constant Gardener* about the immorality of drug companies, but, other than that, it was not a subject I'd studied. I felt there would be legitimate arguments on both sides but a debate was not on the agenda. Pellowe and his associates were only interested in their own set ideas.

The point was, whether their beliefs were right or wrong, the way they were carrying them out was unacceptable and I was there to stop them.

'I guessed you weren't at DRP just to do a radio programme,' said Alison, 'so it didn't take much to realise you might be on to me.'

'Is that why you let me think James Kanlan was the man I should be looking for?'

'Partly, but James did seem to be avoiding you of his own accord anyway.'

'So where does he fit into your little set-up?'

She looked surprised. 'James? He's nothing to do with us.'

'Are you sure?'

'Of course.'

'Then why has he gone missing?'

'His girlfriend has been murdered. Haven't you read the papers?'

'And you think he's killed her?'

'Why else would he be missing?'

'Maybe he's been killed too.'

'Then why weren't they found together? Anyway, who'd want to kill both of them? James hasn't done anything wrong and his girlfriend's a normal girl in an ordinary job. I mean, I can understand a man killing his partner, or vice versa, a crime of passion and all that. But two of them? Doesn't make sense.'

'You know James pretty well, Alison,' I said. 'Do you think he's the type of person who would commit murder?'

'No, not on the surface. He's a nice guy, but the nicest people can be driven to kill can't they? Besides, how well can one really know another person?'

'Let us get back to the matter in hand, please.' Justin Pellowe rose to his feet and stood in the middle of the room. 'Do you intend turning us in to the authorities, Mr. Ace?'

'I only report to Ms Lorenzo at El Greco Detection but ultimately, I would imagine it is up to your respective companies whether they decide to prosecute.'

Guiseppe Roma spoke for the first time. 'Look, we have done nothing wrong, mister. We have stolen no money, taken no goods, hurt no people. All we do is pass on information to help people get better one day.'

'There are four companies in the world specialising in this particular field,' I said. 'Do you have contacts in the other two, in Sydney and Dublin?'

Pellowe lowered his gaze but Alison confirmed that they did.

'I take it they are still working there, undetected?'

'Yes.'

'And how are your experiments proceeding with the benefit of all this pooled knowledge?' I asked Pellowe.

'Slowly. Neurology is a very complex field. All sorts of things like diet, genetics, pollution, cell structures, etc play a part in the formation of the disease.'

I turned back to Alison. 'Where does Rupert Routledge figure in all this? I ask because he didn't seem too keen on allowing me to instigate this investigation.'

'That's strange,' said Alison. 'Knowing how Rupert loves profit, I'd have thought he'd have been only too keen to plug any leak that might cost him money.'

'So would I but he wasn't. Do you think the anonymous letters he received could have had anything to do with it?'

'I don't know.'

Another thought struck me. 'What about Derek Routledge? You were very fond of the old man. Had he any idea what was going on here?'

Alison looked sheepish. 'No, of course not, but I like to think he'd be with us in spirit. Derek was a man who cared.'

Not to the extent that he'd ruin his own company, I thought.

I said, 'Have you ever heard of an organisation called SHAT?'

'Yes. They're an extremist group of Animal Rights protestors. Why do you ask?'

'Have they been involved in any way with DRP at all?'

This time her reply was more guarded. 'There was some trouble with them a couple of years ago.'

'What sort of trouble?'

'When Rupert took over the company, he instigated experiments with dogs and cats instead of the mice we'd been using under Derek.'

'And?'

'SHAT mounted demonstrations outside the factory. The staff had to fight their way past people carrying banners, shouting abuse, that sort of thing.'

'You never mentioned them before.'

'You never asked.' Hardly a satisfactory answer but I let it pass for the moment.

'How long did that go on for?'

'Weeks. It was terrible. They moved on to smashing windows and putting firebombs through the letterboxes. We had to have them all sealed up. In the end, Rupert had to hire a team of security guards.'

'And did that stop them?'

'No. What stopped them was he got rid of the dogs and cats.'

Not good news for the mice then.

'Could it have been SHAT who sent Rupert the threatening letters?'

'Possibly. It was around the same time but I'd have thought they would have signed them. Anonymity was hardly their style.'

Strange that Alison had never given a hint of the SHAT involvement when she first told me about the letters. I could only think that her reason for mentioning the letters to me in the first place was to divert my questions about the industrial espionage. But why had Rupert Routledge never said a word about his run in with SHAT when I confronted him.

What was he hiding?

Chapter Twenty-Eight

Justin Pellowe was becoming tired of the conversation. 'Forget all that. What are we going to do with him?' He pointed at me.

'Before you decide,' I said, 'I should tell you that my partner knows exactly where I am and has complete details of this investigation to date including the fact that I saw Alison at this house when I called earlier. There's no going back for you now. It's over.'

It was a bluff. They weren't to know I hadn't really called in on the mobile, although now I wished I had. Not that I thought that I was in any real danger from them but it was as well to forestall any trouble just in case they were considering disposing of me.

Roma spoke up. 'Look, we're finished as far as any future communications are concerned. I can't go back to the Alicante factory.'

'Guiseppe's right,' agreed Alison. 'And I shan't be able to stay at DRP after this, so it's all finished anyway. You've done your job, Johnny. You've stopped the leaks. Why take it any further?'

'Something called justice might come into it,' I said. 'An old fashioned notion, I know. In the end, though, it depends on what your respective employers want to do.'

'Come on,' said Alison. 'You said yourself Rupert wasn't all that bothered.'

'Like I say, the decision isn't mine. I just tell them what I know and the rest is up to them.'

Alison Whyte and Guiseppe Roma both looked grim. I wasn't sure about Routledge but I couldn't see Roma's employers failing to take action against him after they'd gone to the expense of hiring El Greco Detection. Their bill, with all these European flights, was unlikely to be insubstantial.

'What about you?' I said to Pellowe. 'I take it you're still in contact with the Sydney and Dublin operatives and they're still feeding you the information?'

Pellowe was defiant. 'So? They're nothing to do with The El Greco agency and your investigation.'

'I'm sure the companies they work for would be interested to know about their extra-curricular activities though.'

I wasn't prepared for what happened next. Pellowe let out a roar, charged across the room and smashed me on the jaw with a single blow.

I was off guard and in the split second that I realised what was happening it was too late. I was out cold.

I must have been unconscious for three or four minutes. When I came round, I was lying on the carpet in an empty room. I rose slowly to my feet and staggered into the kitchen where I splashed cold water over my face. I had the mother of headaches but, apart from that, I was OK.

Out of the kitchen window I could see the garage doors were open and no vehicle was there. I did a tour of the house but they were all well away.

I used the phone in the front office to ring Spain. I knew the El Greco office would be shut on Sundays but Gabrielle had given me her mobile number. I just hoped her phone was switched on.

It was. She was on a beach at Altea where it was hot and sunny. I was glad for her. I was in Liverpool where it was raining and I had a sore head. I told her the news and she was delighted to hear that I'd located the miscreants, although less so to learn that they'd got away.

'Keep somebody there to make sure they don't come back for anything. I'll get the first flight over. I shall have to go through their hard drives. The information on them could provide us with vital evidence. I'll ring you when I arrive.'

I needed somebody to stay here and guard the house and decided on Geoffrey. It would be a change from his property duties and give him a bit of overtime into the bargain.

Geoffrey lives with his mother in Aintree and isn't much of a social animal. He's only in his thirties but girls and nightclubs seem to have passed him by. He isn't gay, more the eternal bachelor. Looking after my houses is his life but I wasn't complaining about that.

'Great, boss,' he said, when I asked him. 'Is there likely to be lumber?'

Feeling the bruise on my jaw I told him it was a possibility.

'I'll bring some gear then. How long do you want me there.'

I didn't know how quickly Ms Lorenzo would get a flight to Manchester so I told him to come prepared to stay the night.

Jim wasn't thrilled with the news of Pellowes' escape when I rang him next.

'I hope El Greco will still pay us,' he grumbled. 'A right cock-up this. Fancy letting them get away.'

'There were three of them, Jim, and only one of me.' The fact that Alison was a girl, five foot one in stilettos, Roma was not much taller and Pellowe was middle-aged with glasses and a paunch should have swayed the odds more in my favour. It just shows, surprise is the keynote of victory.

'All the same, that Ms Lorenzo won't be happy at you letting them go.'

'She wasn't but what else could I have done, even supposing they hadn't slugged me. I'm not the police. I couldn't arrest them.'

'I suppose not,' said Jim, grudgingly. 'So what are you doing now?'

'I'm waiting till Geoffrey gets here to guard the place until Ms Lorenzo arrives from Spain, then I'm going home to cook a meal for Maria and Victoria. They're due back late this afternoon.'

'I'll see you at the office in the morning then.'

'Not until I get back from Cheshire. I'm going to talk to Derek Routledge again first.'

I was curious to know what Rupert's father would have to say because I was convinced he knew more than he had let on.

Geoffrey drew up in his battered old BMW half an hour later and I left him in the lounge watching an old Stewart Granger film on TV.

'There's plenty of food in the house,' I told him. 'You just help

182

yourself. If you bolt the front door at night and maybe put a table or something behind it, you'll be able to hear anyone if they try to break in.'

I took the country road out of Hightown to Blundellsands. I realised I still hadn't eaten but it was a bit late now for lunch. Several horseboxes passed me on the narrow road, on their way back from a pony show in Little Crosby.

Weird to think that an investigation that started in a factory in Alicante should wind up here in the English countryside, but although the initial investigation appeared to be tied up, all the spin-offs from it were far from being solved.

Our second case, Ms Grove's stalker (and killer?), was no nearer a solution. Selina Stark's murder was still a mystery, as was the death of Lisa O'Donoghue and the disappearance of James Kanlan. And we were still no nearer understanding how the violent SHAT organisation fitted into it all. Yet SHAT were connected with everything else in the case in one way or another which I felt must mean something.

I let myself into the flat and ran a hot bath. Maria was right. We did need a bigger place. What had been a flat for a single girl now had to accommodate two adults, a baby and a boisterous dog. The sooner we moved to Sefton Park the better.

I didn't know how Hilary would take that. I decided my best plan with her would be to let things lie dormant for a while. Jim wasn't wrong. I couldn't keep the two of them going, yet twenty-five years was a long time to sever all ties.

After I'd towelled and shaved, I put on a clean pair of jeans and a sweater and went into the kitchen to start the meal. I decided to make chicken curry because it was easy. I figured if I wanted to learn to prepare something more exotic, I should start watching *Celebrity Chefs* like everybody else.

I poured a jar of Rogan Josh curry into a pan and placed it on the hob. Then I peeled the potatoes, mushrooms, carrots and onions and tossed them into the pan along with two chicken breast fillets, which I cut into cubes, and some sultanas to add to the flavour.

Maria, complete with child and dog, arrived back just as the meal was ready. She seemed unusually quiet but I put it down to the long drive. Victoria was babbling away about her big brother Robbie and Roly immediately launched himself at the kitchen table where I'd inadvertently left the chicken skins.

The meal went down well enough. Maria and I got through a bottle of Merlot between us then she took Vikki up to bed and I started to clear the table. When she came back, I was in the kitchen filling the dishwasher. She'd stopped at the door and I felt her staring at me. I turned round to see a vehement expression on her face.

'You bastard! You told me you weren't seeing Hilary any more.'

I was totally unprepared for the outburst. It might not have been quite the same as the blow to the head from Pellowe but the effect was just as great.

'I'm not.'

'Don't fucking lie to me, Johnny. You were with her last night.'

'I wasn't.' Maria had been in Bakewell. Hilary and I had not run into anybody we knew. Maria must be guessing. She couldn't know. 'I was with Tommy McKale last night on that SHAT case.'

'You were on television,' she screamed. 'at the Grand National with *her*. You and that slag, arm in arm, all lovey-dovey. Well that's it for me, Johnny. You can get out. Go back to your precious bloody Hilary.'

'Hang on, Maria...'

'Take her to your flat to shag her did you? Thought you were being clever cos I was away?' Her voice deepened. 'You didn't bring her here did you? To my flat! Because if you did...'

'No, of course I didn't. Look, I can explain...'

'There's nothing to explain, Johnny. That's it. I don't want to hear any more of your lies, do you hear. Just get out of my life and take your stinking dog with you.'

Roly growled and bared his teeth. At me.

184

Maria stormed into the bedroom and came back with a handful of my clothes which she threw on the floor. 'You can come back for the rest of your things when we're out and leave the key when you've finished.'

It wasn't the moment for further words. Besides, what could I say? Guilty as charged, m'lud. I didn't take Roly. I picked up the clothes, walked slowly out to the car and drove to the Waterloo Dock leaving behind my dog, my daughter and my ex-girlfriend.

It had been a horrendous twenty-four hours. The gun battle in Heswall, the fight at Hightown and now Maria. I'd just about had enough.

And worse was to come.

Chapter Twenty-Nine

'What can you tell me about a man called Justin Pellowe?' I was in Derek Routledge's lounge. Through the French windows, the Welsh mountains were shrouded in mist and drizzle and it was dark enough at ten in the morning to warrant switching on the light.

I wondered if I'd have been better off staying in bed. I'd had very little sleep, my head ached and I had to concentrate hard on the matter in hand but, as all the old troupers tell us, the show must go on.

'Never heard of him. Who is he?'

'He's the man who has been receiving the classified information sent out from DRP.'

'You mean you've solved your case? Have you found out who was sending it?'

'Alison Whyte.'

'My little Alison, I don't believe it.'

'Your little Alison. She did have a soft spot for you.'

'That's because she believed in the patients before the profits like I do. But who is this Pellowe person. Why would she send stuff to him?'

'He says he's a philanthropist who wants to find the cure for Alzheimer's Disease and share it with the world for nothing without the drug companies getting their greedy hands on any of the money.'

'How altruistic of him!' approved Derek Routledge.

I didn't share his sentiments. I'd met people like Pellowe before and I never believed a word any of them said. Somewhere along the line, I was sure Pellowe had another agenda. Whether Alison and Guiseppe Roma knew of it was debatable. I liked to think they didn't.

'Alison wasn't the only one,' I continued. 'A man called Guiseppe Roma was doing the same thing from a company in Alicante.'

'I know them. They're our competitors.'

'And I think Pellowe has tie-ins with Dublin and Sydney too.'

'Is Rupert going to prosecute?'

'I haven't told him yet.'

'I see.'

I looked him in the eye. Time to get down to business.

'Mr. Routledge, when I asked you the other day about your son receiving death threats, you pretended you didn't know anything about them. You also never mentioned an organisation called SHAT.'

Suddenly, the old man looked all of his seventy years.

'You'd better sit down,' he said. 'I'll get my daily to make some coffee and I'll tell you the whole story.

I wasn't so keen on the coffee but it wasn't the time to argue about it. The days when tea was the universal English drink seem to have long gone.

I looked around the room. The moose heads looked threatening in the gloom and I felt like putting a match to the logs in the fireplace to bring some cheer to the room. It might have been a magnificent house but it was hardly homely.

Derek came back in, we sat down and he began his tale. 'I think I told you last time that I gave up running the business when my wife became ill. Unfortunately, she died shortly afterwards but by then my son had taken over the company and, although I didn't like the way he was changing things, it was too late for me to get back to taking over the reins.'

'What was he doing that you didn't approve of?'

'For a start, he introduced dogs and cats for vivisection purposes which I thought unnecessary. This brought out the animal rights protestors in force and we had terrible trouble from this group calling themselves The Society for Humane Animal Treatment, the one you refer to as SHAT. There was violence at the works, people threatened and intimidated and Rupert received these death threats. In the end, Rupert had to revert to mice for his research experiments.'

'And he wasn't pleased?'

'Rupert is a very vindictive man. He has always been like that, even as a young boy. When he was thirteen, we bought him a watch and some bully at school made him take it off his wrist and he smashed it into pieces. Rupert did nothing then but when the class were next out on the playing field, Rupert didn't play games, he went into the classroom and set fire to the lad's schoolbooks. That boy had to write out a whole term's work in his spare time.'

A lady came into the room bearing a silver tray. She was about the same age as Routledge and wore a beige woollen skirt with matching top and a string of pearls that looked more Boodle and Dunthorne than Stanley Market. I noticed her affectionate glance at her employer as she set out the cups and I surmised that she might be more than just the cleaner.

'So you're telling me he tried to exact some revenge on the people at SHAT?' I asked, as we sipped our coffee. 'What exactly did he do?'

'I don't know, I swear. But it had something to do with James and that's why I'm afraid.'

James! SHAT's Garth Greer had been the last person to call James Kanlan on his phone at home. Now Kanlan was missing and in danger and I knew only too well what happened to people who upset the men running SHAT.

I asked Derek Routledge, 'Why James?'

'He and my son always got on well. James would do anything to help Rupert.'

'Even if it meant risking his life?'

'Surely you don't think he's in any danger?' he asked anxiously.

'His girlfriend has been murdered, Mr. Routledge. What do you think?'

'What about Rupert?'

'I don't know. Maybe they are after him too. I'm going to see him right now and warn him if he doesn't already know.'

Derek Routledge looked very sad. 'Greed,' he murmured. 'That's the cause of it all. Rupert will do anything for money and heaven help people who stand in his way.'

I left him to his reflections. It was still raining as I found my way to the M56 and followed it to Runcorn then over the bridge and on to Speke.

On the way I rang Geoffrey on his mobile. All was quiet at the Pellowe house.

Rupert Routledge was not in at DRP. Nobody knew where he was. I carried on to the Office.

'Any news?' I said to Jim.

'Ms Lorenzo is landing at two at Manchester. She wants you to meet her and take her to Pellowe's house.'

'I'd better go now then. Wouldn't do to miss her.'

'How did the interview go with old man Routledge?'

'Nothing sensational. He just confirmed they'd had trouble with SHAT and Kanlan might have been helping Rupert in some way to get rid of them.'

'So SHAT are still the most likely ones to be chasing Kanlan?'

'So it would appear.'

'Did you see Rupert Routledge to tell him about Alison?'

'He wasn't in.'

'You look rather withdrawn, Johnny, if I may say so. Is anything the matter?'

I didn't really want to tell him. He'd only gloat and say "I told you so" which was not what I wanted to hear, if only because I knew it was true. But I knew I'd have to tell him sometime and, besides, Maria might leave a message.

'Maria's thrown me out. She saw me with Hil on TV at the National on Saturday.'

'What did I tell you.' Gloat gloat.

'Yeah, well, my own fault I know.'

'I've said it all along. Like a time bomb waiting to go off. That reminds me, Hilary rang.'

'What did she want?'

'Asked if everything was OK now after the Battle of Heswall on Saturday. And she wants you to ring her.'

'Later.'

Jim knew when to pry no further. 'What are you going to do now?'

'I'm going to Manchester Airport or I'll be late for the sodding plane.'

How long before it became the Liam Gallagher Airport?

The arrivals lounge was crowded as ever. I parked in the short stay bay and grabbed a polystyrene cup of tea and a sandwich.

The Alicante plane was twenty minutes late, sending the car parking charge through the roof. Sometimes I think they publish the wrong arrival times to extract extra money from the car parks as people are forced to hang around for hours waiting for planes that aren't really due.

Gabrielle Lorenzo swept through the gates like she was on the catwalk at Milan rather than a grey provincial airport in England. She kissed me on both cheeks and said how pleased her company was with our efforts. She didn't seem too upset that I hadn't apprehended Pellowe and his associates.

'We've stopped the leaks, that's the important thing and, as for Pellowe and Co, that part of the operation is, how do you say in England, your buzzard Mr. Ace?'

'Pigeon,' I corrected her.

'Meanwhile, their computers should tell me how much information they've passed on and maybe the names of the spies in the other countries.'

As soon as we arrived at Hightown, Gabrielle made a beeline for Pellowe's computer.

Geoffrey was relieved to see us. 'If I have to watch any more daytime television, boss, I'll go crazy. It's non-stop cooking and confession programmes.'

'You might as well go home now, Geoffrey and I'll see you at Aigburth Road tomorrow.' I wondered if I should mention that my plans for the Sefton Park house were looking decidedly dodgy but decided against it. Maria might come round.

Gabrielle was already zapping through the files on the computer. I made us both a cup of tea - Pellowe's kitchen was surprisingly well stocked - and watched her for awhile then, 'I'm afraid I'll have to leave you to it,' I told her. 'I've got a radio programme to do.'

'That's fine by me. This will keep me occupied for some time.'

'Where are you staying?'

'I'm booked into the Thistle Hotel in town but, don't worry, I'll ring for a taxi to take me there when I've finished.'

'Are you sure?'

'Perfectly. I'll come to your office tomorrow and apprise you of my findings.'

I drove straight to the radio station. Ken was waiting for me in the foyer, a triumphant glint of superiority in his piggy eyes that told me he had bad news for me and didn't it serve me right?

'You're suspended,' he announced. He paused to let it sink in. Another bloody gloater. 'After last Friday's fiasco.'

'Not again.'

'For a month. And when you do come back, you're not to have any more live guests in the studio.'

'No problem, I'll start inviting dead ones,' I replied. 'Tell Creegan I'll arrange a phone-in with Peter Sellers and, with a bit of luck, I might set up an exclusive discussion between Marc Bolan and a well-known tree surgeon.'

Ken snorted.

'Ricky's still shagging Jeanne from the Newsroom then?'

I tried to peer through the plate glass window into the studio to see who was in my chair but nobody had arrived yet.

'It's not Jeanne. Shady Spencer's back.'

'No!' He'd probably been thrown out of Tescos for playing something too controversial like a James Last track.

'God, more of that bloody awful poetry for my listeners to suffer. Just after I'd given them the 33-1 winner of the National too. There'll be a public outcry over this.' I only wished there would be.

I left the station and drove straight to Goodison Park where I managed to find a parking space down a side street half a mile away. I shuddered to think what parking would be like if Everton ever moved to the Kings Dock.

It was the return match against Manchester City. I was early for the kick-off so I queued up for a plate of Scouse and a pint of beer and chatted to Ritchie who ran a carpet shop in town. Over the years I'd bought a few rolls of cord from him for the flats.

'They'll go back down again, City,' he declared. 'They're not up to Premiership standard.'

I wasn't at all sure Everton were either but it wasn't a time for voicing doubts.

City had beaten us 5-0 earlier in the season and had our old manager, Joe Royle, in charge, a man who once likened the Everton team to 'dogs of war', not the most appropriate epitaph for a club that used to be known as 'the school of science'. It promised to be a spicy occasion.

And so it proved, with a penalty for Everton, a man on each side sent off for fighting, a costly cock-up by their goalkeeper and The Blues finally running out 3-1 winners.

After the game, I stopped off at the Winslow for a half and realised I wasn't looking forward to going back to an empty flat. I'd not heard from Maria all day. I didn't really expect to but perhaps I'd hoped she might call.

In the end, I finished my drink, exchanged opinions about the game with a few fans then drove over to the Bamalama Club. The place was still filling up and the dance floor was only half full of people, swaying to an old Barry White hit.

'Jonas has given up with the Scrumpy Jack, Johnny,' apologised Shirley behind the bar. 'I think you were the only one drinking it.'

'Back to the moonshine is it, Shirl?' There was more profit in the moonshine. She filled me a pint glass. 'How's Winston?' I asked her.

'He's fine. That's one eighty, please Johnny.'

I gave her two pounds and told her to keep the change. 'He's lasting well. A year now is it?'

I downed half the glass in one gulp. I was thirsty. Probably due to the Scouse being too salty.

She smiled. 'Fifteen months but who's counting?' Winston

was the eldest son of Jonas who owned the Bamalama. Shirley lives in one of my flats in Princes Avenue and she and I have had an on-off relationship for years. I wondered if Winston would cause it to become a permanent off.

'How's things with Hilary and Maria?'

'Don't ask,' I said.

'Still turbulent eh?' Shirley laughed. I've always said she looks like Mary Wilson of The Supremes but I saw Mary Wilson last year, in concert with Martha Reeves and Edwin Starr, and I reckon Shirley is prettier. Doesn't sing as well though.

'How's Kenny Leatherbarrow,' I asked her, 'have you heard?' Kenny's a drummer from the Merseybeat days who used to drink himself senseless in the Bamalama most nights until he had a stroke a couple of years back.

'Still in the nursing home and he still can't talk though they say he grunts more than he did. Jonas took him some bongos at Christmas so he plays those all day now with his good hand. And he's only in his fifties too! Isn't age frightening, Johnny?'

I finished the drink and got her to pour me another. Then I wandered off into the club. Being Monday there was no group on, just records. The DJ was black, as were most of the punters.

'He's leaving this week; you don't want a job do you, Johnny?' Jonas sidled up to me. 'You'll have better records than he has, he's only young.'

I was about to say I didn't do live gigs and he couldn't afford me anyway but then I remembered I wasn't going to have a lot to do any more at nights and staying in on my own wasn't the number one option.

'You serious?'

He nodded. 'I'd regard it an honour for you to play here.'

'Bullshit,' I said, 'but why not? OK, Jonas, you're on. Say a month's trial.'

We shook hands and he took me to the bar to buy me another drink. I don't remember too much more after that.

I awoke to find myself on a couch in a room that reminded

me of a French brothel and realised I was on a settee in Shirley's front lounge in Princes Avenue.

'Hey, you awake?' Shirley, resplendent in a red and black silk kimono adorned with gold dragons, put a large mug on the coffee table. 'I've brought you some tea.'

'What happened?' I struggled to a sitting position. What sounded like an interminable Yes drum solo was pounding between my ears and my mouth was dry as sandpaper. I thankfully gulped the tea.

Shirley grinned. 'Too much moonshine. I just hope nobody was expecting you home last night though from what you were babbling on about, I guess they weren't.'

I groaned. 'I don't want to know what I said or did last night. Where's Winston?'

'In bed and dead to the world.'

'He's a nice lad, Winston, Shirl. You could do worse.'

'He's twelve years younger than me, Johnny.'

'What difference does that make. You're young at heart.'

Shirley looked embarrassed and changed the subject so I knew it must be serious.

'So tell me, how are things are in the world of great sleuths.'

'So-so. I've just uncovered an international industrial spy ring.'

'Single handed?'

'Of course.'

'That it?'

'No. I'm also trying to find out who shot an old lady called Dorothy Grove and who killed the glamorous Selina Stark, probably with the same gun.'

'Selina Stark. That was ages ago. I thought they had somebody for that.'

'They've changed their minds. He didn't do it after all.'

'I remember meeting Selina Stark once,' mused Shirley. 'She came to our club with her group, believe it or not, when they first started out. She had a little puppy with her she'd got from a rescue place. Very big on Animal Rights was Selina.'

I sat up. 'Say that again.'

'You know, fight against fur, never eat anything that once had a mother, that sort of thing.'

'None of that was ever in the papers was it?'

'She liked to keep it quiet. She didn't want to antagonise the meat eaters or get involved in the leather shoe debate.'

'The what?'

'You know the argument; if you don't believe in killing animals you shouldn't wear leather. At the time she needed all the fans she could get.'

'Shirley,' I said and I reached up and kissed her. 'You're wonderful. You could have just given me the break I've been looking for.'

Chapter Thirty

I phoned Jim immediately with the news. 'Get on to Mike Bennett and ask him whether SHAT were mentioned in Selina Stark's will.'

'He's already told us, she left her money to friends and family.'

'Well get him to check again. If I remember rightly, he said there were no unusual bequests. Well a charity isn't unusual and it needn't have been one of the main beneficiaries, the amount of money she would leave.'

'If you say so.'

'If she has left anything to SHAT, that would give us the first link we've had between her and Ms Grove.'

'I'll do it, Johnny. Where will you be?'

'I'm going to DRP to see if Rupert Routledge is in this time.'

'Why don't you ring to find out?'

'No. I want to catch him unawares. Ring my mobile if there's any news.'

This time when I arrived at the Speke factory, Rupert Routledge was in his office. I was able to inform him we had traced the person responsible for the leaks from his company. He looked pale and anxious, the face of a haunted man, rather than the recipient of glad tidings.

'Alison Whyte, eh? I'd never have thought it.'

'It wasn't personal,' I assured him. 'I think she had an over-developed social conscience.'

'A misguided one more like. So that's the end of it?'

'It's up to you whether you press charges and we haven't caught her yet.'

'I'll have to consider it.'

'Mr. Routledge, I want to talk to you about your association with an organisation called the Society for Humane Animal Treatment.'

'What?' The question jumped from his lips. He was rattled.

'I'm told you had a bitter dispute with them when you took over the company from your father.'

'Where did you hear that?' he demanded angrily.

'Several people including your father and Alison Whyte.'

'It was nothing.'

'Forgive me, but that isn't true. According to what I've been told, there were firebombs, picket lines and it's very likely that the death threats you received at the time probably came from them.'

'It was all sorted, it's in the past.' He was adamant.

'No it's not, Mr. Routledge. James Kanlan is still missing and I believe his disappearance is connected with it. His girlfriend has already been murdered and I think he could be in grave danger.'

At this, Rupert Routledge suddenly crumbled. 'Find James for me,' he pleaded. 'I'll hire you, I'll pay you, just find him.'

'Tell me what part he played in all this and then I might be able to help you.'

But the boss of DRP would not be drawn. 'Nothing. He's just a valuable employee, that's all. No, more than that. He's a friend too. Just find him.'

If that was the way he wanted it, I thought, that was fine by me. There were other avenues I could explore but first of all I drove to Aigburth Road to see Geoffrey.

He was glad to be back in his rightful domain although he said he'd enjoyed his weekend on minder duties. 'All on course for your Sefton Park place, boss.'

'Good,' I said, although, as things stood, it was odds on I might never live there. But it would still be a suitable home for Maria and Victoria and I was quite happy for them to have it. They could always use the recording studio as a games room.

Jim had news from Mike Bennett when I got back to Dale Street. 'Another blank I'm afraid,' he said. 'Selina Stark was indeed a member of SHAT. She paid a monthly fee, just like Ms Grove, but she didn't leave them a penny in her will so that's their motive gone. She was worth more to them alive than dead.'

'But someone killed her and Ms Grove, Jim, and I've changed

my mind now. I think it *was* the same person who killed both of them and I know it's all tied up somehow with SHAT. What we've got to find out is who did it, and why.'

Neither of us had an answer to that so we decided to go for lunch.

A local architect called Ken Martin had recently opened an art gallery in Hanover Street called The View. As well as exhibits of paintings, sculptures, ceramics, textiles, jewellery, and so on, they held live jazz evenings and served food and drink at lunchtimes. I'd been meaning to check it out for ages but I'd never got round to it. This seemed as good a time as any.

But, at that precise moment, the phone rang and The View was off the agenda.

For the caller was James Kanlan and, suddenly, it was all systems go.

'They're after me,' he said. He sounded breathless. 'How quickly can you get here?'

'Who are *they*?'

'It's an animal rights group.'

'SHAT?'

'You know them?'

'Yes, but never mind that now. Whereabouts are you?'

He was in a call box on the Dock Road in Bootle close to Ensor Street. He'd made it as far as the Merton Hotel on Friday but he'd seen one of SHAT's thugs hanging around the car park so he didn't dare go in. Instead, he found this disused building down the road from a scrap metal yard, and he'd been holed up there ever since.

'Why didn't you ring back earlier. It's been three days.'

'I was terrified. I knew they'd killed Lisa and they were going to kill me.'

'Are you near there now?'

'Yes. Look, they know I'm around here somewhere and they're cruising around in an old dark blue Jag. They won't give up.'

'Stay right where you are. We'll be there in ten minutes.'

It was an optimistic estimate but, luckily, I'd parked the RAV4 just across the road from the office and we were on our way within ninety seconds.

'Double back up Tithebarn St and take Vauxhall Road and Bankfield Lane,' said Jim. 'It'll save the lights.'

I did as he said. We reached Ensor Street, wasted a good minute searching for the phone box but found it at last, and there was James Kanlan, leaning over the phone, shaking. With his hair tousled, his clothes torn and filthy, he looked a far cry from the debonair figure I'd seen at DRP.

'Thank God,' he burbled as we ushered him to the car. 'It's been a nightmare.'

'Where shall we take him?' Jim asked as we set off back towards town. 'Bit risky going to the office and his flat will be a non-starter.'

'What about a hotel? Give him a chance to freshen up and have something to eat while we decide what to do.'

He certainly needed freshening up, preferably with carbolic.

Ultimately, of course, we'd hand him over to DI Warnett or whoever was handling the Lisa O'Donoghue murder enquiry but first I wanted to see exactly where he fitted into the jigsaw.

'How do you know it was the SHAT people who killed Lisa?'

'They sent a message for me to meet them. I turned up with Lisa, didn't know what they wanted. Turned out they wanted to kill me but now they had two of us to deal with.'

'How many of them were there?'

'Four.' Probably the same four that had attacked us at Hilary's cottage.

'They dragged us both into their car, the blue Jag that was following me just now.'

'So how did you escape?'

'They did an emergency stop by Princes Park to avoid this kid who'd run into the road and we managed to jump out. We split up. I ran into the Park, Lisa ran the other way. I never saw her again. It was only the next day when I read in the paper I realised they'd killed her.'

That could explain why Lisa had not been shot in cold blood like the others. Her killing hadn't been planned. It was a struggle they hadn't bargained for and maybe they weren't carrying guns. But the end result was the same. Lisa O'Donoghue was dead.

'Why didn't you go to the police?'

'Because they caught up with me and took me to this house in Bootle, I think it was in Kings Road. They held me there overnight. I could hear them arguing about how to get rid of me. Next morning, Friday, I managed to get out through a bedroom window and jumped into the garden. Nearly broke my leg too. I got as far as the Strand Centre, which was when I rang you. I had your number from when you came to DRP. Alison gave it to me.'

We were coming up to the Pier Head. 'How about the Thistle?' Jim suggested.

'Gabrielle Lorenzo is in there. Best not to complicate things. Try the Campanile by the Queens Dock.'

We settled for that.

Jim turned round to look out of the back window. 'Do a detour, Johnny. I want to make sure we're not being followed.'

I swung the car into Lord Street, hit a left into Fenwick Street and pulled into an empty meter bay, a rare sight in Liverpool.

I let seven or eight cars pass until I was sure we were in the clear then I resumed our journey and once we reached the hotel, Jim waited in the car park for a full five minutes whilst I took Kanlan into the reception to check him in.

'Can't be too careful,' Jim explained when he finally joined us. 'I think we're safe now though.'

'You couldn't get me a change of clothes could you?' Kanlan asked, pointing to his torn and muddy suit and scuffed shoes.

'I think so. What size are you?'

'38 regular. Eight and a half shoes.'

'We'll check you in and you can have a shower and get something to eat and in the meantime we'll sort out something for you to wear.'

We saw him to his room and told him not to answer his phone and to admit nobody until we returned.

'What do you think?' asked Jim as I drove back to the office. 'Why do SHAT want to kill him?'

'I don't know but hopefully we'll find out soon. This could be the break we've been waiting for.'

Jim smiled ironically. 'And how many times have we said that in this case?'

The phone was ringing as we walked into the office. It was Rupert Routledge.

'I've just thought where you might find James,' he said. 'I remembered he has an aunt who lives in Windle, just opposite St Helens Crematorium. He might be hiding there.'

'You're all right,' I reassured him. 'We've already found Mr. Kanlan and it appears we were right, it was the people from the animal rights group who were after him. But he's safe now.' I explained what we'd done with James. 'I'll let you know the outcome when we've had a chance to talk to him.'

Rupert Routledge said he was very grateful to us for setting his mind at rest and asked us to get James to contact him.

'I'll go to Littlewoods to kit him out,' I said to Jim. 'I'll be able to get everything under one roof and it won't cost the earth.'

I bought socks, underwear, a casual shirt that didn't need buttoning as I didn't know Kanlan's neck size, a pair of loafers and a jacket and slacks.

'That should do,' approved Jim when I returned. 'I was frightened you'd be going to some designer store in Bold Street.'

Jim always had an eye on the budget and, in this case, he was possibly right. We didn't know who'd be reimbursing us as James Kanlan didn't come strictly under the auspices of the DRT secrets enquiry.

'There was a message on the answerphone from this morning.' he went on. 'Alison Whyte.'

'No? That's a turn up. Did she leave a message?'

'She was concerned about you, wanted to know if you were all right and she was sorry you got hurt. She said Pellowe didn't mean to hit you so hard and that you needn't worry about her. She's with Roma and Pellowe and they're fine.'

'Where was she ringing from.'

'According to the call display, an 01524 paybox number. That's Lancaster.'

'Did she say what she was doing there or where they were headed for?'

'No. It was twelve o'clock when she called.'

'Mmm. 01524. Could have been Morecambe.'

'Why Morecambe rather than Lancaster?'

'Morecambe's on the way to Heysham where the Isle of Man boat sails from. Safer to board it there than from Liverpool where they might be spotted.'

'But Lancaster is on the main London to Scotland railway line. They could have jumped on a train and be in Inverness or anywhere by now.'

'I don't think so, Jim. They could drive to Inverness easily enough and if they'd wanted to catch the train, Preston station's nearer than Lancaster so why would they go another forty miles for no reason?' I felt like Sherlock Holmes. 'No, my bet's on the Isle of Man. I wonder if she'll ring back.'

'Why are you so concerned about Alison?'

'Apart from the fact that it's our job to catch her and her chums on behalf of El Greco Detection you mean?' I felt I ought to make the point. 'The thing is, Jim, I'm worried that Pellowe isn't what he pretends to be. I think he could be using Alison and Roma on the pretext of being a humanitarian, or whatever they call themselves, like they are.'

'But all the time he means to sell the secrets on, is that what you're saying?'

'Yes. And if he's recruited people in the other two companies in Dublin and Sydney then he's got the lot. But if Alison found out his real intentions, I'm sure she'd be horrified in which case, she'd be a liability to him.'

'And you think he might harm her?'

'If he thinks she would shop him, yes I do.'

'What about Roma?'

'The same goes for him.'

'Well, there's nothing we can do about it at the moment, Johnny. First of all, we've got to get these togs to Kanlan and hear what he's got to say. Maybe he'll throw some light on it.'

'You're right. He'll be wondering what's happened to us, we've been gone nearly two hours.'

It was two miles at the most to the Campanile Hotel but, in the busy afternoon traffic, the journey took us fifteen minutes.

In the event, as we found out later, it wouldn't have mattered if we'd have travelled there by helicopter.

Because James Kanlan had already been dead for half an hour when we arrived.

Shot in the head by a single bullet.

Chapter Thirty-One

'Just what's going on?' Detective Inspector Warnett was in a belligerent mood. 'Are you both here because you think there is a connection between this death and Dorothy Grove's murder?'

Warnett had arrived half an hour after the squad car by which time the SOC officers, forensic people and the pathologist were fighting to get inside the small hotel room. He took us out into the lounge area and sat us down around a low coffee table. The young WPC Hagen was by his side.

'What's this got to do with Ms Grove?' I asked innocently.

'I don't know. Yet. Right. Start from the beginning. I want to know everything that's happened here.'

So did we.

'Nothing much to tell,' I said. 'We received a phone call from the dead man around lunchtime.'

'Did you know who he was?'

'He told us his name was James Scanlan.' I emphasised the "s".

'Had you met him before?'

'Never spoken to him in my life before today,' I answered truthfully. I'd never had the opportunity, he'd always been careful to avoid me. Now I might never find out the reason.

'Then how did he know to ring you?'

I looked pained. 'We are a detective agency, Inspector. I like to think we get some feedback from the Yellow Pages advert. We pay enough for it.'

He conceded the point. 'Did he say what he wanted?'

'He was ringing from a public phone box in Bootle. Said some men were after him, could we come and rescue him. Probably a mugging or a car-jacking we thought. Anyway, we drove over there...'

'Where was that exactly?'

'Near Ensor Street off Derby Road. We found him, picked him up and brought him to this hotel for sanctuary.'

'Why here?'

'Cheaper than the Adelphi. We work to a budget.'

Warnett was becoming impatient. 'I mean, why a hotel? Why not your office?'

'Company policy,' I said. 'Keep things in neutral territory in case of problems.'

'What were you going to do with him?'

'Find out what his problem was, but first we went to buy him some new clothes. His own, as you will have seen, were in a mess. We told him to have a shower and get something to eat and we'd be back later, but when we returned, a couple of hours down the line, we found him dead.'

'Killed by a single shot as you can't have failed to notice. Just like Dorothy Grove.'

'Quite a coincidence,' I agreed and Warnett's face contorted like he was in the throes of a *petit mal*.

'I'm not sure it was. I'll need a statement from you at some point.'

'Certainly,' I promised. 'How are you progressing with Dorothy Grove's murder by the way?'

Warnett did not answer but stomped out of the lounge back to the scene of the crime.

'I'm out of here,' I said to Jim.

We hurried to the car park and sped back to the office.

'What next?' he said when we were safely there.

I didn't know. On the face of it, it looked very much like James Kanlan had been killed by the same person who had seen off Dorothy Grove and Selina Stark. They'd probably even used the same gun. Yet I still couldn't fathom a motive.

Everything pointed to Greer, Leech and Mason at SHAT being the likely suspects but what had they to gain?

'Why do you think James Kanlan's girlfriend was killed?' I asked Jim.

'Probably she'd seen too much for her own good. You notice she was strangled not shot.'

'You mean it could be a different killer?'

205

'Maybe.'

I couldn't think much more. I still didn't know where I'd be spending the night. I guessed it would be at my flat because I hadn't heard from Maria all day. I debated whether to ring her but decided against it.

Instead, I went back to the flat to see if there was any message from her on the answerphone. There wasn't. I microwaved myself a Marks's meal and opened a can of Scrumpy Jack. Just the one. I didn't want a repeat of the previous night.

At nine o'clock, the phone rang. I jumped to answer it thinking it might be Maria but it was Gabrielle Lorenzo.

'Are you busy?' she asked.

I said I wasn't and she asked me to come along to the Thistle Hotel for a drink and a chat.

I met her in the lounge. She was sitting at the bar, looking cool and sophisticated in a navy pinstripe suit and ultramarine blouse. She rose to her feet when she saw me come in and we again exchanged kisses on both cheeks.

'Let me get you a drink,' she said, 'cider wasn't it?'

I smiled. 'You have a good memory.'

We took our drinks to a table in the corner and she lit a cigarette which she placed in a holder, like a movie star in a thirties film. I hadn't seen that done in years.

She offered me the packet, Sobranie Kings, but I shook my head.

'You don't mind if I do?'

I did but I wasn't going to say so. I just wished the government would hurry up with the cigarette ban in public places to save everyone from the twin hazards of choking to death on smoke or risking a smack in the mouth for voicing their objections.

She told me she'd had a busy day working on Justin Pellowe's computer at Hightown but it had been fruitless. Pellowe had been careful to wipe the hard disk on his computer before he left and she'd been able to glean nothing from her trawl through his files. What she was looking for was confirmation

206

that the data sent by Alison and Guiseppe had been received by Pellowe.

'He'll have it somewhere,' she said. 'Either on floppy disk or CD Rom. My guess is he'll have a laptop with him and he'll be using that.'

'So we still need to find him?'

I pointed out that she had stopped the leaks and exposed the culprits so, as far as her client at the Alicante drug company was concerned, the job had been carried out satisfactorily.

'If they want to institute proceedings against Guiseppe Roma, the extra evidence would come in useful.'

'You already have the files from his computer showing he sent the classified material.'

'True, but to have it appear at the other end, on Pellowe's machine, completes the proof.'

'Do you think they'll prosecute?' I couldn't see it myself. The leak had been stopped so they had nothing to gain by going to court and risking lost confidence in the company. 'I'd say they'd be glad to pay El Greco's fee and pretend the whole thing never happened.'

Gabrielle thought the same. 'But I'd still like to catch them,' she added. 'if only for my personal satisfaction. And if we can find the names of the people sending information out of Sydney and Dublin, we can warn the companies there.'

'Who should reimburse you accordingly?'

Gabrielle smiled. 'Well the kudos certainly won't do us any harm. So, Johnny, have you any idea where they might have gone?'

'The Isle of Man's a possibility.' I told her about Alison's phone call from the Morecambe area.

'I'm not going back to Spain immediately so keep me posted as soon as you hear any more. Don't worry about further expenses; I'll pass those on to our client.'

We finished our drinks and I bought another round. The Thistle hotel bar was less lonely than my flat. We talked about cases we'd solved and what life was like on the Costa Blanca. She made it sound really attractive. Little did I know I would soon find out for myself.

A waiter came over to clear the empty glasses and Gabrielle ordered another round of drinks, which she had charged to her room.

'We are discussing business so the client should expect to pay,' she said. A sentiment of which Jim would have approved. 'Have you any other interesting cases on at the moment?'

'We've got three bodies with an identical bullet in each,' I said, 'and somewhere along the line there is a link to Derek Routledge Pharmaceuticals through this organisation called The Society for Humane Animal Treatment.

'Really?' Gabrielle leaned forward, her interest aroused. 'Tell me more.'

I ran through an outline of events to date.

'This is really scary,' she said. 'I've never heard of SHAT but we have similar organisations in Spain.'

I mentioned Vicky Moore, a local girl, who'd led a campaign against bullfighting there.

'I think she was protesting against cruelty to donkeys too,' said Gabrielle. 'But the traditions are deeply ingrained in the Spanish way of life.'

We tossed the subject back and forth without coming up with any new ideas. By eleven o'clock we were running out of conversation.

'I'd better be going,' I said. 'Busy day tomorrow.'

'Are you married, Johnny?'

'No. I live down the road in a flat at Waterloo Dock.'

'On your own?'

'Yes.'

'Me too, but I like my own company. I don't think I would like to have somebody around all the time because there are times when I want to be alone. At least when you live on your own, you do have the choice.'

I disagreed. 'You only have the choice, Gabrielle, if the person you want to be with wants to be with you. Otherwise, you're lonely.'

'You can be just as lonely with another person, Johnny, especially if they're not the one you want to be with.'

I pondered her words as I walked back to the flat. Who did I want to be with, Maria or Hilary? But I already knew the answer. Both. Unfortunately, it was no longer an answer.

I wondered if Gabrielle had been making a pass at me. I didn't think so but women seemed to make all the running these days. However, the last thing I needed at the moment was more complications in my life and not doing it with the clients was written in stone, alongside not doing it with the tenants. More likely, Gabrielle was just being friendly.

I slept fitfully, dreaming of Maria and waking in a cold sweat. I finally got up at seven, had a long soak and watched the TV news over breakfast. The Kanlan murder made the regional news bulletin but, needless to say, it was front page headlines in the *Daily Post*.

I reached the office at nine and Jim arrived a few minutes later.

'What's the plan for today?' he asked.

'Ms Lorenzo has given us an open chequebook to go after Pellowe but first I thought we might pay a visit to the SHAT headquarters.'

'Are you mad. After the other night?'

'They're our last chance to solve this case, Jim. Kanlan and his girlfriend are dead, we've got all we can out of the Routledge's, Pellowes gone AWOL so who's left? And we know they're in it up to their necks.'

'What are you going to say?'

'Don't know. We'll play it by ear.'

Reluctantly, Jim walked with me through Williamson Square, past Central Station and up Bold Street. When we turned into Newington Street he hesitated.

'There could be trouble here, Johnny.'

'They wouldn't dare try anything,' I promised. 'Trust me.'

Never trust anyone who says "trust me".

I opened the door to the SHAT office, Jim behind me. Garth Greer wasn't there, probably nursing his broken arm somewhere. Jake Leech was at the desk. When he realised who we were, he let out an almighty bellow, charged round the desk and hurled himself at us.

I didn't see him pick up the knife on the way but he must have done so. He probably kept it on his desk as a safeguard against an unexpected attack.

But that was not important. What was important was where the knife ended up.

Embedded in the chest of Jim Burroughs who collapsed in a heap to the floor.

Chapter Thirty-Two

I didn't move quickly enough. Leech pulled out the knife from Jim's chest, wheeled round and slashed at me. I jumped back and as his arm cut an arc in front of me I kicked out with my right foot and knocked the knife from his hand.

He hardly hesitated but threw himself at me but I was ready for him and stepped aside then turned quickly and hit him as hard as I could in the kidneys with my fist.

He hardly flinched but I gave him an extra push, catching him off balance, and he fell forwards onto his knees.

Before he could get up, I snatched the knife from the floor and, with my left hand, grasped him by the hair and pulled his head back, exposing his Adams Apple to the razor sharp blade.

I was tempted to slit his throat there and then but I could see it might cause trouble for me later on. Some judges might not believe it was an accident. The important thing was, none of his cronies were in the building with him. I wouldn't have fancied my chances against more than one.

Even with the one I had a problem. I needed another pair of hands. I didn't dare let Leech go whilst I attended to Jim but I couldn't hold him like this indefinitely.

Leech made the decision for me. He kicked backwards with his foot, catching me in the groin and causing me to let the knife drop. He turned and swung a fist at me. I ducked in time but he carried on and hit me with his other fist, only a glancing blow but enough to make my nose bleed.

I back-pedalled across the room, almost tripping over Jim who was still not moving. It was then my eye caught sight of a black cast iron doorstopper in the shape of a cat. I leaned down and picked it up by the head and, as Leech came hurtling towards me, I smashed it against his temple.

He dropped like a stone.

I felt Jim's pulse. It seemed regular, if a little weak, but his

211

breathing was laboured. The knife had missed his heart, it was higher up towards his shoulder, but what about his lungs? I wasn't sure where they were. Not for the first time in my life, I wished I'd joined the St John's Ambulance Brigade when I was a kid. Only a small amount of blood was oozing out, which I took to be a good sign, but he was still unconscious. Possibly shock, I thought.

I ran to the desk, picked up the phone and dialled for an ambulance. I told them a man had collapsed, possibly with a cardiac arrest. I thought that might encourage them to put their foot on the throttle.

I didn't know the layout of the office but it didn't take me long to find a storeroom with a key in the lock. I opened the door, dragged Leech inside and locked him in.

The ambulance arrived within ten minutes but I wasn't there to greet it. I watched from further down the street as the paramedics ran in through the front door that I'd left open and I waited until I saw them carry him out on a stretcher.

I'd left a note on the desk, unsigned, advising the police to check the DNA of the man they would find locked in the storeroom for a possible match with DNA found on the body of the murdered girl, Lisa O'Donoghue.

I'd also been careful to bring the knife out with me and I dropped it down a drain after carefully wiping off my fingerprints. The police car was not long in coming, blue lights flashing, siren blazing, as if they were racing back to the station for an early lunch. Two uniforms got out and ran into the SHAT office.

I'd only seen one person carried to the ambulance so that meant Leech was still in there. Possibly one of the paramedics had stayed behind. I hadn't counted them. If so, the officers would have been given full details of Jim's injury, which meant they'd be holding Leech for questioning. All supposing Leech was still alive, that I hadn't hit him too hard. The odds were he was, even now, giving the police some cock and bull story about the morning's events. I wondered if he'd mention me or leave me for his henchmen to deal with at a later date.

I didn't hang around to see what happened next, I could read about it later in the *Echo,* but I was worried about Jim so I rang Rosemary on my mobile and told her what had happened.

'You ought to be with him,' I said. 'He's probably been taken to Fazakerley but if you ring A & E they'll tell you.'

Rosemary was angry. 'For God's sake, Johnny. What have you got him into now?'

'I'm sorry Rosemary. I'd no idea anything like that would happen. In broad daylight in the middle of town.'

'That's when people do get attacked in Liverpool.' Rosemary had long wanted Jim to relocate them to a retirement flat in West Kirby.

I didn't argue with that although I knew that street crime in the city was no worse than other urban areas. Try walking home through Oldham or Burnley at two in the morning.

I asked Rosemary to phone my mobile when she had any news and she reluctantly promised to do so. I also made her give me her mobile number, just in case I couldn't get any information about Jim out of the hospital.

I walked across to Bold Street and went into Waterstones for a quiet cup of tea whilst I worked out what to do next.

I knew I would still have Mason and Greer to deal with but I didn't know where to find them. But Tommy McKale might. Luckily, I had his number programmed into my mobile so I dialled him and tried to explain what I wanted but he couldn't hear me.

'I'm in a bookshop,' I said, in a loud whisper. 'I can't shout.' Bookshops are like libraries, you feel you have to whisper in them in a way you never do in a record shop or a supermarket.

'For fuck's sake, Johnny. Get yourself down to the Leisure Club, and tell me the tale.'

I picked up a cab outside Central Station. Tommy was waiting in the reception area of his club. It was hard to believe, looking round the plush fittings, that this had once been Dennis's old gymnasium where local villains would play snooker and knock shit out of the punchbags and each other while planning their latest jobs.

'I take it you're on the run?' said Tommy, matter of factly.

'I guess so.'

'You get into more trouble than me. I'm not sure I should let you in here. You'll be giving the place a bad name.'

I doubted it. Half the gangsters in the city still worked out here, which, if nothing else, showed that crime did pay.

'Do you like the new name by the way? We've refurbished the place and called it The Fitness Palace.'

'Very swish. Did it need refurbishing? I thought you only did it up last year.'

'Punters like to see change happening, otherwise they think you're falling behind. We have a policy of constant upgrading.'

'A bit like painting the Forth Bridge really,' I said but Tommy didn't seem impressed with the comparison.

'Garth Greer,' I said, as I followed him to the upstairs bar. 'Where can I find him?'

Tommy went behind the bar, nodded to his West Indian barman, and poured us each a glass of freshly squeezed orange juice.

'What do you want him for?'

'I think him and Leech between them, and probably Kevin Mason, could have murdered four people.'

'Only eleven to go then and they'll have caught up with the Wests.'

'Selina Stark was one of them.'

'*The* Selina Stark? You're joking?'

'Deadly serious.'

'I think you'll find you're a bit off beam there, my old son.'

'How do you mean?'

'I thought you'd have known. Kevin Mason and Selina Stark were once an item.'

I was shocked. Why had nobody ever mentioned it before? Probably because they either didn't know or didn't make the connection. 'When was that?'

'A long time before she hit the big time.'

It all fitted in with what Shirley had told me about Selina and animal rights but I needed time to work out the implications.

'Who are the others they're supposed to have stiffed?'

'A client of ours called Dorothy Grove. Old lady. Shot in the head off Queens Drive a fortnight ago.'

'I remember reading about it in the *Post*. Single gunshot in the head. I thought at the time it was a professional job.'

'Precisely. Just like Selina Stark and James Kanlan.'

'Hang on, Kanlan. Wasn't there something about him on the wireless this morning?'

'That's him. Shot in the head, exactly the same, at the Campanille Hotel. He'd been hiding from the SHAT crowd. It was Jim and I who took him there for safety.'

'Remind me not to hire you out as a bodyguard. You said they'd done four people, who was the other?'

'Kanlan's girlfriend, found strangled near Princes Park.'

'Makes a change, I suppose. Perhaps they'd run out of bullets. So what's happening now?'

'This morning, Jim and I went up to SHAT's office in town.'

'And?'

'Leech stuck a knife into Jim.'

'Fuck me! Is he OK?'

'I hope so. It was in his chest but I think it missed his heart. I'm going to ring the hospital later.'

'Where's Leech now?'

'Either in hospital or police custody.' Or the morgue.

'Things happen when you appear on the scene, Johnny, and no mistake. You act as a magnet for bother. I don't know about Greer but Mason lives in Gatacre, I believe, in a big house round the corner from the Bear and Staff. I don't know the number but it's painted yellow, you can't miss it.'

'He's obviously done all right out of his charity lark then. I wonder how much of the money went on the rescued animals?'

'Probably none of it. He'd have had them shot, sold the skins for a fortune and exported what was left to restaurants and take-aways in Korea.'

'I get the picture, thanks. Dog and rice twice with mushy peas.'

Tommy looked serious for a moment. 'I'm puzzled, Johnny. 'Why don't you just tell the Old Bill what's happened and let them get on with it?'

I didn't really know the answer to that myself. Stubborness? Wanting to finish the job I'd been hired to do. Or mistrust of the police after previous experiences with them and frightened of being framed for something I hadn't done? It had happened before. Or was I just chasing the glory?

'There's so many strands to this case, Tommy, and I know they're all connected. If I stop working on it now, there's a good chance the people concerned will get away with it.'

It sounded rather presumptuous the way I said it. After all, I still had no idea who had pulled the trigger of the gun that had killed Selina Stark, Ms Grove or James Kanlan.

I said, 'I wonder if Mason was one of the men in the car last Saturday?' but Tommy said not.

'The monkey in the brown suit that Alec booted in the bollocks was Humphrey Grable, better known as Betty. A nasty piece of work. He's spent most of his life working the doors when he's not been inside.'

'What about the driver?'

'Probably some gash hand they'd picked up to ferry them around.'

'I still can't see how they got to Kanlan. We were so careful to make sure we weren't followed when we drove him from Bootle to the Campanille.'

'And nobody but you and Jim knew you'd taken him there?'

'Not a soul.' And then it hit me. Someone else did know. Somebody who'd rung up our office and I had told him that we had hidden James Kanlan in the Campanille Hotel.

Rupert Routledge!

Chapter Thirty-Three

But why would Rupert Routledge want to harm James Kanlan? They were supposed to be friends. Hadn't Derek Routledge said James would do anything to help his son?

Could James have somehow double crossed him?

I knew it had something to do with SHAT. Routledge had had a run in with SHAT and Kanlan had been kidnapped by them.

So why would Routledge kill Kanlan? It didn't make sense whichever way I looked at it.

'This single bullet business bothers me,' Tommy was saying. These cowboys from SHAT, they're rough and ready types. Planned cold-blooded killings are not their style.'

'We've no other leads though, Tommy, that's why Jim and I went to see them.'

'Fucking stupid thing to do, if you don't mind me saying so,' said Tommy. 'Even if they had killed all these people, do you think they'd tell you?'

He had a point.

'I think I was hoping they would tell me they hadn't and then I could eliminate them from the equation and start looking for somebody else.'

'Like who?'

I was saved from answering by the sound of Mozart's 40th Symphony coming from my pocket. I've tried to get the ring-tone of *Pledging My Love* for my mobile but I've never seen it advertised so I have to make do with Wolfgang. It's better than high pitched bleeping but I must say I'd rather listen to Mozart when the Liverpool Philharmonic play it.

'Johnny Ace.'

'Johnny, it's Alison. Alison Whyte.' She sounded anxious and, if I wasn't imagining it, a little frightened.

'Alison. Where are you?'

'On the Isle of Man. Johnny, I need your help.'

217

'What's the matter?'

'It's Justin Pellowe. Johnny, we've been duped.'

'What do you mean?' But I knew quite well what was coming. It was what I'd suspected all along.

'He's got all the information he wanted from us, now he's selling it on. Can you believe that?'

'Who's he selling it to?'

'I don't know but we need to stop him.'

'What does Roma say about all this?'

'Guiseppe's gone.'

'Gone where?'

'I don't know. He's let me down badly, Johnny. I thought he cared like I do but he was only in it for the money too. Pellowe paid him off in Lancaster and that was the last we saw of him. He said something about going to London. We left him at Lancaster station.'

'Has Pellowe not paid you?'

'I didn't want money. I thought I was helping a cause.'

I remembered what Gabrielle's notes had said. Alison Whyte was "idealistic". Sadly, such people were ripe for exploitation. It's a cynical world.

'Did Guiseppe know about Pellowe's plans?' Not that it mattered any more. He was out of the picture.

'I can't say. I don't think so but perhaps that's because I don't want to think he did.'

So naive and trusting, yet she was not necessarily wrong in this instance. Roma could well have wanted to help the cause but at the same time expect some remuneration for his efforts, which had cost him his job.

'So how come you end up on the Isle of Man with Pellowe?'

'He said he wanted me to help him correlate the stuff he was expecting from Sydney and Dublin.'

'And what does he expect you to do after that, when your work with him is finished? He must know you can't go back to DRP.'

'The original intention was that I would go back there but that was before you came along and scuppered everything.'

'So what does he think you'll do now?'

'Find another job, I suppose.'

Happy in the knowledge she'd struck a blow against wicked capitalism. And why not? She had a good track record. Another company would take her on after Rupert Routledge quietly disposed of her services.

On the other hand, if Pellowe realised she'd rumbled him, I didn't give much for her chances. He'd be under no illusions that she wouldn't shop him so he'd have to silence her.

'When did you find out he was selling on the information?'

'Not until today. We came here yesterday afternoon on the boat from Heysham.'

'How did you find out?'

'I read some of his e-mails by accident when he left me alone with his laptop. Look, can you get over here?'

'Whereabouts are you?'

They were hiding out in a holiday cottage that Pellowe had booked in Port Erin, on the south-western tip of the island. Alison had come out on the pretext of buying food but, otherwise, Pellowe had not let her out of his sight.

I said, 'We can get the 6.30 SeaCat from Liverpool so we should be with you by ten.' It was lucky I hadn't the show to do.

'Who's *we*?'

'I thought I'd bring Gabrielle Lorenzo along. She's back in Liverpool.'

'Right. I quite liked her when she was at our place. Of course, we didn't know she was a detective at the time.'

'These gumshoes get everywhere, Alison. Listen, are you sure you're safe? Pellowe doesn't suspect you at all does he?'

She hesitated. 'He seems a bit wary but I don't think he does.'

'Only, someone suspected that Ms Lorenzo was an informer when she worked at DRP and they took a shot at her.'

'You're kidding?' For the first time, Alison sounded genuinely scared.

'I'm not, I assure you. How long is he expecting you both to stay on the island?'

'Only another day. Justin is waiting for one more bit of

information from Sydney and he's finished. He's already got what he needed from the company in Dublin. It'll then be a case of, bring on the highest bidder.

'He still hasn't got a cure for Alzheimer's though, has he?'

'No, but he'll have the data from all four companies, all of it different but working towards the same goal which means that whoever buys it will be leading the race, to use your terminology, Johnny.'

'Unless, of course, he's already working for somebody, who hired him to set this whole thing up in the first place.'

Alison accepted that this was a possibility.

I said, 'You'd better tell me where you'll be tonight.'

She gave me the precise location of the cottage and I warned her to be careful of Pellowe. I was sure he would go to any lengths to make sure his plan wasn't thwarted.

I rang Gabrielle at the Thistle and brought her up to date. She was very excited by the news. 'I'll ring up my boss in Alicante and tell him. What time will you pick me up?'

'Half past five should give us enough time.' I was glad to be getting out of the country for a short time. It would give me some breathing space before the police came looking for me to ask more questions.

'It's non-stop in your life, isn't it?' commented Tommy McKale, who had been listening to the conversations. 'Will you need any help?'

'I don't think so,' I said.

'Pity. I could have let you have Dolly. She was born over there, you know, near Sulby Glen. Belonged to an old Manx family. She came over between the wars and married my grandfather who was working on the docks.'

'Who came from an old Liverpool family?'

'Indeed. Although the McKales started out in Ireland, of course, originally. But that was much too far back for me to know about it. We're seven generations of Scousers now.'

I thanked him for his help and said I'd be calling on Kevin Mason when I returned from the Isle of Man.

I left the RAV4 in the Fitness Palace car park and strolled up to Queens Square to the Italian Kitchen for some lunch. The whole area was buzzing, new trendy wine bars, designer shops and a four star hotel, a far cry from the Great Charlotte Street Market days.

On my way back to the river, I walked up Bold Street and along Slater Street, past the Jacaranda Club where Allan Williams and Lord Woodbine used to pay The Beatles to back the strippers. Now it's part of the Liverpool Musical Mystery Tour and quite rightly so. The real mystery is why it took the city so long to cash in on its heritage.

I collected the car and drove back to the flat to pack for the trip. I'd not been to the Isle of Man for four years but I didn't imagine it would have changed much except there'd probably be a few thousand more financiers in situ and a glut of million pound mansions desecrating the countryside.

Before anything else, I rang Rosemary on her mobile to see how Jim was. It was reassuring news. The knife had missed any vital organs and, although he was sedated after suffering from shock, he was expected to make a full recovery.

'The police have been to see him, Johnny. They want to talk to you.'

'I know, Rosemary. I'm seeing them later.' Much later if I had anything to do with it. 'Right now, I'm off to the Isle of Man. Tell Jim I'll be in to see him in a couple of days when I get back.'

Just as I was preparing to leave, the phone went. I thought it might be Maria but it was Hilary.

'You never rang me back,' she said accusingly.

'Jim's been rushed to hospital.' As if that was the reason. 'He was stabbed by one of those men who was at yours on Saturday.'

'No! Is he all right?'

'Yes. He's in Fazakerley. It's shock as much as anything. He was lucky. It missed his heart and lungs.'

Hilary sighed. 'Things were much simpler when you were just a DJ, Johnny.'

And when I didn't have Maria as well.

'I've been suspended from the radio again,' I said, 'because of Garth Greer's outburst last Friday.'

'It's all bad news isn't it? How do you fancy taking me to the pictures tomorrow night, cheer yourself up? We could go on to the Masquerade afterwards, we've not been there together for ages. Then perhaps we could go back to your flat?'

She said it teasingly and I was tempted to tell her Maria had thrown me out but thought it best to wait. Maria might phone although it was looking less likely by the minute. It was three days now since the row. I was worried, too, about how Victoria and Roly were getting on. I missed them all.

At the same time, I'd never felt more in need of Hilary's company. She was always cheerful and had a knack of making me forget my troubles.

What Alan Hansen on *Match of the Day* would call a "no win situation".

'I'd have loved to but I'm just leaving for the Isle of Man, on this case. I'll ring you as soon as I get back.'

For a moment, I thought she was going to offer to come with me but she was on duty at the hospital.

At five thirty I called for Gabrielle at the Thistle. 'I've booked us two rooms at the Royal Hotel in Port Erin,' I said. 'It's facing the sea and handy for where we're going.'

She was wearing jeans and a sweater under her anorak. 'I thought we may be in for a rough night,' she explained.

We boarded the SeaCat at Princes Landing Stage at the Pier Head without any trouble. I'd been half afraid DI Warnett would be waiting at the quayside but he wasn't. We parked the RAV 4 below decks and headed upstairs to the bar.

Luckily, the Irish Sea was free of unexpected tempests for once and we made good time into Douglas, knocking ninety minutes off the normal ferry crossing.

I rang Rosemary again before we docked. She had good news. Jim was being kept in overnight as a precaution but she hoped to take him home in the morning.

'He told me to tell you to be careful,' she added.

After the events of the past few days, I didn't need reminding.

'How long now?' asked Gabrielle as I drove off the ferry and swung the car onto the road towards Ronaldsway Airport. Probably soon to be renamed Norman Wisdom Airport?

'Twenty minutes if we're lucky.'

As we passed the Fairy Bridge, I muttered a greeting to the fairies under my breath, adding a quick wish that Alison would be safe.

I'd read Joe Cooper's book on the Cottingley Fairies and I had to say I didn't really believe in them but Manx legend has it that if you don't say *Laa Mie* (Hello) to the fairies, you'll have bad luck so I felt it did no harm to hedge my bets.

If I'd thought about it, I could have asked the fairies to get Maria to speak to me again as well. And perhaps they could tell me who killed Ms Grove, Selina Stark and James Kanlan too. I wasn't getting far by any other method.

I turned off the main road before we came into Castletown and headed towards Port St. Mary. On the way, we passed a neon lit car showroom full of expensive limousines run by the Sutton Brothers, two ex-Merseybeat guitarists, whom I'd called to interview when I was last on the island, when I was investigating the murder of pop star Bradley Hope.

Port Erin was deserted as we drove through the centre. I turned right up towards Bradda Head, past the stately Victorian hotels on our right which loomed over the dark waters of the Irish Sea on our left.

'That's our hotel, the white one on the corner,' I said. 'They say you can see Ireland from the upstairs windows on a clear day.'

'Do you think we should go and check in first? We don't know how long we're going to be and they might lock the doors at midnight.'

'You're right, but let's make it quick.'

I parked right outside the entrance and we rushed up the steps, collected our keys, dumped our cases in our respective rooms and were back in the car again within five minutes.

We proceeded up into the hills and I found the cottage without too much trouble from Alison's directions. It was a white-painted single storey building tucked away at the bottom of a grass-verged lane. I pulled up past the door and we walked back towards the front door.

The place was in darkness. An old blue Almera stood in the drive.

I peered through the front window but the curtains were drawn. I hesitated. I was frightened of what I might find.

Gabrielle took matters into her own hands. She marched up to the front door and gave a resounding knock. No answer.

'I think the big boot, Johnny,' she suggested.

'You could be right.' I just hoped we'd got the right cottage. I didn't fancy being confronted by a family of happy holidaymakers emerging from their bedroom.

I stepped back and kicked the door, just under the lock, with the heel of my shoe. The frame splintered and the door caved in.

We stepped inside the hallway. All was quiet.

'Doesn't seem like anyone's in,' I said and then I opened the door to the front room.

There was Alison Whyte. Sprawled backwards across a settee, with a single bullet hole in her forehead.

Chapter Thirty-Four

I felt her pulse. Nothing. 'She's still warm,' I said.

After all that, we were just minutes too late. I knew I would always blame myself. If only we hadn't stopped at the hotel. If we'd taken a plane across from Liverpool instead of driving up to Heysham to catch the SeaCat, would we have got there any sooner?

Gabrielle Lorenzo rushed out of the room to the cloakroom under the stairs and I could hear her vomiting into the sink. I looked down in dumb horror at the petite figure of Alison Whyte and asked myself, what could I have done to prevent her death?

I'd known she would be in mortal danger if Pellowe realised she had learnt of his plans. I should have told her to run away, get on a bus to Douglas. Anywhere. Hide, until we came over to the island to rescue her.

Too late. The clock can never be turned back. Alison was a girl with good intentions who been exploited by Pellowe. Whether her beliefs were right or wrong was irrelevant. Maybe what she'd done was morally wrong, even against the law, but I couldn't regard her as a crook. To me, she was a sweet, well-meaning girl who'd been led up the wrong path. Who says the meek inherit the earth?

If Pellowe had been in the house, I think I could have killed him with my bare hands.

And then I suddenly realised the implications of that bullet hole. Selina Stark, Dorothy Grove, James Kanlan, and now Alison Whyte had all been killed by a single shot, almost certainly fired by the same person.

Could that really have been Justin Pellowe?

Looking at the way Alison's body was lying, I couldn't see any signs of a struggle as I would have expected if she'd confronted Pellowe about her suspicions.

Also, I couldn't begin to think what motive Pellowe would have for such a train of destruction.

On the other hand, he'd certainly had the opportunity when the first two were killed as he'd been living in Hightown at the time.

But when Kanlan was shot, Pellowe had been on the boat to the Isle of Man with Alison and Roma.

Pellowe could not have killed James Kanlan.

Ergo, if my theory was correct, he did not kill Alison Whyte.

But if Pellowe hadn't killed Alison, who had? And where was Pellowe now?

Gabrielle came back into the room, having composed herself. 'Sorry, it caught me off guard. I should be used to things like that in this job.' She quickly regained her professionalism. 'No sign of a laptop, I take it?'

I glanced round the room. 'Not in here.'

'He'll have taken it with him. He could be anywhere.' She took a closer look at the dead girl. 'At least she didn't suffer. By the look of surprise on her face, she probably never knew what hit her.'

'I don't think Pellowe killed her,' I said. 'I think the murderer is the same person who shot the other four people, a professional hit man.'

And we were no nearer to finding him now than we were on the night Dorothy Grove was killed, when I must have been within a hundred yards of him. Since then, he had killed another two people. How many more before we caught him? Indeed, had there been others before Selina Stark?

Gabrielle listened whilst I outlined my theory. 'You could be right,' she said. 'But if it was a contract killing, the big question is, who signed the contract?'

'That's the million dollar question and the answer's got to be Pellowe. He's the only one who knew where she was.'

'Not necessarily,' said Gabrielle. 'They might have been meeting somebody else here by prior arrangement or maybe they just told someone where they were going.'

'In which case, of course, Pellowe might not have been party to Alison's murder at all?'

'It's a possibility. He may not even have been here when she was killed or, if he was, been too frightened to prevent it.'

'They'd have killed him too if that was the case. Professional killers don't leave witnesses.'

'I guess not.' She sighed and looked down again at the body. 'This is too serious for us to handle on our own. We should bring in the Isle of Man police and arrange for them to liase with the officers on Merseyside.'

I had to accept she was probably right. If we'd let them handle things earlier, would Alison Whyte now be lying dead? Possibly not, but, at the same time, I didn't see what the police could have done to stop it.

Before we got chance to find out, we heard an engine start up outside. I ran to the front door in time to see the blue Almera pull out of the drive and take off down the road.

'It's Pellowe,' I shouted. 'He must have been here all the time. Let's go.'

I jumped over the flattened front door and ran to the RAV4. Gabrielle was right behind me. We were facing the wrong way so I had to reverse into the drive, which took valuable seconds, but the tail lights of the Almera were still visible in the distance as we set off in pursuit.

A light rain had started to fall and I switched on the wipers as we hurtled down the hill back through Port Erin. It was closing time and a cluster of young people were standing in the drizzle outside the Falcon's Nest. Eleven o'clock and nowhere to go. This was the Isle of Man not New York or London. The twenty-four hour day hadn't arrived here yet and would probably be a long time coming.

The Almera was a good half mile ahead of us as we headed back towards Castletown but I was catching up. Pellowe bypassed the town centre and took the Douglas road. For a moment, I thought he was making for the airport but he kept going.

It was at Ballasella I nearly lost him. Instead of taking a right turn and keeping on the main road, he carried on straight ahead then took a side turning.

'Hold tight,' I shouted to Gabrielle as I swung the wheel round. 'I think he's heading for Silverdale Glen.'

'What's that?'

'It's an old fashioned pleasure ground with a boating lake, a craft centre and a café, very Edwardian.'

'My father used to take us to a boating pond when we were little, to sail model yachts.'

'They have radio controlled boats here too,' I said.

'Oh no, not radio ones. Ours had big white sails and you had to hope it was a windy day or your yacht would just sit there on the water.'

The Almera lights went in and out of view as the road twisted and turned. 'The glen leads out into the open countryside. He could be headed for the hills.'

'It looks pretty bleak in those hills.'

'It does, and Pellowe's hardly the rugged outdoor type who'd survive for long without food and shelter.'

I was not far behind him as he hung a left into the car park and screeched to a stop outside a red phone box behind the café.

'This could be a trap,' said Gabrielle, nervously.

'An ambush, you mean? Like in Westerns?' I realised I should have considered that possibility but it was too late for that now. I recalled the battle with SHAT outside Hilary's. Where did SHAT fit into all this? I wondered, but no solution came to mind. 'We'll soon find out.'

I leapt out of the car and started after Pellowe who was already running round the side of the lake.

It was deathly quiet apart from the sound of the water swishing against the sides in the breeze, rocking the pedal boats moored at the end. A full moon, half hidden by cloud, shone eerily through the trees. At any moment I expected to see Vincent Price emerge out of the trees with a raven on his shoulder.

Pellowe had a good two hundred yards start on me but he wasn't fit. Years of sitting at a desk staring at a computer screen wasn't the best way to keep the cardiovascular system in tip top condition. I was gaining by the yard.

He reached the point where the lake narrowed into a stream, running out towards the fields beyond with paths on either side. He turned, saw me and put on a spurt, but it didn't last. He had travelled less than ten yards down the muddy path when I launched myself into a rugby tackle and brought him to the ground.

Before he had the chance to struggle to his feet, I hit him hard on the nose, enough to fracture the bone, and again on the jaw. It put him out. I felt I owed him that.

As he sagged to the floor, I took hold of his collar and dragged him backwards along the path.

'Need any help?' Gabrielle came running up.

'An umbrella would have been nice.' The rain was coming down quite hard now. 'Otherwise, no. Let's get him to the car.' She lifted his feet, I took his shoulders and we carried him to the RAV 4 and manoeuvred him onto the back seat. Gabrielle sat in front in the passenger seat and I got in beside Pellowe who was starting to come round.

'Right,' I said. 'I'm not asking these questions twice, Justin, so listen carefully. Did you kill Alison?'

He started to cry. 'No, no I didn't.'

'Then who did?'

'I don't know.'

I hit him lightly across his nose, which I decided was definitely broken. It was still bleeding slightly and seemed to hang at a distorted angle.

'Don't hit me. I'll tell you everything.'

'Start at the beginning then and leave nothing out.'

'Can I have a towel or something to clean up my face?'

Gabrielle passed over some tissues and he wiped the blood from his nose and coughed up an unpleasant looking clot.

'I think I need a hospital,' he said.

'All in good time. When you've finished your story.'

It was much as I would have predicted. When Pellowe had been working as a research scientist in Germany, he had come across people on the Internet who shared his beliefs about free information of experiments.

Over a period of time, he recruited people from each of the four companies engaged in this particular study of Alzheimer's Disease, including Alison Whyte at DRP and Guiseppe Roma in Alicante.

However, somewhere along the way, his philanthropic motives were compromised when he met a man who was prepared to pay him two hundred and fifty grand to hand over the information he'd collected.

'Every man has his price,' I murmured.

He didn't tell his little group about this new arrangement but let them go on believing they were working unselfishly for a common cause.

I interrupted him here. 'I thought Roma got paid,'

'He'd lost his job because they were on to him and he had to flee the country. He wanted reimbursing. I paid him off in case he made trouble.'

So, to all intents and purposes, Roma had blackmailed Pellowe. I wondered where he was now and if he intended to ask for future payments.

Alison Whyte, of course, didn't ask for money and neither, declared Pellowe, did his contacts in Dublin and Sydney.

'Where do SHAT come into this?' I asked.

'SHAT? They don't. SHAT are a bunch of rent-a-mob thugs who come along and destroy property for the fun of it.'

'I think you'll find they're more than that,' I said, 'and somehow they're connected with Alison's death.'

'I don't see how.'

'Then who did kill Alison? You?'

'No, no, of course not. I liked Alison.'

'But you were in that house with her when she died, you let someone else kill her.'

'I wasn't there when it happened, I swear.' Pellowe choked and coughed up some more blood. 'Look, I'd spent all afternoon working on the laptop.'

'Waiting for the final piece of information from Australia?' Pellowe looked surprised. 'Alison rang me. She'd read some of your e-mails and found out you were selling the information. She wanted to stop you.'

'I wondered why you came to be over here.'

The other man had arrived at the cottage at nine o'clock. Pellowe could not say how he had travelled. It was only later, as he went to his car, that he realised there was no other vehicle there.

I asked who the man was.

'He said his name was Carlos Botago. He was Spanish. Dark skinned with jet black hair and a bushy moustache. He looked like the guy from *Magnum* on TV. Tom Selleck was it?'

'I believe so.'

'Whatever. He seemed quite a cultured man. He said he collected antiques and his command of English was excellent.'

'Hold on,' broke in Gabrielle. 'Carlos Botago, you say? I know that name. There's a wine merchant in Javea called Carlos Botago. He lives in a palatial villa outside town. I know the police have been suspicious for a long time how he has been able to afford such luxury.'

'This could be the answer then. He moonlights as a hitman.'

Pellowe had given Botago numerous pages of the vital information he had collected from his four sources all printed out and indexed.

'Months of work had gone into those figures. He took them from me, merely glanced through them in a perfunctory way before putting them in his briefcase. Then he handed me a cheque for a a quarter of a million pounds, told me my work was finished and I should pack my things and leave immediately.'

I couldn't believe there any chance that Pellowe was ever intended to cash that cheque. Botago was there for one purpose only; to collect the goods and get rid of the evidence.

'Where was Alison whilst all this was going on?'

'In the kitchen making coffee. I don't know why, I suddenly felt apprehensive. It seemed too easy, two hundred and fifty thousand pounds, just like that. I just wanted to get away so I took my laptop and my printer out to my car. I was on my way back into the house when I heard the shot.'

Realising what had happened and rightly fearing he'd be next, Pellowe fled for cover but, at that moment, before the Spaniard had time to come looking for him, Gabrielle and I had driven up in the RAV4.

'Which meant Botago had still been in the house when Gabrielle and I went inside and discovered her body?'

'I suppose so.'

'No suppose about it.' Had we arrived three or four minutes earlier and caught him, gun in hand, it was odds on Gabrielle and I would have been shot too.

Pellowe continued. 'I waited until you'd both gone in then I jumped into my Almera and drove away. The rest you know.'

'All except one thing,' I reminded him. 'The man you were working for, who wrote that cheque. The man who hired Carlos Botago to kill for him. The man behind all this. What's his name, Pellowe?'

He lowered his eyes and put his hand up to his damaged face.

'Rupert Routledge.'

Chapter Thirty-Five

'Rupert Routledge?' I couldn't get my head round this. 'But he was one of the people whose secrets you were stealing. Or rather, Alison was.'

'Yes, but he wanted the lot. Being one of the victims, as it were, was a good cover for him.'

I cast my mind back to when I first visited Derek Routledge Pharmaceuticals. No wonder Rupert hadn't been so keen when I approached him about the leak from his company. He was the one who was profiting from it.

'Probably it was Botago who shot at me to warn me off,' said Gabrielle.

'I wouldn't know about that,' said Pellowe. 'I only met Routledge once and I never went near his factory.'

I asked him, 'Why would Routledge have Selina Stark and Dorothy Grove killed?'

I was sure it would have been Botago who had pulled the trigger on his behalf but I couldn't for the life of me work out what Routledge's motive could have been.

Neither could Justin Pellowe.

'You'll have to ask him that when you find him.'

That was a point. Where was Botago now? Had he had his own car parked away from the cottage? Could he have followed us here to Silverdale and be waiting for us even now outside the car park, ready to shoot?

I couldn't see how he could have left the island, unless he had a private jet waiting at the airport. That's the thing about islands. When you're being pursued, you can't get off them too easily. The scales are tilted in favour of the seeker not the hider. All the same, I thought it was time to move on.

'Shouldn't we go to the police?' asked Gabrielle.

She was right, of course, but all my instincts just told me to get the hell out of there and go back to the mainland.

'I think I prefer the boat option.'

'But there won't be a ferry till morning.'

'The early SeaCat leaves for Liverpool at seven o'clock, we can be on that. In the meantime, I suggest we go back to Port Erin and the Royal Hotel. I don't know about you but I need some sleep.'

'What about me?' objected Pellowe. 'I need a hospital.'

'You'll keep. A broken nose never did Jack Palance any harm. I've got some rope in the back,' I said to Gabrielle. 'I'll tie him up and keep him in my room. There's a SeaCat leaving Douglas at seven in the morning for Liverpool. We'll go back on that.'

'Before we go,' said Gabrielle. 'I want to get that laptop from his car. That's the proof I need for my client.' She went across to the Almera, which was unlocked, and brought back Pellowe's computer.

'Can you drive,' I asked her, 'and I'll stay in the back with the patient. And don't forget we drive on the left here.'

'What if someone discovers Alison's body?' queried Gabrielle, as she started the engine and slowly edged out of the car park, turning left down the one way road. I couldn't see another car lurking in the shadows.

'A chance we have to take but I think it's unlikely. That cottage was at the end of a cul-de-sac. I don't imagine anyone is likely to be around before eight o'clock, by which time we'll be halfway across the Irish Sea. All we've got to do is make sure that we don't oversleep and miss the boat.'

'He doesn't seem bothered about the bodies being found, does he?' You say that Selina Stark and Dorothy Grove had both been left in the street, and James Kanlan in his hotel room.'

'That's because the victims don't know him and have no connections with him. There's no weapon left behind, no witnesses and he hasn't touched the victims to leave any DNA.'

'What about Mr. Kanlan at the Campanile? Someone must have seen Botago go into his hotel room. The receptionist would have given him the keys for a start.

'No, no, Gabrielle. Nothing simpler. Think about it. Botago

comes in, quiet and polite. The receptionist is busy on the phone. He pretends to take a brochure, glances at the guestbook to find out the right room number then ambles through and knocks on the door. Kanlan shouts out "who is it?", Botago says "room service" or even just "it's me". Kanlan opens the door and, bang, who's first for the mortuary? And, before you ask, he uses a silencer.'

We came back into Port Erin, quiet as the grave. I advised her to park round the back of the hotel, just in case Botago was driving around looking for us. He might have clocked the RAV4 from an upstairs window while we were in the cottage.

We each grabbed an arm and frog-marched Pellowe into the hotel but all resistance was now gone from him. I think Alison's death had shocked him. Perhaps he hadn't realised before the kind of people he was dealing with and the knowledge had horrified him.

Or maybe he just thought he was safer with us than chancing his luck on the empty streets with Botago hunting him down.

I took the rope with me and secured him to a wicker chair in my room then I boiled a kettle and made us each a mug of hot chocolate from the hospitality tray.

Pellowe sipped his and looked at me with a worried expression.

'What will happen to me?'

'Probably fifteen years locked up in a tiny prison cell with male rapists and perverts and an open communal lavatory in the corner.'

He was German and wouldn't know better. In real life, of course, British prisoners watched colour TV, went home at weekends and were invited to study for PhDs in flower arranging. Those, that is, who weren't running multi-million pound drug rings from the comfort of their cells.

I set my alarm for half past five to make sure we got to the landing stage at Douglas in time, which meant we got four hours sleep. Better than nothing and, if you believed Mrs Thatcher, as much as anyone needs anyway.

I had one thing only on my mind and that was to get my hands on Rupert Routledge.

Gabrielle was up and ready when I knocked on her door. 'What are we going to do with Pellowe?' she asked.

'I thought we'd leave him safely tied up in my room.'

'You'd better put a gag on him in case he tries to scream.'

'Good thinking. When we get to Liverpool, I'll ring the Isle of Man police from a phone box and tell them where to find him. I'll say he's involved in the murder of a young woman whose body they can find at the cottage in Port Erin. That should keep them busy for a while.'

'Will you say who you are?'

'Not then. Not until I've got Routledge. Then I'll inform the officer dealing with events in Liverpool and get him to liase with the island.'

I went back to my room to secure Pellowe and pack my case. 'Don't worry,' I told him. 'Someone's coming for you soon.' I put the *Do Not Disturb* sign on the door as I went out.

Gabrielle met me in the hall. 'All done,' I said. 'He won't get away.' I looked enviously across to the deserted dining room. 'Pity we're too early for breakfast. I was looking forward to the Manx kippers.'

We reached Douglas before six thirty and boarded the SeaCat without any trouble. The vessel was only half full of passengers but I saw no sign of the Botago.

The Spaniard, I reckoned, was in a dilemma. Did he stay on the island, hoping to track down and silence Pellowe, who was the only living witness to his crimes, or get the hell out of it before the police found him? He was not to know we hadn't called them.

'Do you think Botago will be on this boat?' asked Gabrielle, as if reading my thoughts.

'I'd say it's more likely he flew over and hired a car at the airport which means he'll probably take a plane out although where he'll fly to is anybody's guess. He might think Liverpool is too dangerous for him. There's a flight to Heathrow at seven, he could be on that and on his way to Spain by the time we get to Liverpool.'

When the bar opened, we ordered tea and sandwiches which turned out to be a bad move. Force seven south-westerly winds and driving rain buffeted the vessel which rolled from side to side for most of the journey making us feel quite nauseous.

I'd never been gladder to see the towers of the Royal Liver Buildings as I was when finally we turned into the Mersey Estuary.

As we neared the shore, I gave Rosemary a ring and found out she was at the hospital, collecting Jim to bring him home.

'Mind if we come round?' I asked her. 'We've got a lot to tell him.' I explained Gabrielle would be with me. She reluctantly said it would be all right but we 'hadn't to excite him'.

As soon as we disembarked, I drove onto the dock road and parked up by a phone box. The Isle of Man police were surprised to receive my call. I briefly told them where to find Pellowe and the body of Alison and rang off as soon as they started asking personal questions.

We reached Jim's house at half past ten. The timing was good. They had arrived home themselves just five minutes earlier.

Rosemary put the kettle on and Jim led us through to the lounge. I didn't like the look of him. His skin had a grey pallor and his face was strained.

'How are you feeling?' I asked him.

'A bit groggy. Nothing to worry about though. I'll be right as rain with a couple of days rest. Who's going to run the office while I'm stuck here though?'

'All taken care of Jim. I'm back now.' Although I didn't intend going anywhere near the office for the moment. I had other things to do, not least of which was confronting Rupert Routledge.

I put Jim in the picture about the Isle of Man trip. He was shocked to hear of Alison Whyte's death.

'How many more?' he asked wearily.

'Hopefully, none. I'm on way to Speke right now to sort out Routledge.'

'Be careful, Johnny. Why don't you leave it to the police now? You've got enough on Routledge for them to go and arrest him.'

'Call me stubborn, Jim, but I want to see this through and I'm very nearly there. Also, I want to know why Dorothy Grove was killed. She's our original client, remember?'

'Remember?' He grimaced. 'I don't think I'll forget that night at the Simply Single club in a hurry.'

Gabrielle had her piece to say. 'I've done all that my client in Alicante asked me to do but it would be nice to go back with the jigsaw complete.'

Jim knew when he was beaten.

Rosemary brought us in some tea and a couple of slices of toast and marmalade as well.

'He's having a week off, Johnny. Doctor's instructions. You sometimes forget about his heart condition.'

'A week off's fine,' I said. 'Good job you've no gigs, Jim.'

Gabrielle looked surprised. 'I didn't know you were a musician, Jim.'

'One of Merseybeats forgotten heroes is Jim.' I gave her a potted history of The Chocolate Lavatory's inauspicious career but it lost some of its impact when Gabrielle reminded us she wasn't born when The Beatles came on the scene and was more aware of Madonna and Mary J. Blige.

'Time to go,' I said, when the tea and toast had been consumed. 'I want to get to Routledge before he skips the country.'

'Do you think he will?'

'Once he knows the game is up, he'll know he can't afford to hang around.'

'Where do you think he'll go?'

'Your guess is as good as mine but I'd say Spain's favourite.'

'We've come to see Mr. Routledge,' I said to the Asian receptionist when we arrived at the DRP building. I noticed she had a different jewel in her nose, a blue one.

'I'm afraid he's not in.'

'Oh dear,' said Gabrielle. 'Have we just missed him?'

'No, he's away at a conference today. Can I give him a message?'

'No thanks,' I said and asked if we could go up to the Research Dept.

'You know the way,' she smiled.

Leroy Holden met us up there. I noticed Gabrielle take on an almost kittenish air.

'Is Dr. Schneider not here?' I asked.

'She's taken the day off. A family bereavement.'

'So there's only you left in the department?'

'Fraid so. Alison's on holiday and you know about James of course?'

'Yes.'

'It was a terrible shock, I mean, shot! Why would anyone shoot James? Alison's going to be so upset when she hears.'

There was no point in hiding it from him. 'Alison's dead,' I said, gently.

'Dead? What do you mean? She can't be. She was here on Friday. She was looking forward to her week off.'

'She was murdered, I'm afraid. By the same person who killed James Kanlan.'

Leroy looked frightened. 'You're joshing me? Oh Lord! Is this to do with work? Does this mean I'm in danger?'

'No, not at all. Alison was leaking secret information from your experiments. She was killed to silence her.'

'And what about James? Is that why he was killed?'

'No. I don't know the reason for his death, unless…' A thought struck me. 'What do you know, Mr. Holden, about an organisation called SHAT, the Society for Humane Animal Treatment.'

Leroy's face clouded over. 'Those bastards! I can tell you things about them.'

'In that case, Leroy, go ahead. I want to hear all you know.'

Chapter Thirty-Six

Leroy had been an enthusiastic supporter of Rupert Routledge's methods when Rupert took over the company from his father. Leroy approved of vivisection and felt he was making real progress with his experiments, especially after Rupert introduced dogs and cats into the laboratory.

He was thus very annoyed when the protests started from animal rights groups.

'We were trying to find a cure for an illness that affects thousands of people in the most dreadful way yet these ignorant thugs came along threatening us and, in the end, put a stop to the experiments.'

'What was Routledge's reaction to SHAT's persecution of his company?'

'He was livid, obviously. He went round to their office to sort them out but I think he bit off more than he could chew there. He didn't come into the office for a couple of days afterwards and the general opinion here was that they'd roughed him up a bit.'

Gabrielle asked, 'And did he retaliate?'

'No, just the opposite. He backed down. That was when he got rid of the cats and dogs and left me with just the mice to experiment on.'

'And that was the end of it?'

'Not quite. A few weeks later, I was at the Waterloo Cup out at Altcar.'

Gabrielle looked puzzled. 'Hare coursing,' I explained. 'The Waterloo Cup is the biggest event in their calendar.'

Leroy agreed. 'That's right. Well, it always attracts an army of animal rights protestors but amongst the yobs waving their banners was James.'

'Kanlan?'

'Yes. I was surprised to see him there. He'd not mentioned at work he was going and with the protestors as well. But the strange thing was, when I walked across to talk to him, to ask him what the hell he was doing there, someone else in front of me went up to him and said "How's it going, Pete."'

'Perhaps they got his name mixed up.'

'No, I don't think so because James saw me and he shook his head as if to warn me off. So I backed away.'

'Did he not mention it when you saw him back at work the next day?'

'No, but I did. I asked him what he was doing with that shower and he just said it wasn't what it seemed and left it at that. He wouldn't be drawn anymore.'

'So what conclusion did you come to?'

'This seems preposterous but I thought he'd infiltrated the organisation in order to get back at them for Rupert. Rupert and James were very friendly.'

It didn't seem preposterous to me. Derek Routledge had hinted at something similar. If Kevin Mason and his cronies at SHAT had got wind that James Kanlan was a fifth columnist in their midst, that would account for the reason they were after him.

All this tied in with everything that Kanlan had told us.

Summoned by SHAT to a meeting, James turns up with Lisa, unsuspecting, and finds out his cover has been blown. Before he can do anything, they're both bundled into a car. They manage to jump out at Princes Park which is when they split up. Kanlan is caught and brought back but when they catch up with Lisa, she struggles and is killed. I could see it might well have been an accident but, if Greer and Leech were the men involved, nothing could be certain.

Either way, Lisa's dead.

Kanlan escapes and keeps out of their clutches over the weekend until Jim and I pick him up in Bootle and take him to the Campanille Hotel.

Whereupon Botago shoots him.

This is the bit that doesn't ring true. Why should Botago

shoot him if Botago is working for Routledge and Kanlan is Routledge's friend.

Leroy didn't know either.

'Have you heard of a man called Carlos Botago?' Gabrielle asked him. 'Spanish. Sallow skin, black hair and moustache.'

'I didn't know his name but a man of that description has been to the office a few times to see Rupert. Who is he?'

'If I'm right, he's the man who killed Alison and James.'

'Good Lordy.'

'Do you remember when it was that you first saw him?'

He thought. 'I can't tell you exactly but it was months ago.'

'Before or after the trouble with SHAT?'

'After. Rupert took a couple of weeks off and went over to Spain for a holiday. He has a villa there on the Costa Blanca. I presume he met this Botago on that trip because the first time I saw Botago was a short while after he'd returned.'

'By which time, your experiments had been stopped?'

'Yes.'

So? Had Botago been brought in to fight the war against SHAT? If so, why kill Kanlan who was on the same side?

Leroy was never going to provide me with an answer to that but I thanked him for his help and we took our leave.

On the way past the front desk, I stopped for a word with the receptionist. 'This conference that Mr. Routledge is attending, where is it being held?'

At the back of my mind I was I was thinking I might go along there and confront him but I wasn't expecting the answer she gave me.

'It's in Valencia.'

'What now?' asked Gabrielle as we walked back across the car park.

'You mentioned Carlos Botago's villa earlier, Gabrielle. Do you know the address?'

'It's near Javea. I can get it easily enough. Why?'

'I don't believe there is a conference. I think Routledge has done a runner and my guess is he's with Botago.'

'It's possible. Valencia airport isn't much further from Javea than Alicante.'

'He must have realised we'd be on to him. He probably caught the first plane out that he could get.'

'So what's your next move?'

'When had you planned to return to Spain?'

'Any time now. My investigation is complete. I'm ready to report back to the Alicante company.'

'Give me today to sort things out at this end and I'll travel back with you.'

There were a few things I needed to tidy up before I left. For a start, I knew I must contact DI Warnett and put him in the picture with regard to recent events both in Liverpool and the Isle of Man.

Then there was Maria. I still hadn't heard from her and, the longer it went on, the worse the situation would get. I was missing her, not to mention Victoria and Roly.

Gabrielle came back with me to the office and I checked the flights to Alicante on the Internet.

'There's one leaving tomorrow afternoon from Manchester,' I said.

'Book us on it.'

She was still booked into the Thistle Hotel so I arranged to pick her up there the next morning.

'What are you doing for the rest of the day?'

'Looking round your city,' she replied. 'I've not had time to get to know Liverpool yet. I want to see the Walker Art Gallery and the Tate.'

'The Tate's in the Albert Dock and while you're there it's worth going to the Liverpool Life and the Maritime Museums, not to mention The Beatle Story.'

If I ever gave up being a private eye, I could always get a job as a tour guide.

After Gabrielle had left, I phoned Jim to see if Warnett had been in touch.

'Has he been in touch? Is the Pope a Catholic? He's looking

243

for you, Johnny', was the answer. 'If I see you I have to tell you to contact him immediately.' Jim gave me the number. 'Any developments?'

'Routledge has done a bunk to Spain with Botago. I'm flying out there tomorrow with Ms Lorenzo.'

'Lucky sodding you. I trust your little excursion is chargeable to her account.'

'Of course.'

'What will you do with him when you get there?'

'If there's a warrant out for him in England, I'll get the Spanish police to extradite him.'

'That's up to Warnett. You'd better ring him.'

'When I've had some lunch.'

I went across to Richie's Butty Bar. Maria served me. 'Have you seen anything of *my* Maria?' I asked her but she hadn't.

'She's not been near the place for weeks, Johnny.'

I had a toasted teacake filled with cheese and a mug of strong tea. After the early morning sea crossing, I couldn't face anything more substantial.

D.I. Warnett didn't sound too delighted to hear from me when I rang him. He went on about tinkering with evidence, obstructing the police in the execution of their duty, harbouring wanted criminals and failing to report crimes.

When he shut up, I told him I could solve the case for him if he'd like to come down to my office and replaced the receiver before he could argue.

He arrived within ten minutes, accompanied, as always, by WPC Hagen. This time she favoured me with a nervous smile as if she knew something unpleasant was going to happen to me and she was feeling sad about it.

'We are dealing here with a serial killer…' Warnett began.

'His name is Carlos Botago,' I cut in. 'Resident of Javea on the Costa Blanca. Employed as a contract killer by Rupert Routledge, managing director of Derek Routledge Pharmaceuticals in Speke. Killer of Selina Stark, Dorothy Morton nee Grove, James Kanlan and, recently on the Isle of Man, Miss Alison Whyte.'

That shut the tosser up. WPC Hagen's smile broadened. She obviously regarded her superior as a pain in the ass too.

'What about Lisa O'Donoghue? You missed her out.'

'That one's down to Jake Leech and Garth Greer though it could have been an accident.'

Knowing the past records of the SHAT organisers, I was sure that every effort would be made to hang a murder charge on both of them. Clean up the streets, improve the crime statistics and do no harm to the old promotion prospects. The Wayne Paladin syndrome was alive and well.

'You've no right to interfere in police business,' he protested, lamely.

'Routledge and Botago have fled to Spain,' I continued, ignoring his feeble protestations. 'I'm going there myself tomorrow. If I find them, I'll hand them over to your Spanish counterparts and you can take it from there. Oh, and while you are about it, you might get the Fraud Squad to look at SHAT's books. Could be a little hokey-pokey going on there.'

'What was that about the Isle of Man?' Warnett didn't miss a trick.

'Alison Whyte, a female employee of DRP, was shot by Botago in Port Erin last night. She'd been involved in selling classified information from her company. The operation was masterminded by Rupert Routledge but the person who collected the information for him worldwide was a Mr. Justin Pellowe, a German gentleman residing in Hightown, who is currently in the custody of the Isle of Man police nursing a broken nose.'

At least, I hoped he was. I had secured the knots pretty tight.

WPC Hagen looked very excited and for one startled moment I thought she was going to clap.

'As for the charges of industrial espionage,' I went on, 'I presume that will depend on the companies concerned but a Ms Gabrielle Lorenzo, who is currently staying at the Thistle Hotel, will fill you in on the details should you want them. She is employed by the El Greco Detection in Alicante and she was a witness to events in the Isle of Man.'

'What's the motive for all these killings?'

This time, Warnett's tone was more serious, as if he'd accepted I was on his side and he genuinely wanted to know. Yet here, I had to confess I was lost.

'Alison's death was to keep her quiet but, as for the other three, I truly don't know. I'm as much in the dark as you are.'

But I intended to find out as soon as I reached Javea and Rupert Routledge.

Chapter Thirty-Seven

Warnett couldn't think of anything else to say. WPC Hagen looked positively radiant. I felt exhausted.

What would happen to DRP now? I wondered, but I knew the answer. Derek Routledge. The old man would seize his chance to take over the running of his company again.

'I'll need a full statement from you, Mr. Ace,' said Warnett.

'No problem, Inspector. I'll pop down to the station later.' Like when I returned from Spain.

When the two officers had gone, I called Maria. She answered on the third ring.

'Maria, it's me,' I said.

She put the phone down.

I rang back but this time she let the answerphone pick it up. I didn't want an argument with a machine so I hung up. I felt very dispirited.

I locked up the office, automatically looking for Roly on his usual blanket under the desk. I wondered if he'd noticed my absence. And what about Victoria? Had she been asking for me?

How had I got into this? This was what happened when you allowed yourself to have attachments. It was a mistake for me to ever get involved. I collected the car and drove furiously to the flat.

I checked my own answerphone. There was a message from Shirley asking if I was OK. Badger had rung about the noise from the flat below his penthouse caused by Pat Lake, the tenant there, who had recently discovered the music of Kid Rock and was playing his CDs at 200 watts. Geoffrey's voice informed me that the architect had completed the revised plans for the Sefton Park house. Great but would I ever get to live there myself?

No word from Maria or from Hilary. I rang Hil. I needed a carefree night out after all the strain of the last few days. But Hilary couldn't make it.

'I'm sorry, Johnny. I've arranged something for tonight.'

Was she seeing her doctor friend? And, if she was, who could blame her?

'Never mind. It was just on the off chance,' I said.

'How about tomorrow? I'm off at eight.'

'I've got to go to Spain tomorrow.' She didn't ask why. 'With this case.'

'Not to worry. Ring me when you get back.'

I put the phone down. Maybe a long hot bath and an early night would do me more good. This wasn't likely to be a fun holiday.

I couldn't be bothered to go out to eat so I put a Billie Holiday CD on the hi-fi, phoned for an Indian takeaway and opened a couple of cans of Scrumpy Jack.

I was in bed by nine and slept for a good ten hours. Obviously I needed the rest. I awoke to more gales blowing in from the Mersey and rain lashing against the windows. April in Liverpool. Someone should write a song about it.

In less than ten hours I'd be in the Mediterranean sunshine but I'd also be in gave danger if things didn't go to plan.

And I still hadn't decided what the plan was.

It was also Friday the thirteenth, not perhaps the most auspicious day to track down a mass murderer. Good job I wasn't superstitious.

The plane was due to take off at one o'clock which meant we had to be at Manchester Airport for eleven. I called for Gabrielle at the Thistle at nine thirty, knowing that there could be heavy traffic on the M62 and M6.

'You'll be glad to be getting back to your family,' I said to her, as I negotiated the traffic along Edge Lane leading to the motorway.

'My family are all in Madrid. My father runs a catering business there. But I have friends, of course, in Alicante.'

'Have you never been married?'

'No.' Her abrupt answer brooked no encouragement for me to enquire further. 'My job leaves little time for a social life,' she added, as if she realised she had sounded a little curt.

'Me too,' I said. If only, I thought.

We made the airport in plenty of time. I parked the car in the long stay car park and we took the shuttle to the departure lounge. I rang Jim from a call box. He said he was feeling better and might look in at the office the next day but he didn't sound over enthusiastic.

'Wait till Monday,' I told him. 'You might as well have the rest of the weekend off and get properly better.' The doctor had said a week but Jim was obviously fed up of being stuck at home under Rosemary's feet.

The two hour flight to Alicante was uneventful. After we'd collected our luggage, passed through customs and queued for a taxi, Gabrielle suggested I accompany her to the El Greco office to meet her boss, Paulo Romero.

The office was on the fourth floor of a block in the middle of town. Romero turned out to be a personable man in his early fifties, running a little to fat but possessed of charming manners.

'So good to meet you, Mr. Ace. Can I offer you a sherry or perhaps you prefer whisky?'

I said a sherry would be fine. When in Spain.

He poured three sherries and held up his glass for a toast. 'Here is to crime. Without it we should all be out of business.' We all drank to that then Romero's voice took on a serious tone.

'This investigation, Mr. Ace, has escalated in a way I never dreamt possible. What was a routine case of a foolish local employee selling a few company secrets has become a quite exceptional major murder enquiry stretching over continents.'

If you counted the Sydney drug company in that description, I suppose he was right, but I preferred to think of Rupert Routledge as a one man megalomaniac working out of Liverpool. I tried to put that view across.

'Well, of course, the Alicante connection turned out to be only a small part of the operation, Mr. Romero. The real Mr. Big, if I can call him that, operated in Britain. It was there that all the murders were committed.'

'But the actual killer, he was from Spain.'

The Spanish Liquidator, I thought. Good title for a film.

'Maybe, but I think you could describe Carlos Botago as a global mercenary. He might well live on the Costa Blanca but he was an assassin for hire. Have gun will travel. He could just as easily have resided in New York or Paris.'

'I wonder how Routledge came across him?' mused Gabrielle.

I offered them my reading of the situation. 'He came to Costa Blanca after he'd been worked over by the SHAT mob. He would be thinking of ways to get back at them. Routledge wasn't one to take defeat lying down. He probably met Botago in some bar one night and they got talking. Routledge would tell him of the trouble he was having with these animal rights people. Botago would say this was war and, like any general in conflict, he should use soldiers to fight on his behalf.'

'Go on,' said Romero. 'This is fascinating.'

'It would be an idea that Routledge would find attractive. He wasn't cut out for rough stuff but he understood that money could buy you anything. "Where would he find such men?" He would ask Botago.'

'Funny you should say that.' Romero finished the sentence and threw his hands up in the air. 'Perfect.'

'The only flaw in the argument,' I said, 'is that Botago killed the wrong people. Leech, Greer and Mason, the animal rights people, were unharmed. He killed a singer who was a household name and an old woman who thought he was a stalker.'

'Why was that?'

'I don't know but either Botago or Routledge is going to tell me.'

Romero was able to give me the address of the villa where Botago lived.

'How many men do you want?' he asked.

'None. I'm better on my own. We don't want a shoot out.'

Gabrielle set about hiring a car for me and Romero poured us another sherry. By now we were Paulo and Johnny and old mates.

The car was a silver Mercedes. Funny how Mercedes are

thought of as chauffeur driven limos in England yet, on the Continent, every taxi driver and his dog owns one.

'Ring us immediately if you need any help,' they both insisted as I prepared to set off on the forty-minute drive up the coast to Javea. They had supplied me with a road map and Gabrielle had drawn directions to Botago's villa which was close to the mountain known as Montgo.

I took the quick route, the inland motorway, from Alicante to Javea, by-passing Benidorm and Altea on the coast. The weather was hot and sunny, a welcome change from the rain and gales I'd left behind.

I found a hotel in Port Javea, the Mirimar, which was close to the beach. They had a single room vacant, overlooking the sea, which suited me fine. After I'd had a shower and put on a clean T-shirt and jeans, I ventured out to suss out the area and find somewhere to eat.

I ended up in a district called The Arenal at the Valanta Chinese Restaurant. When in Spain! The food was good and plentiful and I worked out the cost to be just £6 for a banquet while my bottle of wine cost less than a glass at home. Prices here were unbelievable. No wonder pensioners came to Spain for the winter. It cost them less than living in England and, as a bonus, they didn't get mugged, the buses ran on time and, if they were ill, they went straight into hospital to be mended.

On the downside, it was a long way from Goodison Park.

I figured the best time to negotiate with a cold blooded killer was when he was half awake so I decided I'd go round to Botago's villa early next morning.

I took a walk up to the Old Town for a look round before retiring. I set the alarm for 5am.

At five to six next morning, I glided up to the front door of the villa in the Mercedes. There was no traffic around and the sun was still low in the sky although it was already much warmer than the UK.

Gabrielle had described Botago's residence as palatial and that was a good adjective for it. It looked like it had been built for an oil sheik and I could understand why the police had been suspicious of a local wine merchant's ability to afford such splendour.

I marched straight up to the front door and gave a thunderous knock, almost enough to wake the dead.

Nothing happened. I walked round the side of the building and tried a gate leading to the back. It was unlocked. The path led to a patio and a huge swimming pool.

I couldn't miss the body lying beside the water's edge. It was Carlos Botago. I went over and felt his pulse but the body was cold. He'd obviously been dead some time and it didn't take much to see what had killed him. I'd looked down on a bullet hole like that three times before; after our night at the singles club in an empty street off Queens Drive, at the Campanille Hotel last Tuesday and the day after in the cottage at Port Erin.

Killed by a single shot.

Lying before me now was the man who had pulled the trigger on each of those occasions. A case of the biter bit, but who bit him? The answer was obviously Rupert Routledge but where was Routledge now?

The corpse was fully dressed so I felt in his pockets hoping to find something that might help me and I struck gold. In his inside jacket pocket was a leather wallet containinng a Transavia Airlines ticket from Alicante to Amsterdam Schiphol. The flight time was 20.50 on Saturday April 14th. Tonight.

My guess was that the two men had planned to flee the country but only one of them was going to get the trip and that man was Rupert Routledge. I had about twelve hours to make sure he never reached the plane.

Chapter Thirty-Eight

My first thought was to get away from the scene of the crime. Let somebody else discover this body. I wiped my prints from the latch after I'd closed the side gate behind me and ran back to the Merc.

I drove back to Javea and to the hotel in time for breakfast in the dining room. Most of the other guests were just getting up but already some people were strolling on to the beach in the sunshine. As soon as nine o'clock came, I rang El Greco Detection and spoke to Paulo.

'Botago's dead,' I informed him and told him what I'd seen at the villa, adding that I'd hopefully left the scene of the crime without being observed.

Paulo approved. 'You did right. Leave him for the servants to find.'

'I found a ticket in Botago's wallet for a flight to Amsterdam from Alicante tonight. I think Routledge could be on that plane.'

'Why Amsterdam I wonder?'

'Schipol is a hub airport, gateway to long haul destinations. I guess he's heading for somewhere like Brazil.'

'So what do you want to do?'

'I want to get to him when he's checking in and speak to him. He won't be armed because of airport security but I suggest you have a couple of your people standing by in case he makes a run for it. After I've finished with him, we can hand him over to the police.'

'Why not just have him arrested?'

'Because, Paulo, I want to ask him some questions of my own first.' I needed to know why he'd had Selina Stark and Ms Grove and James Kanlan murdered.

'OK. No problem. Say 18.50 at Alicante Airport.'

'18.50 it is.' Which meant I had the whole day in front of me. I wandered out of the hotel and took a stroll round Port Javea.

Across from the hotel was a second hand bookshop called Polly's with a stock of hundreds of English paperbacks. I came across a copy of a Stuart Pawson mystery I hadn't read and a new edition of Colin Wilson's *The Killer,* which I'd lent to someone years ago and never got back.

I paid for those then strolled further up the road to a gift shop that sold newspapers. I picked up the morning's edition of the *Daily Telegraph,* printed in Spain, and went back to the Mirimar where I sat for half an hour on the terrace with a pot of tea, doing the crossword. To my left, boats were leaving the nearby Marina, sailing off towards the Mediterranean.

I don't know what made me look up when I did.

Across the street, Rupert Routledge was getting into a black Lexus. I immediately jumped up and ran to my own car parked a few yards down the road.

He didn't move off straight away, giving me time to take Mike Bennett's recording device from the glove compartment and fix it inside my shirt.

He didn't see me as he pulled out and drove away from the port and I was careful to keep a couple of cars behind him.

We passed the Arenal and the Chinese restaurant. Routledge kept going. I had a quick look at the map Gabrielle had given me. As far as I could make out, we were headed towards an area called Cabo de Nao but it didn't appear to lead anywhere. I decided this must be the region where Routledge had his villa and I was proved right when he stopped outside the opulent two-storey building and climbed out of the car.

I drew up alongside him and, before he could move, leapt out of the driver's seat and threw him against the wall.

'Enjoying your holiday, Rupert,' I smiled as he struggled to regain his balance. He looked as flabby and repulsive as ever.

A look of sheer panic crossed his face but I held my hand against his chest to stop him from bolting.

'How much do you want?' Rupert all over. No stomach for a fight but always ready to buy himself out of trouble.

'I can give you ten thousand now. In cash.' His voice was

almost falsetto. More Frankie Valli than his usual Gene Pitney. It must have taken some doing, I thought, for him to kill Botago. Desperation was my guess. The last witness, the last obstacle to his escape. He had reckoned without me.

'Nice little place you've got. Shall we go inside?' As I spoke, I frisked him. He was clean. I wondered what had happened to Botago's gun.

He opened the front door and I pushed him inside in front of me. Beads of sweat covered his head, sticking his thin strands of hair to his white skull, as he stumbled forward obediently, like a rabbit hypnotised by a car's headlights.

'Make it twenty. I can give you twenty,' he pleaded.

'Tell me why you had Selina Stark killed, Rupert.'

'I didn't, I...'

I hit him hard on the nose, just like I'd hit Justin Pellowe. The blow landed with a satisfying crunch and a rivulet of blood ran down his face. I raised my fist again and noticed a damp patch appear on his trouser leg. He was wetting himself. Good job, I thought, that the villa had air conditioning.

I thought of poor Alison Whyte and hit him again. He screamed and fell backwards onto a settee.

'Now listen to me because I'm only going to say this once. If you don't want to be permanently disfigured, sit down and tell me the whole story, the murders, the stolen information, the lot.'

'All right, all right. Don't hit me.'

He wiped his face with a handkerchief and started his tale. I was gratified to hear that I had guessed a lot of it correctly.

Rupert Routledge had taken over Derek Routledge Pharmaceuticals with the prime objective of making as much money as possible.

To accelerate progress towards finding a cure for Alzheimer's Disease, he introduced the use of cats and dogs in experiments which aroused the ire of animal rights organisations, in particular a militant group known as the Society for Humane Animal Treatment.

SHAT mounted a terror campaign against DRP, forcing them to discontinue the policy of vivisection.

Rupert was furious at this and went round to the SHAT offices to confront them but he was beaten up and sent on his way.

The beating served only to make him seek revenge another way and I remembered the story his father had told me about his young son setting fire to his tormentor's books when he was bullied at school.

Realising he couldn't beat the SHAT leaders by force, he persuaded James Kanlan to join the organisation under an assumed name to try and find out how they were financed. Rupert's plan was to destroy them by cutting off their money supply.

No wonder he hadn't told me anything about SHAT when I first asked him about the anonymous letters.

'James found out that it was Selina Stark who'd bankrolled the operation. She was having a relationship with one of the directors.'

'Kevin Mason.'

'Whoever. I thought if we removed her from the picture, they'd struggle to keep going.'

'Which is where your friend Carlos Botago came in. How did you find him?'

'I used to buy wine from him and we became friendly. When I came over here after the trouble with SHAT, I told him of the problems I'd had and he said if I ever needed anyone removing, that's how he expressed it, removing, then he would be happy to oblige at a price.'

'And a few weeks later, when James had discovered that Selina Stark was SHAT's benefactor, you decided she'd be easier to "remove" than Leech, Greer or Mason?'

He nodded. 'I'd always learnt to attack the enemy at their weakest point.'

'How lucky for you that the police stuck the killing on an innocent man.'

'Yes, wasn't it?' He almost smirked. No remorse for Wayne Paladin.

'So having got rid of Selina Stark, why did you have Dorothy Grove killed?'

'Mrs. Morton, you mean? Because SHAT didn't fold, as I thought they would, when the girl died, then James found out that this old woman had baled them out. Furthermore, she was keeping them going with regular hand-outs.'

'So she had to go too?'

'I thought that would finish them.'

'But it didn't because, thanks to the Internet, they'd built up an effective subscription scheme. And, of course, she left them a small fortune in her will which they wouldn't have got if she'd not died.'

Rupert snarled, causing bubbles of congealing blood to form on his nostrils. 'The whole set-up was a scam. They were coining it and feathering their own bloody nests.'

'How reprehensible of them.' I couldn't keep the sarcasm out of my voice. 'But at least they didn't go in for wholesale slaughter.'

A thought suddenly struck me. 'Was it you driving the Lantra that picked up Botago after he'd shot the old lady?'

'What if it was?'

'Action man eh? Did it give you a thrill?"

He ignored my taunting and I moved closer to him.

'Why did James Kanlan have to die? I take it Botago shot him on your instructions?'

'Yes. I was sorry about that but I was frightened. When you rang me and told me what had happened to him, that the SHAT heavies were after him, I was afraid they'd get it out of him that it was me who'd had the two women killed.'

'So to make sure he didn't land you in the shit, you had your friend shot. You are scum, Routledge,' and I smashed my fist again into his face, fracturing his cheekbone.

I regretted it when I'd done it because I knew the reason why I'd lost control. It was guilt because it was I who had told Routledge that James Kanlan was hiding out at the Campanille Hotel and, by doing so, had unknowingly signed his death warrant.

Routledge was whimpering now, in pain. I pressed on.

'And Alison Whyte had to die for the same reason? She knew too much.'

'Yes.'

Routledge had recruited Pellowe to collect secrets from the other companies under the pretext of by-passing the profit motivated drug companies, but all the time fully intending to use them for the benefit of DRP.

Once his work was completed, Pellowe was always going to be disposed of. Alison had to go once she could finger Pellowe in case the trail led back to Routledge. Guiseppe Roma was lucky; he jumped ship.

'You may not have killed any of these people yourself,' I said, 'although I'm sure there's enough evidence to prove you were behind the murders. However, one murder that can be pinned on you is Botago. Why him?' But I didn't even need to ask the question. "Seal every possible leak" seemed to be the Routledge motto.

'He was the only person left who could connect me with anything. Once he'd gone, I was free.'

Deranged was more how I would have described it. Surely he couldn't have thought for a moment he'd get away with it.

'What are you going to do now?'

'Take you to the police station and turn you in. What did you do with the gun after you shot Botago?'

'It's in the drawer over there.'

I went over to the sideboard he was pointing to but as I was about to open the drawer, he shoved his hand down the side of the settee and pulled out the gun.

His face contorted into a twisted smile as he waved it at me but I didn't give him time to aim. I launched myself across the room and grabbed hold of his arm that held the gun, twisting it until the barrel was pointing against his own temple.

'Go on, Routledge,' I said. 'Do us all a favour. Shoot.'

The blast nearly blew me across the room. A round hole appeared at the side of Routledge's head and most of the contents spilled out at the back.

'Oh Christ!' I exclaimed aloud.

Rupert Routledge was dead but I had his confession on tape. The case was over.

Chapter Thirty-Nine

I rang Paulo and Gabrielle at El Greco Detection with the news.

'Forget about the airport,' I said. 'Routledge won't be needing his ticket', and I told them what had happened.

Paulo, who was on good working terms with the local police, said he would arrange for an ambulance and the police to come out to the villa straight away.

'When they've finished, come on over,' he said. 'We should celebrate. How about a meal this evening?'

'Fine.'

The ambulance and police arrived within a quarter of an hour. Rupert's body was taken away and I drove back to the police station with the officers to make a statement.

I didn't mention the tape. I was saving that for DI Warnett but I did tell the officer in charge to liase with Warnett at Merseyside Police who would fill them in with details of the crimes Routledge and Botago had committed in England.

I learned that Botago's body had already been discovered and reported.

After I'd answered all the questions, I asked to use the phone and I rang Derek Routledge to tell him of his son's death. I somehow felt I owed it to him. The old man was very upset yet not wholly surprised. Rupert had never been the son he had wanted him to be. As I'd expected, he intended to take over the reins of his company again. I gave him the number of the local police and hospital so he could ring and make arrangements to bury his son.

I then rang Jim Burroughs at his home. 'Good news, Jim. It's all over. Botago's dead.'

He sounded as if he'd been asleep but that woke him up. 'What happened?'

'Rupert Routledge shot him but Routledge is dead too.'

'Who shot him?'

'I suppose I did, in a manner of speaking.'

Jim groaned. 'You're not under arrest are you?'

I laughed. 'No, nothing like that. Look, I'll give you a ring on Monday when you're back in the office. How are you feeling?'

'A bit shaky but otherwise I'm OK. No permanent damage.'

I was worried. He didn't sound his usual self or was it my imagination?

It was past noon when I took leave of the police and set off in the Mercedes for Alicante.

I decided to take the coast road instead of the motorway and stopped off to have a look at Calpe where crowds of shoppers thronged the streets for the Saturday market. At one stall I saw a denim waistcoat which I fancied but it was 16000 pesetas. Then I saw the same waistcoat at another stall for only 7500. I went back to the first stall and offered them 3000 and, after a bit of haggling, we settled on 4000 which was about £16.

I stayed in Calpe for a vegetable pizza and cider at the Capri Restaurant then drove on to Altea where I walked up to the church high on the cliffs looking down on the village and the sea.

Benidorm was the next town but I'd seen enough of that on television holiday programmes to know I wouldn't like it so I kept driving until I reached Alicante.

Paulo and Gabrielle were highly satisfied with the conclusion of the case. 'You've done a good job, Johnny. Make sure you include all your expenses when you send us your bill.'

'Jim handles all that but, don't worry, he will.'

That evening, Paulo took us both out to dinner at an exclusive restaurant just outside of town. His wife came along, an elegant woman who was quite charming, although she spoke little English.

'When are you going back to England, Johnny?' Gabrielle asked, after we'd finished the meal.

'I'm not sure.' There was no reason for me to stay in Spain any longer. All the loose ends of the case had been tied up. 'I thought I'd hang around for a couple more days in the sun.'

Days to think about Maria, and if she would have me back. Did I want the family life? And Hilary. Could we reinvent our relationship to become just friends? Without the inverted commas! And would even that be acceptable to Maria?

'Why not?' agreed Paulo. 'You've earned it.'

When the waiter came back, he ordered liqueurs but I declined.

'I'd better be on my way soon,' I said. 'I've got to drive back to Javea yet.'

'You can stay the night with us, Johnny, we'll put you up.'

I thanked him but said I needed to get back to the Mirimar because I was expecting phone calls early the next morning.

In truth, I wanted to be on my own.

I thanked them for their hospitality, promised to keep in touch then walked out into the warm night air and to my waiting car. I felt free.

I stayed around the hotel most of Sunday, venturing as far as the paper shop to buy *The Sunday Times*. The TV in my room picked up BBC1, BBC2 and Sky so I was able to keep up with English news and the football. In fact, it wasn't much different than a lazy Sunday at home.

Monday morning I called Jim. He was back in the office.

'How's the chest?'

'Mending slowly. I go back to the hospital tomorrow for a check-up.' He hesitated. 'Look, I know it's not the best time to tell you this, with you being in Spain, like.'

'What are you talking about?'

'But I thought I should let you know as soon as I'd made my mind up.'

'Made your mind up about what?'

'I told you the other day about Mike Bennett starting up this security company.'

'The surveillance company, you mean?' I knew what was coming.

'Well, he wants me to go in with him.'

'And?'

'It's not that I haven't enjoyed working with you, Johnny...'

'Come on, Jim. Cut the bullshit. It's me you're talking to. Listen, I understand, OK? You don't have to make excuses.'

'I know, I know. You're right.' He sounded relieved. 'Anyway, I said I'd take it. It's in the office, you see, no outside work. In fact, it's just paperwork really but I think I'm getting a bit long in the tooth for this detective caper. Especially with my ticker the way it is. Rosemary said...'

I stopped him. 'Jim, I told you, I understand.' How else could I take it? He wasn't going to change his mind. Besides, I knew he'd really be better off with a desk job.

'It's for the best, Johnny.'

'You'll be in competition with Tommy McKale.' I warned him, half jokingly.

'Yes but ours'll be on the right side of the law. I'm glad you're taking it like this, Johnny.'

'Don't worry, Jim. The agency will survive. I think I'll make Roly a partner.' He laughed.

I didn't laugh. Mentioning Roly brought back home to me my situation. I hadn't even got Roly at the moment. Did one get custody of dogs? Custody? I wasn't even married to Maria. But it had seemed like a marriage and wasn't it a marriage, in all but name?

'I'll still do the odd gig with the band.' Jim said.

'In that case, I might even come and drum for you again one day if you're stuck.'

He laughed. 'How about Crosby Comrades Club on the 27th. We're on with Kingsize Taylor.'

'Yeah, I heard he'd made a comeback.'

'He was on the Marconi the other night, I believe, with Faron, The Undertakers and Carl Terry. What a bill. Legends all of them and they were all brilliant.'

'And every one of them should have made it in the sixties.' They never would now. Nineteen was too old to break into today's record market never mind sixty.

'Luck of the draw, Johnny. Right place, right time. Take Rory

263

Storm, He was Rod Stewart before Rod Stewart was, if you know what I mean. Did you ever see his act? Broke his leg jumping off the balcony at the Birkenhead Empire. The ultimate showman Rory was.'

I remembered him before he died when he'd given up trying to make it as a singer and was DJ-ing at posh Jewish barmitzvahs.

'Hey, I take it you'll be home by the 27th, despite all that Spanish sunshine?'

'Yeah, of course.' The 27th was almost a fortnight away.

'I'll stop on in the office, of course, till you get back.'

'I'd appreciate that, Jim.'

'When do you think you'll be back?'

He was fishing. He could sense something was not right.

'It depends. I just need a little time to myself.'

'You've not heard from Maria then?'

'No.'

There was nothing more to say. Partnership dissolved. End of an era. Time to move on.

Chapter Forty

We said our goodbyes and I put the phone down and dialled Maria's number. She answered on the second ring.

'Hi, it's me,' I said. 'I'm in Spain.'

The line went dead. She'd hung up again. I'd not even been allowed a word with Roly.

Was I too late to make it up with Maria? Did I really want to? And what about Hilary? I rang her number and got the answerphone.

'This is Hilary Taylor. I'm away for the weekend, please leave a message.'

Away with her doctor? Maybe.

Would I see her again? Would it bother me if I didn't? Right now I wasn't sure. In some ways, it was even a relief, but I knew in the future there'd be times when I would need her.

I put down the phone. The time bomb waiting to happen had exploded good style. It was inevitable, I knew, but none the less startling and upsetting when it did. Until now, by some miracle, I'd always managed to put it off, but not this time.

I knew I'd have to go back to England at some time to sort things out once and for all. Or was it already too late? Maybe the decision been taken out of my hands.

I was fifty-three, a time for reflection. Did I relish the prospect of spending the rest of my life on my own?

I picked up the paper. There was an advert for a jazz night at the 121 Club. I figured I might go along.

Back home it was the derby match at Goodison Park and I was going to miss it for the first time in years. Everton badly needed a win but Liverpool were striving to qualify for the Champions League. It was going to be tight.

I spent the rest of the day hanging around the hotel then set off about eight thirty for the 121. The club was situated in a white-painted hut a few miles out of town. I parked round the back and walked through some bushes to the front entrance. Already, at nine o'clock, the place was crowded. On the walls were sepia photographs of a British air force base with Lancasters and Spitfires lined up on the runways and fresh-faced boys in RAF uniform. Memories of England Past.

A jazz band was playing in a corner, trombone, trumpet, bass, drums and sax, all men who wouldn't see fifty again, but they were swinging with the sheer joy of playing. I'd not heard such exuberance from a band since I saw The Beatles at Litherland Town Hall in 1961, that famous gig when they'd just returned from Hamburg and everyone in the audience thought they were German.

I went to the bar, bought myself a cider, and found an empty seat to sit down and listen.

Two women were sitting in a corner chatting and watching the band. They were both in their forties, I guessed, and one of them was particularly attractive with long dark hair and ultra-marine eyes. She wore a white top with a scoop neck showing a generous cleavage and a black skirt that covered her knees.

Perhaps she felt me looking at her because she glanced up. I smiled and she smiled back. Straight out of *South Pacific* - 'Some enchanted evening'. A stranger across a crowded room.

The band took a break and I got chatting to the drummer at the bar. He was in his sixties and it turned out he'd played in a jazz band in Liverpool in the late nineteen fifties, in the days when The Cavern was a jazz club, Brian Epstein ran NEM's Record Shop and skiffle groups like The Swinging Blue Jeans were about to metamorphose as rock'n'roll outfits.

He remembered Jim Turner running The Odd Spot Club, Hank Walters singing country with The Dusty Road Ramblers, The Royal Caribbean Steel Orchestra backing the strippers at the Jacaranda and Stuart Sutcliffe playing with The Beatles at the Casbah Club in Pete Best's cellar.

Is there a city in the world recognised all over the globe as much as Liverpool?

I bought him a pint and he went back onstage for the next

set. The woman was still there with her friend. Half an hour later, I'd finished my third cider and was on my way to the bar for another when she got up and walked over.

I smiled again as she reached the bar. 'Hi.'

She smiled back. 'I haven't seen you in here before.' She had a Northern accent. Not quite Geordie but close.

'It's the first time I've been here,' I said.

'You don't live here in Spain then?'

'No, just visiting. I live in Liverpool. What about you?'

'I live over here now but originally I come from a village in Cumbria called Kirksanton. You won't have heard of it.'

'Yes I have. It's on the road from Millom to Whitehaven.'

'Fancy you knowing that.'

'Back in the sixties I used to play drums in a band called The Cruzads and we played a few times in Millom.'

'Not the Cumbria Club by any chance?'

'You know it?'

'Of course.'

'A fellow called Jack Usher used to run it.'

'That's right. Jack's still around but the club's closed down now, though I'm told someone's bought it and they're doing it up.' She laughed. 'My Mum keeps me up to date with all the news from home.'

I remembered the Cumbria well. 'They used to have Bingo on early in the evening. The group would arrive at ten to set up and when the bingo finished, the kids would all stream in and we'd play till one in the morning. But there were these four old dears who'd get on the fruit machines when the bingo finished and still be there when we came off at the end of the night.'

She laughed. 'Sounds like Millom. Las Vegas of the North.'

'We used to play the Ritz as well. That could be rough. I remember the night two topless dancers were on and things got a bit out of hand. I don't think the locals had seen anything like that before. The bouncers were dragging the troublemakers downstairs by their ankles, bouncing their chins on every one of the stone steps all the way down.'

'The Ritz is called Amnesia now. Funny name for a club isn't it?'

'Probably because the punters drink so much they forget where they've been.'

She grinned. 'Early Alzheimer's Disease you mean?'

And Rupert Routledge not yet in his grave. Seems I couldn't get away from it.

The barmaid came over. 'Let me get you a drink,' I offered.

'Thanks, I'll have a lager.'

'And another cider for me,' I looked over to the table where she had been sitting. A tall, brown haired man was talking to her friend. 'Looks like your friend has got herself fixed up.'

'That's her husband. He usually picks us up and takes us home.'

'What about you then, have you…'

'My husband died two years after we came out here. Heart attack. He was only 47.'

'And you stayed on your own?'

'We'd made a lot of friends here.'

'But no boyfriends?'

'No permanent ones. I have my own villa just outside Denia, with views over the bay. It's quite enchanting really.' She gave me that intimate smile again. 'You must come and see it sometime if you're going to be around for a while.'

'I'd like that.' I took a sip of cider.

'How long are you over here for?'

'I'm not sure. I'm having a rest between jobs.'

'What do you do?'

'I'm in property.'

'In Liverpool?'

'Yes.'

She hesitated before asking, 'Are you on your own too?'

'Yes.'

'Where are you staying? With friends?'

'No. I'm at the Mirimar in Javea."

'I know it. By the beach.'

'That's the one.'

We looked at each other but without any feeling of embarrassment or any need to make small talk. The band started up the old Chris Barber hit, 'Petite Fleur'. I asked her, 'Shall we have a dance?'

'Why not?' She stood up and let me lead her through the crowd.

'My name's Mary,' she said. She looked at me as she spoke and I noticed the softness in those bright blue eyes. 'What's yours?'

'It's Johnny,' I said, as we stepped on to the dance floor. 'Johnny Ace.'

Outside, a full moon bathed the blossom on the orange trees with a gentle light, the same moon that would be shining on the waters of the River Mersey but, right now, I was quite content to be on the Costa Blanca.

Sure I had problems to sort out but they could wait. For the moment, Liverpool was a million miles away.

I slipped my arms around her. She held me tight and we moved together to the music.

And the band, as they say, played on.